The Arabia

Alibaba and Forty Thieves

--Story of Treasure

Contents

I. Alibaba and Forty Thieves

II. Sindbad the Seaman and Sindbad the Landsman
- The First Voyage of Sindbad Hight the Seaman
- The Second Voyage of Sindbad the Seaman
- The Third Voyage of Sindbad the Seaman
- The Fourth Voyage of Sindbad the Seaman
- The Fifth Voyage of Sindbad the Seaman
- The Sixth Voyage of Sindbad the Seaman
- The Seventh Voyage of Sindbad the Seaman

III. Aladdin, or The Wonderful Lamp

IV. The Ebony Horse

I.   Alibaba and Forty Thieves

In days of yore and in times and tides long gone before, there dwelt in a certain town of Persia two brothers, one named Kasim and the other Ali Baba, who at their father's demise had divided the little wealth he had left to them with equitable division, and had lost no time in wasting and spending it all. The elder, however, presently took to himself a wife, the daughter of an opulent merchant, so that when his father-in-law fared to the mercy of Almighty Allah, he became owner of a large shop filled with rare goods and costly wares and of a storehouse stocked with precious stuffs, likewise of much gold that was buried in the ground. Thus was he known throughout the city as a substantial man. But the woman whom Ali Baba had married was poor and needy. They lived, therefore, in a mean hovel, and Ali Baba eked out a scanty livelihood by the sale of fuel which he daily collected in the jungle and carried about the town to the bazaar upon his three asses.

Now it chanced one day that Ali Baba had cut dead branches and dry fuel sufficient for his need, and had placed the load upon his beasts, when suddenly he espied a dust cloud spiring high in air to his right and moving rapidly toward him, and when he closely considered it, he descried a troop of horsemen riding on amain and about to reach him. At this sight he was sore alarmed, and fearing lest perchance they were a band of bandits who would slay him and drive off his donkeys, in his affright he began to run. But forasmuch as they were near-hand and he could not escape from out the forest, he drove his animals laden with the fuel into a byway of the bushes and swarmed up a thick trunk of a huge tree to hide himself therein. And he sat upon a branch whence he could descry everything beneath him whilst none below could catch a glimpse of him above, and that tree grew close beside a rock which towered high abovehead.

The horsemen, young, active, and doughty riders, came close up to the rock face and all dismounted, whereat Ali Baba took good note of them, and soon he was fully persuaded by their mien and demeanor that they were a troop of highwaymen who, having fallen upon a caravan, had despoiled it and carried off the spoil and brought their booty to this place with intent of concealing it safely in some cache. Moreover, he observed that they were forty in number. Ali Baba saw the robbers, as soon as they came under the tree, each unbridle his horse and hobble it. Then all took off their saddlebags, which proved to he full of gold and silver. The man who seemed to he the captain presently pushed forward, load on shoulder, through thorns and thickets, till he came up to a certain spot, where he uttered these strange words: "Open, Sesame!" And forthwith appeared a wide doorway in the face of the rock. The robbers went in, and last of all their chief, and then the portal shut of itself.

Long while they stayed within the cave whilst Ali Baba was constrained to abide perched upon the tree, reflecting that if he came down, peradventure the band might issue forth that very moment and seize him and slay him. At last he had determined to mount one of the horses and driving on his asses, to return townward, when suddenly the portal flew open. The robber chief was first to issue forth, then, standing at the entrance, he saw and counted his men as they came out, and lastly he spake the magical words, "Shut,

Sesame!" whereat the door closed of itself. When all had passed muster and review, each slung on his saddlebags and bridled his own horse, and as soon as ready they rode off, led by the leader, in the direction whence they came. Ali Baba remained still perched on the tree and watched their departure, nor would he descend until what time they were clean gone out of sight, lest perchance one of them return and look around and descry him.

Then he thought within himself: "I too will try the virtue of those magical words and see if at my bidding the door will open and close." So he called out aloud, "Open, Sesame!" And no sooner had he spoken than straightway the portal flew open and he entered within. He saw a large cavern and a vaulted, in height equaling the stature of a full-grown man, and it was hewn in the live stone and, lighted up with light that came through air holes and bull's-eyes in the upper surface of the rock which formed the roof. He had expected to find naught save outer gloom in this robbers' den, and he was surprised to see the whole room filled with bales of all manner stuffs, and heaped up from sole to ceiling with camelloads of silks and brocades and embroidered cloths and mounds on mounds of varicolored carpetings. Besides which, he espied coins golden and silvern without measure or account, some piled upon the ground and others bound in learthern bags and sacks. Seeing these goods and moneys in such abundance, Ali Bab determined in his mind that not during a few years only but for many generations thieves must have stored their gains and spoils in this place.

When he stood within the cave, its door had closed upon him, yet he was not dismayed, since he had kept in memory the magical words, and he took no heed of the precious stuffs around him, but applied himself only and wholly to the sacks of ashrafis. Of these he carried out as many as he judged sufficient burthen for the beasts, then he loaded them upon his animals, and covered his plunder with sticks and fuel, so none might discern the bags but might think that he was carrying home his usual ware. Lastly he called out, "Shut, Sesame!" and forthwith the door closed, for the spell so wrought that whensoever any entered the cave, its portal shut of itself behind him, and as he issued therefrom, the same would neither open nor close again till he had pronounced the words "Shut, Sesame!" Presently, having laden his asses, Ali Baba urged them before him with all speed to the city and reaching home, he drove them into the yard, and, shutting close the outer door, took down first the sticks and fuel and after the bags of gold, which he carried in to his wife.

She felt them, and finding them full of coin, suspected that Ali Baba had been robbing, and fell to berating and blaming him for that he should do so ill a thing. Quoth Ali Baba to his wife, "Indeed I am no robber, and rather do thou rejoice with me at our good fortune." Hereupon he told her of his adventure, and began to pour the gold from the bags in heaps before her, and her sight was dazzled by the sheen and her heart delighted at his recital and adventures. Then she began counting the gold, whereat quoth Ali Baba: "O silly woman, how long wilt thou continue turning over the coin? Now let me dig a hole wherein to hide this treasure, that none may know its secret." Quoth she: "Right is thy rede! Still would I weigh the moneys and have some inkling of their amount," and he replied, "As thou pleasest, but see thou tell no man." So she went off in haste to Kasim's home to borrow weights and scales wherewith she might balance the ashrafis and make some reckoning of their value. And when she could not find Kasim, she said to his wife, "Lend me, I pray thee, thy scales for a moment." Replied her sister-in-law, "Hast thou need of the bigger balance or the smaller?" and the other rejoined, "I need not the large scales, give me the little," and her sister-in-law cried, "Stay here a moment whilst I look about and find thy want."

With this pretext Kasim's wife went aside and secretly smeared wax and suet over the pan of the balance, that she might know what thing it was Ali Baba's wife would weigh, for she made sure that whatso it be, some bit thereof would stick to the wax and fat. So the woman took this opportunity to satisfy her curiosity, and Ali Baba's wife, suspecting naught thereof, carried home the scales and began to weigh the gold, whilst Ali Baba ceased not digging. And when the money was weighed, they twain stowed it into the hole, which they carefully filled up with earth. Then the good wife took back the scales to her kinswoman, all unknowing that an ashrafi had adhered to the cup of the scales. But when Kasim's wife espied the gold coin, she fumed with envy and wrath, saying to herself: "So ho! They borrowed my balance to weigh out ashrafis?" And she marveled greatly whence so poor a man as Ali Baba had gotten such store of wealth that he should he obliged to weigh it with a pair of scales.

Now after long pondering the matter, when her husband returned home at eventide, she said to him: "O man, thou deemest thyself a wight of wealth and substance, but lo! thy brother Ali Baba is an emir by the side of thee, and richer far than thou art. He hath such heaps of gold that he must needs weigh his moneys with scales, whilst thou, forsooth, art satisfied to count thy coin." "Whence knowest thou this?" asked Kasim. And in answer his wife related all anent the pair of scales, and how she found an ashrafi stuck to them, and shewed him the gold coin, which bore the mark and superscription of some ancient king. No sleep had Kasim all that night by reason of his envy and jealousy and covetise, and next morning he rose betimes and going to Ali Baba, said: "O my brother, to all appearance thou art poor and needy, but in effect thou hast a store of wealth so abundant that perforce thou must weigh thy gold with scales." Quoth Ali Baba: "What is this thou sayest? I understand thee not. Make clear thy purport." And quoth Kasim, with ready rage: "Feign not that thou art ignorant of what I say, and think not to deceive me." Then, showing him the ashrafi, he cried: "Thousands of gold coins such as these thou hast put by, and meanwhile my wife found this one stuck to the cup of the scales." Then Ali Baba understood how both Kasim and his wife knew that he had store of ashrafis, and said in his mind that it would not avail him to keep the matter hidden, but would rather cause ill will and mischief, and thus he was induced to tell his brother every whit concerning the bandits and also of the treasure trove in the cave.

When he had heard the story, Kasim exclaimed: "I would fain learn of thee the certainty of the place where thou foundest the moneys, also the magical words whereby the door opened and closed. And I forewarn thee, an thou tell me not the whole truth, I will give notice of those ashrafis to the wah, then shalt thou forfeit all thy wealth and he disgraced and thrown into gaol." Thereupon Ali Baba told him his tale, not forgetting the magical words, and Kasim, who kept careful heed of all these matters, next day set out, driving ten mules he had hired, and readily found the place which Ali Baba had described to him. And when he came to the aforesaid rock and to the tree whereon Ali Baba had hidden himself, and he had made sure of the door he cried in great joy, "Open, Sesame!" The portal yawned wide at once and Kasim went within and saw the piles of jewels and treasures lying ranged all around, and as soon as he stood amongst them the door shut after him, as wont to do. He walked about in ecstasy marveling at the treasures, and when weary of admiration, he gathered together bags of ashrafis, a sufficient load for his ten mules, and placed them by the entrance in readiness to he carried outside and set upon the beasts. But by the will of Allah Almighty he had clean forgotten the cabalistic words, and cried out, "Open, Barley!" Whereat the door refused to move. Astonished and confused beyond measure, he named the names of all manner of grains save sesame, which had slipped from his memory as though he had never heard the word, whereat in his dire distress he heeded not the ashrafis that lay heaped at the entrance, and paced to and fro, backward and forward, within the cave, sorely puzzled and perplexed. The wealth whose sight had erewhile filled his heart with joy and gladness was now the cause of bitter grief and sadness.

It came to pass that at noontide the robbers, returning by that way, saw from afar some mules standing beside the entrance, and much they marveled at what had brought the beasts to that place, for inasmuch as Kasim by mischance had faded to tether or hobble them, they had strayed about the jungle and were browsing hither and thither. However, the thieves paid scant regard to the estrays, nor cared they to secure them, but only wondered by what means they had wandered so far from the town. Then, reaching the cave, the captain and his troop dismounted, and going up to the door, repeated the formula, and at once it flew open.

Now Kasim had heard from within the cave the horse hoofs drawing nigh and yet nigher, and he fell down to the ground in a fit of fear, never doubting that it was the clatter of the banditti who would slaughter him without fail. Howbeit, he presently took heart of grace, and at the moment when the door flew open he rushed out hoping to make good his escape. But the unhappy ran full tilt against the captain, who stood in front of the band, and felled him to the ground, whereupon a robber standing near his chief at once bared his brand and with one cut clave Kasim clean in twain. Thereupon the robbers rushed into the cavern, and put back as they were before the bags of ashrafis which Kasim had heaped up at the doorway ready for taking away, nor recked they aught of those which Ali Baba had removed, so dazed and amazed were they to discover by what means the strange man had effected an entrance. All knew that it was not possible for any to drop through the skylights, so tall and steep was the rock's face, withal slippery of ascent, and also that none could enter by the portal unless he knew the magical words whereby to open it. However, they presently quartered the dead body of Kasim and hung it to the door within the cavern, two parts to the right jamb and as many to the left, that the sight might be a warning of approaching doom for all who dared enter the cave. Then, coming out, they closed the hoard door and rode away upon their wonted work.

Now when night fell and Kasim came not home, his wife waxed uneasy in mind, and running round to Ali Baba, said: "O my brother, Kasim hath not returned. Thou knowest whither he went, and sore I fear me some misfortune hath betided him." Ali Baba also divined that a mishap had happened to prevent his return. Not the less, however, he strove to comfort his sister-in-law with words of cheer, and said: "O wife of my brother, Kasim haply exerciseth discretion and, avoiding the city, cometh by a roundabout road and will he here anon. This I do believe is the reason why he tarrieth." Thereupon, comforted in spirit, Kasim's wife fared homeward and sat awaiting her husband's return, but when half the night was spent and still he came not, she was as one distraught. She feared to cry aloud for her grief, lest haply the neighbors, hearing her, should come and learn the secret, so she wept in silence and upbraiding herself, fell to thinking: "Wherefore did I disclose this secret to him and beget envy and jealousy of Ali Baba? This be the fruit thereof, and hence the disaster that hath come down upon me."

She spent the rest of the night in bitter tears, and early on the morrow hied in hottest hurry to Ali Baba and prayed that he would go forth in quest of his brother. So he strove to console her, and straightway set out with his asses for the forest. Presently, reaching the rock, he wondered to see stains of blood freshly shed, and not finding his brother or the ten mules, he forefelt a calamity from so evil a sign. He then went to the door and saying, "Open, Sesame!" he pushed in and saw the dead body of Kasim, two parts hanging to the right and the rest to the left of the entrance. Albeit he was affrighted beyond measure of affright, he wrapped the quarters in two cloths and laid them upon one of his asses, hiding them carefully with sticks and fuel that none might see them. Then he placed the bags of gold upon the two other animals and likewise covered them most carefully, and when all was made ready he closed the cave door with the magical words, and set him forth wending homeward with all ward and watchfulness. The asses with the load of ashrafis he made over to his wife, and bade her bury the bags with diligence, but he told her not the condition in which he had come upon his brother Kasim. Then he went with the other ass- to wit, the beast whereon was laid the corpse- to the widow's house and knocked gently at the door.

Now Kasim had a slave girl shrewd and sharp-witted, Morgiana hight. She as softly undid the bolt and admitted Ali Baba and the ass into the courtyard of the house, when he let down the body from the beast's back and said: "O Morgiana, haste thee and make thee ready to perform the rites for the burial of thy lord. I now go to tell the tidings to thy mistress, and I will quickly return to help thee in this matter." At that instant Kasim's widow, seeing her brother-in-law, exclaimed: "O Ali Baba, what news bringest thou of my spouse? Alas! I see grief tokens written upon thy countenance. Say quickly what hath happened." Then he recounted to her how it had fared with her husband and how he had been slain by the robbers and in what wise he had brought home the dead body. Ali Baba pursued: "O my lady, what was to happen hath happened, but it behooveth us to keep this matter secret, for that our lives depend upon privacy." She wept with sore weeping and made answer: "It hath fared with my husband according to the fiat of Fate, and now for thy safety's sake I give thee my word to keep the affair concealed." He replied: "Naught can avail when Allah hath decreed. Rest thee in patience until the days of thy widowhood be accomplisht, after which time I will take thee to wife, and thou shalt live in comfort and happiness. And fear not lest my first spouse vex thee or show aught of jealousy, for that she is kindly and tender of heart." The widow, lamenting her loss noisily, cried, "Be it as e'en thou please."

Then Ali Baba farewelled her, weeping and wailing for her husband, and joining Morgiana, took counsel with her how to manage the burial of his brother. So, after much consultation and many warnings, he left the slave girl and departed home driving his ass before him. As soon as Ali Baba had fared forth Morgiana went quickly to a druggist's shop, and that she might the better dissemble with him and not make known the matter, she asked of him a drug often administered to men when diseased with dangerous distemper. He gave it saying: "Who is there in thy house that lieth so in as to require this medicine?" and said she: "My master Kasim is sick well nigh unto death. For many days he hath nor spoken nor tasted aught of food, so that almost we despair of his life." Next day Morgiana went again and asked the druggist for more of medicine and essences such as are adhibited to the sick when at door of death, that the moribund may haply rally before the last breath. The man gave the potion and she, taking it, sighed aloud and wept, saying: "I fear me he may not have strength to drink this draught. Methinks all will be over with him ere I return to the house."

Meanwhile Ali Baba was anxiously awaiting to hear sounds of wailing and lamentation in Kasim's home, that he might at such signal hasten thither and take part in the ceremonies of the funeral. Early on the second day Morgiana went with veiled face to one Baba Mustafa, a tailor well shotten in years whose craft was to make shrouds and cerecloths, and as soon as she saw him open his shop she gave him a gold piece and said, "Do thou bind a bandage over thine eyes and come along with me." Mustafa made as though he would not go, whereat Morgiana placed a second gold coin in his palm and entreated him to accompany her. The tailor presently consented for greed of gain, so, tying a kerchief tightly over his eyes, she led him by the hand to the house wherein lay the dead body of her master. Then, taking off the bandage in the darkened room, she bade him sew together the quarters of the corpse, limb to its limb, and casting a cloth upon the body, said to the tailor: "Make haste and sew a shroud according to the size of this dead man, and I will give thee therefor yet another ducat." Baba Mustafa quickly made the cerecloth of fitting length and breadth, and Morgiana paid him the promised ashrafi, then, once more bandaging his eyes, led him back to the place whence she had brought him. After this she returned hurriedly home and with the help of Ali Baba washed the body in warm water and donning the shroud, laid the corpse upon a clean place ready for burial.

This done, Morgiana went to the mosque and gave notice to an imam that a funeral was awaiting the mourners in a certain household, and prayed that he would come to read the prayers for the dead, and the imam went back with her. Then four neighbors took up the bier and bore it on their shoulders and fared forth with the imam and others who were wont to give assistance at such obsequies. After the funeral prayers were ended four other men carried off the coffin, and Morgiana walked before it bare of head, striking her breast and weeping and wailing with exceeding loud lament, whilst Ali Baba and the neighbors came behind. In such order they entered the cemetery and buried him, then, leaving him to Munkar and Nakir- the Questioners of the Dead- all wended their ways. Presently the women of the quarter, according to the custom of the city, gathered together in the house of mourning and sat an hour with Kasim's widow comforting and condoling, presently leaving her somewhat resigned and cheered. Ali Baba stayed forty days at home in ceremonial lamentation for the loss of his brother, so none within the town save himself and his wife (Kasim's widow) and Morgiana knew aught the secret. And when the forty days of mourning were ended Ali Baba removed to his own quarters all the property belonging to the deceased and openly married the widow. Then he appointed his nephew, his brother's eldest son, who had lived a long time with a wealthy merchant and was perfect of knowledge in all matters of trade, such as selling and buying, to take charge of the defunct's shop and to carry on the business.

It so chanced one day when the robbers, as was their wont, came to the treasure cave that they marveled exceedingly to find nor sign nor trace of Kasim's body, whilst they observed that much of gold had been carried off. Quoth the captain: "Now it behooveth us to make inquiry in this matter, else shall we suffer much of loss, and this our treasure, which we and our forefathers have amassed during the course of many years, will little by little be wasted and spoiled." Hereto all assented and with single mind agreed that he whom they had slain had knowledge of the magical words whereby the door was made to open; moreover, that someone besides him had cognizance of the spell and had carried off the body, and also much of gold. Wherefore they needs must make diligent research and find out who the man ever might be. They then took counsel and determined that one amongst them, who should be sagacious and deft of wit, must don the dress of some merchant from foreign parts, then, repairing to the city, he must go about from quarter to quarter and from street to street and learn if any townsman had lately died, and if so where he wont to dwell, that with this clue they might be enabled to find the wight they sought. Hereat said one of the robbers: "Grant me leave that I fare and find out such tidings in the town and bring thee word anon, and if I fail of my purpose I hold my life in forfeit."

Accordingly that bandit, after disguising himself by dress, pushed at night into the town, and next morning early he repaired to the market square and saw that none of the shops had yet been opened save only that of Baba Mustafa, the tailor, who, thread and needle in hand, sat upon his working stool. The thief bade him good day and said: "'Tis yet dark. How canst thou see to sew?" Said the tailor: "I perceive thou art a stranger. Despite my years, my eyesight is so keen that only yesterday I sewed together a dead body whilst sitting in a room quite darkened." Quoth the bandit thereupon to himself, "I shall get somewhat of my want from this snip," and to secure a further clue he asked: "Meseemeth thou wouldst jest with me, and thou meanest that a cerecloth for a corpse was stitched by thee and that thy business is to sew shrouds." Answered the tailor: "It mattereth not to thee. Question me no more questions."

Thereupon the robber placed an ashrafi in his hand and continued: "I desire not to discover aught thou hidest, albeit my breast, like every honest man's, is the grave of secrets, and this only would I learn of thee- in what house didst thou do that job? Canst thou direct me thither, or thyself conduct me thereto?" The tailor took the gold with greed and cried: "I have not seen with my own eyes the way to that house. A certain bondswoman led me to a place which

I know right well, and there she bandaged my eyes and guided me to some tenement and lastly carried me into a darkened room where lay the dead body dismembered. Then she unbound the kerchief and bade me sew together first the corpse and then the shroud, which having done, she again blindfolded me and led me back to the stead whence she had brought me and left me there. Thou seest then I am not able to tell thee where thou shalt find the house." Quoth the robber: "Albeit thou knowest not the dwelling whereof thou speakest, still canst thou take me to the place where thou wast blindfolded. Then I will bind a kerchief over thine eyes and lead thee as thou wast led. On this wise perchance thou mayest hit upon the site. An thou wilt do this favor by me, see, here another golden ducat is thine." Thereupon the bandit slipped a second ashrafi into the tailor's palm, and Baba Mustafa thrust it with the first into his pocket. Then, leaving his shop as it was, he walked to the place where Morgiana had tied the kerchief around his eyes, and with him went the robber, who, after binding on the bandage, led him by the hand.

Baba Mustafa, who was clever and keen-witted, presently striking the street whereby he had fared with the handmaid, walked on counting step by step, then, halting suddenly, he said, "Thus far I came with her," and the twain stopped in front of Kasim's house, wherein now dwelt his brother Ali Baba. The robber then made marks with white chalk upon the door, to the end that he might readily find it at some future time, and removing the bandage from the tailor's eyes, said: "O Baba Mustafa, I thank thee for this favor, and Almighty Allah guerdon thee for thy goodness. Tell me now, I pray thee, who dwelleth in yonder house?" Quoth he: "In very sooth I wot not, for I have little knowledge concerning this quarter of the city." And the bandit, understanding that he could find no further clue from the tailor, dismissed him to his shop with abundant thanks, and hastened back to the tryst place in the jungle where the band awaited his coming.

Not long after, it so fortuned that Morgiana, going out upon some errand, marveled exceedingly at seeing the chalk marks showing white in the door. She stood awhile deep in thought, and presently divined that some enemy had made the signs that he might recognize the house and play some sleight upon her lord. She therefore chalked the doors of all her neighbors in like manner and kept the matter secret, never entrusting it or to master or to mistress. Meanwhile the robber told his comrades his tale of adventure and how he had found the clue, so the captain and with him all the band went one after other by different ways till they entered the city, and he who had placed the mark on Ali Baba's door accompanied the chief to point out the place. He conducted him straightway to the house and shewing the sign exclaimed, "Here dwelleth he of whom we are in search!" But when the captain looked around him, he saw that all the dwellings bore chalk marks after like fashion, and he wondered, saying: "By what manner of means knowest thou which house of all these houses that bear similar signs is that whereof thou spokest?" Hereat the robber guide was confounded beyond measure of confusion, and could make no answer. Then with an oath he cried: "I did assuredly set a sign upon a door, but I know not whence came all the marks upon the other entrances, nor can I say for a surety which it was I chalked." Thereupon the captain returned to the market place and said to his men: "We have toiled and labored in vain, nor have we found the house we went forth to seek. Return we now to the forest, our rendezvous. I also will fare thither."

Then all trooped off and assembled together within the treasure cave, and when the robbers had all met, the captain judged him worthy of punishment who had spoken falsely and had led them through the city to no purpose. So he imprisoned him in presence of them all, and then said he: "To him amongst you will I show special favor who shall go to town and bring me intelligence whereby we may lay hands upon the plunderer of our property." Hereat another of the company came forward and said, "I am ready to go and inquire into the case, and 'tis I who will bring thee to thy wish." The captain, after giving him presents and promises, dispatched him upon his errand, and by the decree of Destiny, which none may gainsay, this second robber went first to the house of Baba Mustafa the tailor, as had done the thief who had foregone him. In like manner he also persuaded the snip with gifts of golden coin that he be led hood-winked, and thus too he was guided to Ali Baba's door. Here, noting the work of his predecessor, he affixed to the jamb a mark with red chalk, the better to distinguish it from the others, whereon still showed the white. Then hied he back in stealth to his company.

But Morgiana on her part also descried the red sign on the entrance, and with subtle forethought marked all the others after the same fashion, nor told she any what she had done. Meanwhile the bandit rejoined his band and vauntingly said: "O our captain, I have found the house and thereon put a mark whereby I shall distinguish it clearly from all its neighbors." But, as aforetime, when the troop repaired thither, they saw each and every house marked with signs of red chalk. So they returned disappointed and the captain,

18

waxing displeased exceedingly and distraught, clapped also this spy into gaol. Then said the chief to himself: "Two men have failed in their endeavor and have met their rightful meed of punishment, and I trow that none other of my band will essay to follow up their research. So I myself will go and find the house of this wight."

Accordingly he fared along, aided by the tador Baba Mustafa, who had gained much gain of golden pieces in this matter, he hit upon the house of Ali Baba. And here he made no outward show or sign, but marked it on the tablet of his heart and impressed the picture upon the page of his memory. Then, returning to the jungle, he said to his men: "I have full cognizance of the place and have limned it clearly in my mind, so now there will be no difficulty in finding it. Go forth straightway and buy me and bring hither nineteen mules, together with one large leathern jar of mustard oil and seven and thirty vessels of the same kind clean empty. Without me and the two locked up in gaol ye number thirty-seven souls, so I will stow you away armed and accoutered each within his jar and will load two upon each mule, and upon the nineteenth mule there shall be a man in an empty jar on one side and on the other the jar full of oil. I for my part, in guise of an oil merchant, will drive the mules into the town, arriving at the house by night, and will ask permission of its master to tarry there until morning. After this we shall seek occasion during the dark hours to rise up and fall upon him and slay him." Furthermore, the captain spake, saying: "When we have made an end of him we shall recover the gold and treasure whereof he robbed us and bring it back upon the mules."

This counsel pleased the robbers, who went forthwith and purchased mules and huge leathern jars, and did as the captain had bidden them. And after a delay of three days, shortly before nightfall they arose, and oversmearing all the jars with oil of mustard, each hid him inside an empty vessel. The chief then disguised himself in trader's gear and placed the jars upon the nineteen mules; to wit, the thirty-seven vessels, in each of which lay a robber armed and accoutered, and the one that was full of oil. This done, he drove the beasts before him, and presently he reached Ali Baba's place at nightfall, when it chanced that the housemaster was strolling after supper to and fro in front of his home. The captain saluted him with the salaam and said: "I come from such-and-such a village with oil, and ofttimes have I been here a-selling oil, but now to my grief I have arrived too late and I am sore troubled and perplexed as to where I shall spend the night. An thou have pity on me, I pray thee grant that I tarry here in thy courtyard and ease the mules by taking down the jars and giving the beasts somewhat of fodder." Albeit Ali Baba had heard the captain's voice when perched upon the tree and had seen him enter the cave, yet by reason of the disguise he knew him not for the leader of the thieves, and granted his request with hearty welcome and gave him full license to halt there for the night. He then pointed out an empty shed wherein to tether the mules, and bade one of the slave boys go fetch grain and water. He also gave orders to the slave girl Morgiana, saying: "A guest hath come hither and tarrieth here tonight. Do thou busy thyself with all speed about his supper and make ready the guest bed for him."

Presently, when the captain had let down all the jars and had fed and watered his mules, Ali Baba received him with all courtesy and kindness, and summoning Morgiana, said in his presence: "See thou fail not in service of this our stranger, nor suffer him to lack for aught. Tomorrow early I would fare to the hammam and bathe, so do thou give my slave boy Abdullah a suit of clean white clothes which I may put on after washing. Moreover, make thee ready a somewhat of broth overnight, that I may drink it after my return home." Replied she, "I will have all in readiness as thou hast bidden." So Ali Baba retired to his rest, and the captain, having supped, repaired to the shed and saw that all the mules had their food and drink for the night, and finding utter privacy, whispered to his men who were in ambush: "This night at midnight, when ye hear my voice, do you quickly open with your sharp knives the leathern jars from top to bottom, and issue forth without delay." Then, passing through the kitchen, he reached the chamber wherein a bed had been dispread for him, Morgiana showing the way with a lamp. Quoth she, "An thou need aught beside, I pray thee command this thy slave, who is ever ready to obey thy say!" He made answer, "Naught else need I." Then, putting out the light, he lay down on the bed to sleep awhile ere the time came to rouse his men and finish off the work.

Meanwhile Morgiana did as her master had bidden her. She first took out a suit of clean white clothes and made it over to Abdullah, who had not yet gone to rest. Then she placed the pigskin upon the hearth to boil the broth and blew the fire till it burnt briskly. After a short delay she needs must see an the broth be boiling, but by that time all the lamps had gone out and she found that the oil was spent and that nowhere could she get a light. The slave boy Abdullah observed that she was troubled and perplexed hereat, and quoth he to her: "Why make so much ado? In yonder shed are many jars of oil. Go now and take as much soever as thou listest." Morgiana gave thanks to him for his suggestion, and Abdullah, who was lying at his ease in the hall, went off to sleep so that he might wake betimes and serve Ali Baba in the bath. So the handmaiden rose, and with oil can in hand walked to the shed where stood the leathern jars all ranged in rows.

Now as she drew nigh unto one of the vessels, the thief who was hidden therein, hearing the tread of footsteps, bethought him that it was of his captain, whose summons he awaited, so he whispered, "Is it now time for us to sally forth?" Morgiana started back affrighted at the sound of human accents, but inasmuch as she was bold and ready of wit, she replied, "The time is not yet come," and said to herself: "These jars are not full of oil, and herein I perceive a manner of mystery. Haply the oil merchant hatcheth some treacherous plot against my lord, so Allah, the Compassionating, the Compassionate, protect us from his snares!" Wherefore she answered in a voice made like to the captain's, "Not yet, the time is not come." Then she went to the next jar and returned the same reply to him who was within, and soon to all the vessels, one by one. Then said she in herself: "Laud to the Lord! My master took this fellow in believing him to he an oil merchant, but lo! he hath admitted a band of robbers, who only await the signal to fall upon him and plunder the place and do him die."

Then passed she on to the furthest jar and, finding it brimming with oil, filled her can. and returning to the kitchen, trimmed the lamp and lit the wicks. Then, bringing forth a large caldron, she set it upon the fire, and filling it with oil from out the jar, heaped wood upon the hearth and fanned it to a fierce flame, the readier to boil its contents. When this was done, she bailed it out in potfuls and poured it seething hot into the leathern vessels, one by one, while the thieves, unable to escape, were scalded to death and every jar contained a corpse. Thus did this slave girl by her subtle wit make a clean end of all, noiselessly and unknown even to the dwellers in the house. Now when she had satisfied herself that each and every of the men had been slain, she went back to the kitchen and, shutting to the door, sat brewing Ali Baba's broth.

Scarce had an hour passed before the captain woke from sleep and, opening wide his window, saw that all was dark and silent. So he clapped his hands as a signal for his men to come forth, but not a sound was heard in return. After a while he clapped again and called aloud, but got no answer, and when he cried out a third time without reply, he was perplexed and went out to the shed wherein stood the jars. He thought to himself: "Perchance all are fallen asleep, whenas the time for action is now at hand, so I must e'en awaken them without stay or delay." Then, approaching the nearest jar, he was startled by a smell of oil and seething flesh, and touching it outside, he felt it reeking hot. Then, going to the others one by one, he found all in like condition. Hereat he knew for a surety the fate which had betided his band and, fearing for his own safety, he clomb onto the wall, and thence dropping into a garden, made his escape in high dudgeon and sore disappointment. Morgiana awaited awhile to see the Captain return from the shed but he came not, whereat she knew that he had scaled the wall and had taken to flight, for that the street door was double-locked. And the thieves being all disposed of on this wise, Morgiana laid her down to sleep in perfect solace and ease of mind.

When two hours of darkness yet remained, Ali Baba awoke

and went to the hammam, knowing naught of the night adventure, for the gallant slave girl had not aroused him, nor indeed had she deemed such action expedient, because had she sought an opportunity of reporting to him her plan, she might haply have lost her chance and spoiled the project. The sun was high over the horizon when Ali Baba walked back from the baths, and he marveled exceedingly to see the jars still standing under the shed, and said: "How cometh it that he, the oil merchant, my guest, hath not carried to the market his mules and jars of oil?" She answered: "Allah Almighty vouchsafe to thee sixscore years and ten of safety! I will tell thee in privacy of this merchant."

So Ali Baba went apart with his slave girl, who, taking him without the house, first locked the court door, then, showing him a jar, she said, " Prithee look into this and see if within there be oil or aught else."

Thereupon, peering inside it, he perceived a man, at which sight he cried aloud and fain would have fled in his fright. Quoth Morgiana: "Fear him not. This man hath no longer the force to work thee harm, he lieth dead and stone-dead." Hearing such words of comfort and reassurance, Ali Baba asked: "O Morgiana, what evils have we escaped, and by what means hath this wretch become the quarry of Fate?" She answered: "Alhamdolillah-praise be to Almighty Allah!- I will inform thee fully of the case. But hush thee, speak not aloud, lest haply the neighbors learn the secret and it end in our confusion. Look now into all the jars, one by one from first to last." So Ali Baba examined them severally and found in each a man fully armed and accoutered, and all lay scalded to death. Hereat, speechless for sheer amazement, he stared at the jars, but presently, recovering himself, he asked, "And where is he, the oil merchant?" Answered she: "Of him also I will inform thee. The villain was no trader, but a traitorous assassin whose honeyed words would have ensnared thee to thy doom. And now I will tell thee what he was and what hath happened, but meanwhile thou art fresh from the hammam and thou shouldst first drink somewhat of this broth for thy stomach's and thy health's sake." So Ali Baba went within and Morgiana served up the mess, after which quoth her master: "I fain would hear this wondrous story. Prithee tell it to me, and set my heart at ease." Hereat the handmaid fell to relating whatso had betided in these words:

"O my master, when thou badest me boil the broth and retiredst to rest, thy slave in obedience to thy command took out a suit of clean white clothes and gave it to the boy Abdullah, then kindled the fire and set on the broth. As soon as it was ready I had need to light a lamp so that I might see to skim it, but all the oil was spent, and, learning this, I told my want to the slave boy Abdullah, who advised me to draw somewhat from the jars which stood under the shed. Accordingly I took a can and went to the first vessel, when suddenly I heard a voice within whisper with all caution, 'Is it now time for us to sally forth?' I was amazed thereat, and judged that the pretended merchant had laid some plot to slay thee, so I replied, 'The time is not yet come.' Then I went to the second jar and heard another voice, to which I made the like answer, and so on with all of them. I now was certified that these men awaited only some signal from their chief, whom thou didst take to guest within thy walls supposing him to he a merchant in oil, and that after thou receivedst him hospitably the miscreant had brought these men to murther thee and to plunder thy good and spoil thy house.

"But I gave him no opportunity to will his wish. The last jar I found full of od, and taking somewhat therefrom, I lit the lamp. Then, putting a large caldron upon the fire, I filled it up with oil which I brought from the jar and made a fierce blaze under it, and when the contents were seething hot, I took out sundry cansful with intent to scald them all to death, and going to each jar in due order, I poured within them, one by one, boiling oil. On this wise having destroyed them utterly, I returned to the kitchen, and having extinguished the lamps, stood by the window watching what might happen, and how that false merchant would act next. Not long after I had taken my station, the robber captain awoke and ofttimes signaled to his thieves. Then, getting no reply, he came downstairs and went out to the jars, and finding that all his men were slain, he fled through the darkness, I know not whither. So when he had clean disappeared I was assured that, the door being double-locked, he had scaled the wall and dropped into the garden and made his escape. Then with my heart at rest I slept."

And Morgiana, after telling her story to her master, presently added: "This is the whole truth I have related to thee. For some days indeed have I had inkling of such matter, but withheld it from thee, deeming it inexpedient to risk the chance of its meeting the neighbors' ears. Now, however, there is no help but to tell thee thereof. One day as I came to the house door I espied thereon a white chalk mark, and on the next day a red sign beside the white. I knew not the intent wherewith the marks were made, nevertheless I set others upon the entrances of sundry neighbors, judging that some enemy had done this deed, whereby to encompass my master's destruction. Therefore I made the marks on all the other doors in such perfect conformity with those I found that it would be hard to distinguish amongst them. Judge now and see if these signs and all this villainy be not the work of the bandits of the forest, who marked our house that on such wise they might know it again. Of these forty thieves there yet remain two others concerning whose case I know naught, so beware of them, but chiefly of the third remaining robber, their captain, who fled hence alive. Take good heed and be thou cautious of him, for shouldst thou fall into his hands, he will in no wise spare thee, but will surely murther thee. I will do all that lieth in me to save from hurt and harm thy life and property, nor shall thy slave be found wanting in any service to my lord."

Hearing these words, Ali Baba rejoiced with exceeding joyance and said to her: "I am well pleased with thee for this thy conduct, and say me what wouldst thou have me do in thy behalf. I shall not fail to remember thy brave deed so long as breath in me remaineth." Quoth she: "It behooveth us before all things forthright to bury these bodies in the ground, that so the secret be not known to anyone." Hereupon Ali Baba took with him his slave boy Abdullah into the garden and there under a tree they dug for the corpses of the thieves a deep pit in size proportionate to its contents, and they dragged the bodies (having carried off their weapons) to the fosse and threw them in. Then, covering up the remains of the seven and thirty robbers, they made the ground appear level and clean as it wont to be. They also hid the leathern jars and the gear and arms, and presently Ali Baba sent the mules by ones and twos to the bazaar and sold them all with the able aid of his slave boy Abdullah. Thus the matter was hushed up, nor did it reach the ears of any. However, Ali Baba ceased not to be ill at ease, lest haply the captain or the surviving two robbers should wreak their vengeance on his head. He kept himself private with all caution, and took heed that none learn a word of what had happened and of the wealth which he had carried off from the bandits' cave.

Meanwhile the captain of the thieves, having escaped with his life, fled to the forest in hot wrath and sore irk of mind, and his senses were scattered and the color of his visage vanished like ascending smoke. Then he thought the matter over again and again, and at last he firmly resolved that he needs must take the life of Ali Baba, else he would lose all the treasure which his enemy, by knowledge of the magical words, would take away and turn to his own use. Furthermore, he determined that he would undertake the business singlehanded; and that after getting rid of Ali Baba, he would gather together another band of banditti and would pursue his career of brigandage, as indeed his forebears had done for many generations. So he lay down to rest that night, and rising early in the morning, donned a dress of suitable appearance, then, going to the city, alighted at a caravanserai, thinking to himself: "Doubtless the murther of so many men hath reached the wali's ears, and Ali Baba hath been seized and brought to justice, and his house is leveled and his good is confiscated. The townfolk must surely have heard tidings of these matters." So he straightway asked of the keeper of the khan, "What strange things have happened in the city during the last few days?" And the other told him all that he had seen and heard, but the captain could not learn a whit of that which most concerned him. Hereby he understood that Ali Baba was ware and wise, and that he had not only carried away such store of treasure, but he had also destroyed so many lives and withal had come off scatheless. Furthermore, that he himself must needs have all his wits alert not to fall into the hands of his foe and perish.

With this resolve the captain hired a shop in the bazaar, whither he bore whole bales of the finest stuffs and goodly merchandise from his forest treasure house, and presently he took his seat within the store and fell to doing merchant's business. By chance his place fronted the booth of the defunct Kasim, where his son, Ali Baba's nephew, now traded, and the captain, who called himself Khwajah Hasan, soon formed acquaintance and friendship with the shopkeepers around about him and treated all with profuse civilities. But he was especially gracious and cordial to the son of Kasim, a handsome youth and a well-dressed, and ofttimes he would sit and chat with him for a long while. A few days after, it chanced that Ali Baba, as he was sometimes wont to do, came to see his nephew, whom he found sitting in his shop. The captain saw and recognized him at sight, and one morning he asked the young man, saying, "Prithee tell me, who is he that ever and anon cometh to thee at thy place of sale?" Whereto the youth made answer, "He is my uncle, the brother of my father." Whereupon the captain showed him yet greater favor and affection, the better to deceive him for his own devices, and gave him presents and made him sit at meat with him and fed him with the daintiest of dishes.

Presently Ali Baba's nephew bethought him it was only right and proper that he also should invite the merchant to supper, but whereas his own house was small, and he was straitened for room and could not make a show of splendor, as did Khwajah Hasan, he took counsel with his uncle on the matter. Ali Baba replied to his nephew: "Thou sayest well. It behooveth thee to entreat thy friend in fairest fashion even as he hath entreated thee. On the morrow, which is Friday, shut thy shop, as do all merchants of repute. Then, after the early meal, take Khwajah Hasan to smell the air, and as thou walkest lead him hither unawares. Meanwhile I will give orders that Morgiana shall make ready for his coming the best of viands and all necessaries for a feast. Trouble not thyself on any wise, but leave the matter in my hands." Accordingly on the next day- to wit, Friday- the nephew of Ali Baba took Khwajah Hasan to walk about the garden, and as they were returning he led him by the street wherein his uncle dwelt. When they came to the house, the youth stopped at the door and knocking, said: "O my lord, this is my second home. My uncle hath heard much of thee and of thy goodness meward, and desireth with exceeding desire to see thee, so shouldst thou consent to enter and visit him, I shall be truly glad and thankful to thee." Albeit Khwajah Hasan rejoiced in heart that he had thus found means whereby he might have access to his enemy's house and household, and although he hoped soon to attain his end by treachery, yet he hesitated to enter in and stood to make his excuses and walk away. But when the door was opened by the slave porter, Ali Baba's nephew seized his companion's hand and after abundant persuasion led him in, whereat he entered with great show of cheerfulness as though much pleased and honored. The housemaster received him with all favor and worship and asked him of his welfare, and said to him: "O my lord, I am obliged and thankful to thee for that thou hast shewn favor to the son of my brother, and I perceive that thou regardest him with an affection even fonder than my own." Khwajah Hasan replied with pleasant words and said: "Thy nephew vastly taketh my fancy and in him I am well pleased, for that although young in years yet he hath been endued by Allah with much of wisdom."

Thus they twain conversed with friendly conversation, and presently the guest rose to depart and said: "O my lord, thy slave must now farewell thee, but on some future day- Inshallah- he will again wait upon thee." Ali Baba, however, would not let him leave, and asked: "Whither wendest thou, O my friend? I would invite thee to my table, and I pray thee sit at meat with us and after hie thee home in peace. Perchance the dishes are not as delicate as those whereof thou art wont to eat, still deign grant me this request, I pray thee, and refresh thyself with my victual." Quoth Khwajah Hasan: "O lord, I am beholden to thee for thy gracious invitation, and with pleasure would I sit at meat with thee, but for a special reason must I needs excuse myself. Suffer me therefore to depart, for I may not tarry longer, nor accept thy gracious offer." Hereto the host made reply: "I pray thee, O my lord, tell me what may be the reason so urgent and weighty." And Khwajah Hasan answered: "The cause is this. I must not, by order of the physician who cured me lately of my complaint, eat aught of food prepared with salt." Quoth Ali Baba: "An this be all, deprive me not, I pray thee, of the honor thy company will confer upon me. As the meats are not yet cooked, I will forbid the kitchener to make use of any salt. Tarry here awhile, and I will return anon to thee." So saying, Ali Baba went in to Morgiana and bade her not put salt into any one of the dishes, and she, while busied with her cooking, fell to marveling greatly at such order and asked her master, "Who is he that eateth meat wherein is no salt?" He answered: "What to thee mattereth it who he may be? Only do thou my bidding." She rejoined: "'Tis well. All shall be as thou wishest." But in mind she wondered at the man who made such strange request, and desired much to look upon him.

Wherefore, when all the meats were ready for serving up, she helped the slave boy Abdullah to spread the table and set on the meal, and no sooner did she see Khwajah Hasan than she knew who he was, albeit he had disguised himself in the dress of a stranger merchant. Furthermore, when she eyed him attentively, she espied a dagger hidden under his robe. "So ho!" quoth she to herself. "This is the cause why the villain eateth not of salt, for that he seeketh an opportunity to slay my master, whose mortal enemy he is. Howbeit I will be beforehand with him and dispatch him ere he find a chance to harm my lord." Now when Ali Baba and Khwajah Hasan had eaten their sufficiency, the slave boy Abdullah brought Morgiana word to serve the dessert, and she cleared the table and set on fruit fresh and dried in salvers, then she placed by the side of Ali Baba a small tripod for three cups with a flagon of wine, and lastly she went off with the slave boy Abdullah into another room, as though she would herself eat supper. Then Khwajah Hasan-that is, the captain of the robbers- perceiving that the coast was clear, exulted mightily, saying to himself: "The time hath come for me to take full vengeance. With one thrust of my dagger I will dispatch this fellow, then escape across the garden and wend my ways. His nephew will not adventure to stay my hand, for an he do but move a finger or toe with that intent, another stab with settle his earthly account. Still must I wait awhile until the slave boy and the cookmaid shall have eaten and lain down to rest them in the kitchen."

Morgiana, however, watched him wistfully and divining his purpose, said in her mind: "I must not allow this villain advantage over my lord, but by some means I must make void his project and at once put an end to the life of him." Accordingly the trusty slave girl changed her dress with all haste and donned such clothes as dancers wear. She veiled her face with a costly kerchief, around her head she bound a fine turban, and about her middle she tied a waistcloth worked with gold and silver, wherein she stuck a dagger whose hilt was rich in filigree and jewelry. Thus disguised, she said to the slave boy Abdullah: "Take now thy tambourine, that we may play and sing and dance in honor of our master's guest." So he did her bidding and the twain went into the room, the lad playing and the lass following. Then, making a low congee, they asked leave to perform and disport and play, and Ali Baba gave permission, saying, "Dance now and do your best that this our guest may he mirthful and merry." Quoth Khwajah Hasan, "O my lord, thou dost indeed provide much pleasant entertainment."

Then the slave boy Abdullah, standing by, began to strike the tambourine whilst Morgiana rose up and showed her perfect art and pleased them vastly with graceful steps and sportive motion. And suddenly, drawing the poniard from her belt, she brandished it and paced from side to side, a spectacle which pleased them most of all. At times also she stood before them, now clapping the sharp-edged dagger under armpit and then setting it against her breast. Lastly she took the tambourine from the slave boy Abdullah, and still holding the poniard in her right, she went round for largess as is the custom amongst merrymakers. First she stood before Ali Baba, who threw a gold coin into the tambourine, and his nephew likewise put in an ashrafi. Then Khwajah Hasan, seeing her about to approach him, fell to pulling out his purse, when she heartened her heart, and quick as the blinding levin she plunged the dagger into his vitals, and forthwith the miscreant fell back stone-dead.

Ali Baba was dismayed, and cried in his wrath: "O unhappy, what is this deed thou hast done to bring about my ruin?" But she replied: "Nay, O my lord, rather to save thee and not to cause thee harm have I slain this man. Loosen his garments and see what thou wilt discover thereunder." So Ali Baba searched the dead man's dress and found concealed therein a dagger.

Then said Morgiana: "This wretch was thy deadly enemy. Consider him well. He is none other than the oil merchant, the captain of the band of robbers. Whenas he came hither with intent to take thy life, he would not eat thy salt, and when thou toldest me that he wished not any in the meat, I suspected him, and at first sight I was assured that he would surely do thee die. Almighty Allah he praised, 'tis even as I thought." Then Ali Baba lavished upon her thanks and expressions of gratitude, saying, "Lo, these two times hast thou saved me from his hand," and falling upon her neck, he cried: "See, thou art free, and as reward for this thy fealty I have wedded thee to my nephew." Then, turning to the youth, he said: "Do as I bid thee and thou shalt prosper. I would that thou marry Morgiana, who is a model of duty and loyalty. Thou seest now yon Khwajah Hasan sought thy friendship only that he might find opportunity to take my life, but this maiden with her good sense and her wisdom hath slain him and saved us."

Ali Baba's nephew straightway consented to marry Morgiana. After which the three, raising the dead body, bore it forth with all heed and vigilance and privily buried it in the garden, and for many years no one know aught thereof. In due time Ali Baba married his brother's son to Morgiana with great pomp, and spread a bride feast in most sumptuous fashion for his friends and neighbors, and made merry with them and enjoyed singing and all manner of dancing and amusements. He prospered in every undertaking and Time smiled upon him and a new source of wealth was opened to him.

For fear of the thieves he had not once visited the jungle cave wherein lay the treasure since the day he had carried forth the corpse of his brother Kasim. But some time after, he mounted his hackney one morning and journeyed thither, with all care and caution, till finding no signs of man or horse, and reassured in his mind, he ventured to draw near the door. Then, alighting from his beast, he tied it up to a tree, and going to the entrance, pronounced the words which he had not forgotten, "Open, Sesame!" Hereat, as was its wont, the door flew open, and entering thereby he saw the goods and hoard of gold and silver untouched and lying as he had left them. So he felt assured that not one of all the thieves remained alive, and that save himself there was not a soul who knew the secret of the place. At once he bound in his saddlecloth a load of ashrafis such as his horse could bear and brought it home, and in after days he showed the hoard to his sons and sons' sons and taught them how the door could he caused to open and shut. Thus Ali Baba and his household lived all their lives in wealth and joyance in that city where erst he had been a pauper, and by the blessing of that secret treasure he rose to high degree and dignities.

II. Sindbad the Seaman and Sindbad the Landsman

There lived in the city of Baghdad during the reign of the Commander of the Faithful, Harun al-Rashid, a man named Sindbad the Hammal, one in poor case who bore burdens on his head for hire. It happened to him one day of great heat that whilst he was carrying a heavy load, he became exceeding weary and sweated profusely, the heat and the weight alike oppressing him. Presently, as he was passing the gate of a merchant's house before which the ground was swept and watered, and there the air was temperate, he sighted a broad bench beside the door, so he set his load thereon, to take rest and smell the air. He sat down on the edge of the bench, and at once heard from within the melodious sound of lutes and other stringed instruments, and mirth-exciting voices singing and reciting, together with the song of birds warbling and glorifying Almighty Allah in various tunes and tonguess-turtles, mocking birds, merles, nightingales, cushats, and stone curlews- whereat he marveled in himself and was moved to mighty joy and solace.

Then he went up to the gate and saw within a great flower garden wherein were pages and black slaves and such a train of servants and attendants and so forth as is found only with kings and sultans. And his nostrils were greeted with the savory odours of an manner meats rich and delicate, and delicious and generous wines. So he raised his eyes heavenward and said, "Glory to Thee, O Lord, O Creator and Provider, Who providest whomso Thou wilt without count or stint! O mine Holy One, I cry Thee pardon for an sins and turn to Thee repenting of all offenses!

"How many by my labors, that evermore endure,
All goods of life enjoy and in cooly shade recline?
Each morn that dawns I wake in travail and in woe,
And strange is my condition and my burden gars me pine.
Many others are in luck and from miseries are free,
And Fortune never load them with loads the like o' mine.
They live their happy days in all solace and delight,
Eat, drink, and dwell in honor 'mid the noble and the digne.
All living things were made of a little drop of sperm,
Thine origin is mine and my provenance is thine,
Yet the difference and distance 'twixt the twain of us are far
As the difference of savor 'twixt vinegar and wine.
But at Thee, O God All-wise! I venture not to rail,
Whose ordinance is just and whose justice cannot fail."

When Sindbad the Porter had made an end of reciting his verses, he bore up his burden and was about to fare on when there came forth to him from the gate a little foot page, fair of face and shapely of shape and dainty of dress, who caught him by the hand saying, "Come in and speak with my lord, for he calleth for thee." The porter would have excused himself to the page, but the lad would take no refusal, so he left his load with the doorkeeper in the vestibule and followed the boy into the house, which he found to be a goodly mansion, radiant and full of majesty, till he brought him to a grand sitting room wherein he saw a company of nobles and great lords seated at tables garnished with all manner of flowers and sweet-scented herbs, besides great plenty of dainty viands and fruits dried and fresh and confections and wines of the choicest vintages. There also were instruments of music and mirth and lovely slave girls playing and singing. All the company was ranged according to rank, and in the highest place sat a man of worshipful and noble aspect whose beard sides hoariness had stricken, and he was stately of stature and fair of favor, agreeable of aspect and full of gravity and dignity and majesty. So Sindbad the Porter was confounded at that which he beheld and said in himself, "By Allah, this must be either a piece of Paradise or some king's palace!"

Then he saluted the company with much respect, praying for their prosperity, and kissing the ground before them, stood with his head bowed down in humble attitude. The master of the house bade him draw near and be seated and bespoke him kindly, bidding him welcome. Then he set before him various kinds of viands, rich and delicate and delicious, and the porter, after saying his Bismillah, fell to and ate his fill, after which he exclaimed, "Praised be Allah, whatso be our case!" and, washing his hands, returned thanks to the company for his entertainment. Quoth the host: "Thou art welcome, and thy day is a blessed. But what thy name and calling?" Quoth the other, "O my lord, my name is Sindbad the Hammal, and I carry folk's goods on my head for hire." The housemaster smiled and rejoined: "Know, O Porter, that thy name is even as mine, for I am Sindbad the Seaman. And now, O Porter, I would have thee let me hear the couplets thou recitedst at the gate anon.' The porter was abashed and replied: "Allah upon thee! Excuse me, for toil and travail and lack of luck when the hand is empty teach a man ill manners and boorish ways." Said the host: "Be not ashamed. Thou art become my brother. But repeat to me the verses, for they pleased me whenas I heard thee recite them at the gate."

Hereupon the Porter repeated the couplets and they delighted the merchant, who said to him: "Know, O Hammal, that my story is a wonderful one, and thou shalt hear all that befell me and all I underwent ere I rose to this state of prosperity and became the lord of this place wherein thou seest me. For I came not to this high estate save after travail sore and perils galore, and how much toil and trouble have I not suffered in days of yore! I have made seven voyages, by each of which hangeth a marvelous tale, such as confoundeth the reason, and all this came to pass by doom of Fortune and Fate. For from what Destiny doth write there is neither refuge nor flight. Know, then, good my lords," continued he, "that I am about to relate the

The First Voyage of Sindbad Hight the Seaman

My father was a merchant, one of the notables of my native place, a moneyed man and ample of means, who died whilst I was yet a child, leaving me much wealth in money and lands and farmhouses. When I grew up, I laid hands on the whole and ate of the best and drank freely and wore rich clothes and lived lavishly, companioning and consorting with youths of my own age, and considering that this course of life would continue forever and ken no change. Thus did I for a long time, but at last I awoke from my heedlessness and, returning to my senses, I found my wealth had become unwealth and my condition ill-conditioned, and all I once hent had left my hand. And recovering my reason, I was stricken with dismay and confusion and bethought me of a saying of our lord Solomon, son of David (on whom be peace!), which I had heard aforetime from my father: things are better than other three. The day of death is better than the day of birth, a live dog is better than a dead lion, and the grave is better than want." Then I got together my remains of estates and property and sold all, even my clothes, for three thousand dirhams, with which I resolved to travel to foreign parts, remembering the saying of the poet:

By means of toil man shall scale the height,
Who to fame aspires mustn't sleep o' night.
Who seeketh pearl in the deep must dive,
Winning weal and wealth by his main and might.
And who seeketh Fame without toil and strife
Th' impossible seeketh and wasteth life.

So, taking heart, I bought me goods, merchandise and all needed for a voyage, and impatient to be at sea, I embarked, with a company of merchants, on board a ship bound for Bassorah. There we again embarked and sailed many days and nights, and we passed from isle to isle and sea to sea and shore to shore, buying and selling and bartering everywhere the ship touched, and continued our course till we came to an island as it were a garth of the gardens of Paradise. Here the captain cast anchor and, making fast to the shore, put out the landing planks. So all on board landed and made furnaces, and lighting fires therein, busied themselves in various ways, some cooking and some washing, whilst other some walked about the island for solace, and the crew fell to eating and drinking and playing and sporting. I was one of the walkers, but as we were thus engaged, behold the master, who was standing on the gunwale, cried out to us at the top of his voice, saying: "Ho there! Passengers, run for your lives and hasten back to the ship and leave your gear and save yourselves from destruction, Allah preserve you!. For this island whereon ye stand is no true island, but a great fish stationary a-middlemost of the sea, whereon the sand hath settled and trees have sprung up of old time, so that it is become like unto an island. But when ye lighted fires on it, it felt the heat and moved, and in a moment it will sink with you into the sea and ye will all be drowned. So leave your gear and seek your safety ere ye die!"

All who heard him left gear and goods, clothes washed and unwashed, fire pots and brass cooking pots, and fled back to the ship for their lives, and some reached it while others (amongst whom was I) did not, for suddenly the island shook and sank into the abysses of the deep, with all that were thereon, and the dashing sea surged over it with clashing waves. I sank with the others down, down into the deep, but Almighty Allah preserved me from drowning and threw in my way a great wooden tub of those that had served the ship's company for tubbing. I gripped it for the sweetness of life and, bestriding it like one riding, paddled with my feet like oars, whilst the waves tossed me as in sport right and left. Meanwhile the captain made sail and departed with those who had reached the ship, regardless of the drowning and the drowned. And I ceased not following the vessel with my eyes till she was hid from sight and I made sure of death.

Darkness closed in upon me while in this plight, and the winds and waves bore me on all that night and the next day, till the tub brought to with me under the lee of a lofty island with trees overhanging the tide. I caught hold of a branch and by its aid clambered up onto the land, after coming nigh upon death. But when I reached the shore, I found my legs cramped and numbed and my feet bore traces of the nibbling of fish upon their soles, withal I had felt nothing for excess of anguish and fatigue. I threw myself down on the island ground like a dead man, and drowned in desolation, swooned away, nor did I return to my senses till next morning, when the sun rose and revived me. But I found my feet swollen, so made shift to move by shuffling on my breech and crawling on my knees, for in that island were found store of fruits and springs of sweet water. I ate of the fruits, which strengthened me. And thus I abode days and nights till my life seemed to return and my spirits began to revive and I was better able to move about. So, after due consideration, I fell to exploring the island and diverting myself with gazing upon all things that Allah Almighty had created there, and rested under the trees, from one of which I cut me a staff to lean upon.

One day as I walked along the marge I caught sight of some object in the distance and thought it a wild beast or one of the monster creatures of the sea, but as I drew near it, looking hard the while, saw that it was a noble mare, tethered on the beach. Presently I went up to her, but she cried out against me with a great cry, so that I trembled for fear and turned to go away, when there came forth man from under the earth and followed me, crying out and saying, "Who and whence art thou, and what caused thee to come hither?" "O my lord," answered I, "I am in very sooth a waif, a stranger, and was left to drown with sundry others by the ship we voyaged in. But Allah graciously sent me a wodden tub, so I saved myself thereon and it floated with me, till the waves cast me up on this island." When he heard this, he took my hand and saying, "Come with me," carried me into a great sardab, or underground chamber, which was spacious as a saloon.

He made me sit down at its upper end, then he brought me somewhat of food and, being a-hungered, I ate till I was satisfied and refreshed. And when he had put me at mine ease, he questioned me of myself, and I told him all that had befallen me from first to last. And as he wondered at my adventure, I said: "By Allah, O my lord, excuse me, I have told thee the truth of my case and the accident which betided me, and now I desire that thou tell me who thou art and why thou abidest here under the earth and why thou hast tethered yonder mare on the brink of the sea." Answered he: "Know that I am one of the several who are, stationed in different parts of this island, and we are of the grooms of King Mihrjan, and under our hand are all his horses. Every month about new-moon tide we bring hither our best mares which have never been covered, and picket them on the seashore and hide ourselves in this place under the ground, so that none may espy us. Presently the stallions of the sea scent the mares and come up out of the water and, seeing no one, leap the mares and do their will of them. When they have covered them, they try to drag them away with them, but cannot, by reason of the leg ropes. So they cry out at them and butt at them and kick them, which we hearing, know that the stallions have dismounted, so we run out and shout at them, whereupon they are startled and return in fear to the sea. Then the mares conceive by them and bear colts and fillies worth a mint of money, nor is their like to be found on earth's face. This is the time of the coming forth of the sea stallions, and Inshallah! I will bear thee to King Mihrjan and show thee our country. And know that hadst thou not happened on us, thou hadst perished miserably and none had known of thee. But I will be the means of the saving of thy life and of thy return to thine own land." I called down blessings on him and thanked him for his kindness and courtesy. And while we were yet talking, behold, the stallion came up out of the sea, and giving a great cry, sprang upon the mare and covered her. When he had done his will of her, he dismounted and would have carried her away with him, but could not by reason of the tether. She kicked and cried out at him, whereupon the groom took a sword and target and ran out of the underground saloon, smiting the buckler with the blade and calling to his company, who came up shouting and brandishing spears. And the stallion took fright at them and plunging into the sea like a buffalo, disappeared under the waves.

After this we sat awhile till the rest of the grooms came up, each leading a mare, and seeing me with their fellow syce, questioned me of my case, and I repeated my story to them. Thereupon they drew near me and spreading the table, ate and invited me to eat. So I ate with them, after which they took horse and mounting me on one of the mares, set out with me and fared on without ceasing till we came to the capital city of King Mihrjan, and going in to him, acquainted him with my story. Then he sent for me, and when they set me before him and salaams had been exchanged, he gave me a cordial welcome and wishing me long life, bade me tell him my tale. So I related to him all that I had seen and all that had befallen me from first to last, whereat he marveled and said to me: "By Allah, O my son, thou hast indeed been miraculously preserved! Were not the term of thy life a long one, thou hadst not escaped from these straits. But praised be Allah for safety!" Then he spoke cheerily to me and entreated me with kindness and consideration. Moreover, he made me his agent for the port and registrar of all ships that entered the harbor. I attended him regularly, to receive his commandments, and he favored me and did me all manner of kindness and invested me with costly and splendid robes. Indeed, I was high in credit with him as an intercessor for the folk and an intermediary between them and him when they wanted aught of him.

I abode thus a great while, and as often as I passed through the city to the port, I questioned the merchants and travelers and sailors of the city of Baghdad, so haply I might hear of an occasion to return to my native land, but could find none who knew it or knew any who resorted thither. At this I was chagrined, for I was weary of long strangerhood, and my disappointment endured for a time till one day, going in to King Mihrjan, I found with him a company of Indians. I saluted them and they returned my salaam, and politely welcomed me and asked me of my country. When they asked me of my country, I questioned them of theirs and they told me that they were of various castes, some being called shakiriyah, who are the noblest of their casts and neither oppress nor offer violence to any, and others Brahmans, a folk who abstain from wine but live in delight and solace and merriment and own camels and horses and cattle. Moreover, they told me that the people of India are divided into two and seventy castes, and I marveled at this with exceeding marvel.

Amongst other things that I saw in King Mihrijan's dominions was an island called Kasil, wherein all night is heard the beating of drums and tabrets, but we were told by the neighboring islanders and by travelers that the inhabitants are people of diligence and judgment. In this sea I saw also a fish two hundred cubits long and the fishermen fear it, so they strike together pieces of wood and put it to flight. I also saw another fish with a head like that of an owl, besides many other wonders and rarities, which it would be tedious to recount. I occupied myself thus in visiting the islands till one day as I stood in the port with a staff in my hand, according to my custom, behold, a great ship, wherein were many merchants, came sailing for the harbor. When it reached the small inner port where ships anchor under the city, the master furled his sails and making fast to the shore, put out the landing planks, whereupon the crew fell to breaking bulk and landing cargo whilst I stood by, taking written note of them.

They were long in bringing the goods ashore, so I asked the master, "Is there aught left in thy ship?" and he answered: "O my lord, there are divers bales of merchandise in the hold, whose owner was drowned from amongst us at one of the islands on our course; so his goods remained in our charge by way of trust, and we purpose to sell them and note their price, that we may convey it to his people in the city of Baghdad, the Home of Peace." "What was the merchant's name?" quoth I, and quoth he, "Sindbad the Seaman," whereupon I straitly considered him and knowing him, cried out to him with a great cry, saying: "O Captain, I am that Sindbad the Seaman who traveled with other merchants, and when the fish heaved and thou calledst to us, some saved themselves and others sank, I being one of them. But Allah Almighty threw in my way a great tub of wood, of those the crew had used to wash withal, and the winds and waves carried me to this island, where by Allah's grace I fell in with King Mihrjan's grooms and they brought me hither to the King their master. When I told him my story, he entreated me with favor and made me his harbor-master, and I have prospered in his service and found acceptance with him. These bales therefore are mine, the goods which God hath given me."

The other exclaimed: "There is no Majesty and there is no Mihgt save in Allah, the Glorious, the Great! Verily, there is neither conscience nor good faith left among men!" Said I, "O Rais, what mean these words, seeing that I have told thee my case?" And he answered, "Because thou heardest me say that I had with me goods whose owner was drowned, thou thinkest to take them without right. But this is forbidden by law to thee, for we saw him drown before our eyes, together with many other passengers, nor was one of them saved. So how canst thou pretend that thou art the owner of the goods?" "O Captain," said I, "listen to my story and give heed to my words, and my truth will be manifest to thee, for lying and leasing are the letter marks of the hypocrites." Then I recounted to him all that had befallen me since I sailed from Baghdad with him to the time when we came to the fish island where we were nearly drowned, and I reminded him of certain matters which had passed between us. Whereupon both he and the merchants were certified of the truth of my story and recognized me and gave me joy of my deliverance, saying: "By Allah, we thought not that thou hadst escaped drowning! But the Lord hath granted thee new life."

Then they delivered my bales to me, and I found my name written thereon, nor was aught thereof lacking. So I opened them and making up a present for King Mihrjan of the finest and costliest of the contents, caused the sailors carry it up to the palace, where I went in to the King and laid my present at his feet, acquainting him with what had happened, especially concerning the ship and my goods, whereat he wondered with exceeding wonder, and the truth of an that I had told him was made manifest to him. His affection for me redoubled after that and he showed me exceeding honor and bestowed on me a great present in return for mine. Then I sold my bales and what other matters I owned, making a great profit on them, and bought me other goods and gear of the growth and fashion of the island city.

When the merchants were about to start on their homeward voyage, I embarked on board the ship all that I possessed, and going in to the King, thanked him for all his favors and friendship and craved his leave to return to my own land and friends. He farewelled me and bestowed on me great store of the country stuffs and produce, and I took leave of him and embarked. Then we set sail and fared on nights and days, by the permission of Allah Almighty, and Fortune served us and Fate favored us, so that we arrived in safety at Bassorah city, where I landed rejoiced at my safe return to my natal soil. After a short stay, I set out for Baghdad, the House of Peace, with store of goods and commodities of great price. Reaching the city in due time, I went straight to my own quarter and entered my house, where all my friends and kinsfolk came to greet me.

Then I bought me eunuchs and concubines, servants and Negro slaves, till I had a large establishment, and I bought me houses, and lands and gardens, till I was richer and in better case than before, and returned to enjoy the society of my friends and familiars more assiduously than ever, forgetting all I had suffered of fatigue and hardship and strangerhood and every peril of travel. And I applied myself to all manner joys and solaces and delights, eating the daintiest viands and drinking the deliciousest wines, and my wealth allowed this state of things to endure.

This, then, is the story of my first voyage, and tomorrow, Inshallah! I will tell you the tale of the second of my seven voyages. (Saith he who telleth the tale): Then Sindbad the Seaman made Sindbad the Landsman sup with him and bade give him a hundred gold pieces, saying, "Thou hast cheered us with thy company this day." The porter thanked him and, taking the gift, went his way, pondering that which he had heard and marveling mightily at what things betide mankind. He passed the night in his own place and with early morning repaired to the abode of Sindbad the Seaman, who received him with honor and seated him by his side. As soon as the rest of the company was assembled, he set meat and drink before them, and when they had well eaten and drunken and were merry and in cheerful case, he took up his discourse and recounted to them in these words the narrative of

The Second Voyage of Sindbad the Seaman

Know, O my brother, that I was living a most comfortable and enjoyable life, in all solace and delight, as I told you yesterday, until one day my mind became possessed with the thought of traveling about the world of men and seeing their cities and islands, and a longing seized me to traffic and to make money by trade. Upon this resolve I took a great store of cash and buying goods and gear fit for travel, bound them up in bales. Then I went down to the riverbank, where I found a noble ship and brand-new about to sail equipped with sails of fine cloth and well manned and provided. So I took passage in her, with a number of other merchants, and after embarking our goods, we weighed anchor the same day. Right fair was our voyage, and we sailed from place to place and from isle to isle, and whenever we anchored we met a crowd of merchants and notables and customers, and we took to buying and selling and bartering.

At last Destiny brought us to an island, fair and verdant, in trees abundant, with yellow-ripe fruits luxuriant, and flowers fragrant and birds warbling soft descant, and streams crystalline and radiant. But no sign of man showed to the descrier- no, not a blower of the fire. The captain made fast with us to this island, and the merchants and sailors landed and walked about, enjoying the shade of the trees and the song of the birds, that chanted the praises of the One, the Victorious, and marveling at the works of the Omnipotent King. I landed with the rest, and, sitting down by a spring of sweet water that welled up among the trees, took out some vivers I had with me and ate of that which Allah Almighty had allotted unto me. And so sweet was the zephyr and so fragrant were the flowers that presently I waxed drowsy and, lying down in that place, was soon drowned in sleep.

When I awoke, I found myself alone, for the ship had sailed and left me behind, nor had one of the merchants or sailors bethought himself of me. I searched the island right and left, but found neither man nor Jinn, whereat I was beyond measure troubled, and my gall was like to burst for stress of chagrin and anguish and concern, because I was left quite alone, without aught of worldly gear or meat or drink, weary and heartbroken. So I gave myself up for lost and said: "Not always doth the crock escape the shock. I was saved the first time by finding one who brought me from the desert island to an inhabited place, but now there is no hope for me." Then I fell to weeping and wailing and gave myself up to an access of rage, blaming myself for having again ventured upon the perils and hardships of voyage, whenas I was at my ease in mine own house in mine own land, taking my pleasure with good meat and good drink and good clothes and lacking nothing, neither money nor goods. And I repented me of having left Baghdad, and this the more after all the travails and dangers I had undergone in my first voyage, wherein I had so narrowly escaped destruction, and exclaimed, "Verily we are, Allah's, and unto Him we are returning!"

I was indeed even as one mad and Jinn-struck, and presently I rose and walked about the island, right and left and every whither, unable for trouble to sit or tarry in ay one place. Then I climbed a tall tree and looked in all directions, but saw nothing save sky and sea and trees and birds and isles and sands. However, after a while my eager glances fell upon some great white thing, afar off in the interior of the island. So I came down from the tree and made for that which I had seen, and behold, it was a huge white dome rising high in air and of vast compass. I walked all around it, but found no door thereto, nor could I muster strength or nimbleness by reason of its exceeding smoothness and slipperiness. So I marked the spot where I stood and went round about the dome to measure its circumference, which I found fifty good paces. And as I stood casting about how to gain an entrance, the day being near its fall and the sun being near the horizon, behold, the sun was suddenly hidden from me and the air became dull and dar! Methought a cloud had come over the sun, but it was the season of summer, so I marveled at this and, lifting my head, looked steadfastly at the sky, when I saw that the cloud was none other than an enormous bird, of gigantic girth and inordinately wide of wing, which as it flew through the air veiled the sun and hid it from the island.

At this sight my wonder redoubled and I remembered a story I had heard aforetime of pilgrims and travelers, how in a certain island dwelleth a huge bird, called the "roc," which feedeth its young on elephants, and I was certified that the dome which caught my sight was none other than a roc's egg. As I looked and wondered at the marvelous works of the Almighty, the bird alighted on the dome and brooded over it with its wings covering it and its legs stretched out behind it on the ground, and in this posture it fell asleep, glory be to Him who sleepeth not! When I saw this, I arose and, unwinding my turban from my head, doubled it and twisted it into a rope, with which I girt my middle and bound my waist fast to the legs of the roc, saying in myself, "Peradventure this bird may carry me to a land of cities and inhabitants, and that will be better than abiding in this desert island." I passed the night watching and fearing to sleep, lest the bird should fly away with me unawares, and as soon as the dawn broke and morn shone, the roc rose off its egg and spreading its wings with a great cry, flew up into the air dragging me with it, nor ceased it to soar and to tower till I thought it had reached the limit of the firmament. After which it descended earthward, little by little, till it lighted on the top of a high hill.

As soon as I found myself on the hard ground, I made haste to unbind myself, quaking for fear of the bird, though it took no heed of me nor even felt me, and loosing my turban from its feet, I made off with my best speed. Presently I saw it catch up in its huge claws something from the earth and rise with it high in air, and observing it narrowly, I saw it to be a serpent big of bulk and gigantic of girth, wherewith it flew away clean out of sight. I marveled at this, and faring forward, found myself on a peak overlooking a valley, exceeding great and wide and deep and bounded by vast mountains that spired high in air. None could descry their summits for the excess of their height, nor was any able to climb up thereto. When I saw this, I blamed myself for that which I had done and said: "Would Heaven I had tarried in the island! It was better than this wild desert, for there I had at least fruits to eat and water to drink, and here are neither trees nor fruits nor streams. But there is no Majesty and there is no Might save in Allah, the Glorious, the Great! Verily, as often as I am quit of one peril I fall into a worse danger and a more grievous."

However, I took courage and walking along the wady, found that its soil was of diamond, the stone wherewith they pierce minerals and precious stones and porcelain and onyx, for that it is a dense stone and a dure, whereon neither iron nor hardhed hath effect, neither can we cut off aught therefrom nor break it, save by means of loadstone. Moreover, the valley swarmed with snakes and vipers, each big as a palm tree, that would have made but one gulp of an elephant. And they came out by night, hiding during the day lest the rocs and eagles pounce on them and tear them to pieces, as was their wont, why I wot not. And I repented of what I had done and Allah, I have made haste to bring destruction upon myself!" The day began to wane as I went along, and I looked about for a place where I might pass the night, being in fear of the serpents, ace for my and I took no thought of meat and drink in my concern for my life. Presently, I caught sight of a cave near-hand, with a narrow doorway, so I entered, and seeing a great stone close to the mouth, I rolled it up and stopped the entrance, saying to myself, "I am safe here for the night, and as soon as it is day, I will go forth and see what Destiny will do." Then I looked within the cave and saw at the upper end a great serpent brooding on her eggs, at which my flesh quaked and my hair stood on end, but I raised my eyes to Heaven and, committing my case to fate and lot, abode all that night without sleep till daybreak, when I rolled back the stone from the mouth of the cave and went forth, staggering like a drunken man and giddy with watching and fear and hunger.

As in this sore case I walked along the valley, behold, there fell down before me a slaughtered beast. But I saw no one, whereat I marveled with great marvel and presently remembered a story I had heard aforetime of traders and pilgrims and travelers- how the mountains where are the diamonds are full of perils and terrors, nor can any fare through them, but the merchants who traffic in diamonds have a device by which they obtain them; that is to say, they take a sheep and slaughter and skin it and cut it in pieces and cast them down from the mountaintops into the valley sole, where, the meat being fresh and sticky with blood, some of the gems cleave to it. Then they leave it till midday, when the eagles and vultures swoop down upon it and carry it in their claws to the mountain summits, whereupon the merchants come and shout at them and scare them away from the meat. Then they come, and taking the diamonds which they find sticking to it, go their ways with them and leave the meat to the birds and beasts, nor can any come at the diamonds but by this device.

So when I saw the slaughtered beast fall (he pursued) and bethought me of the story, I went up to it and filled my pockets and shawl girdle and turban and the folds of my clothes with the choicest diamonds, and as I was thus engaged, down fell before me another great piece of meat. Then with my unrolled turban and lying on my back, I set the bit on my breast so that I was hidden by the meat, which was thus raised above the ground. Hardly had I gripped it when an eagle swooped down upon the flesh and, seizing it with his talons, flew up with it high in air and me clinging thereto, and ceased not its flight till it alighted on the head of one of the mountains, where, dropping the carcass he fell to rending it. But, behold, there arose behind him a great noise of shouting and clattering of wood, whereat the bird took fright and flew away. Then I loosed off myself the meat, with clothes daubed with blood therefrom, and stood up by its side. Whereupon up came the merchant who had cried out at the eagle, and seeing me standing there, bespoke me not, but was affrighted at me and shook with fear.

However, he went up to the carcass and, turning it over, found no diamonds sticking to it, whereat he gave a great cry and exclaimed: "Harrow, my disappointment! There is no Majesty and there is no Might save in Allah with Whom we seek refuge from Satan the stoned!" And he bemoaned himself and beat hand upon hand, saying: "Alas, the pity of it! How cometh this?" Then I went up-to him and he said to me, "Who art thou, and what causeth thee to come hither?" And I: "Fear not, I am a man and a good man and a merchant. My story is a wondrous and my adventures marvelous and the manner of my coming hither is prodigious. So be of good cheer. Thou shalt receive of me what shall rejoice thee, for I have with me great plenty of diamonds and I will give thee thereof what shall suffice thee, for each is better than aught thou couldst get otherwise. So fear nothing." The man rejoiced thereat and thanked and blessed me. Then we talked together till the other merchants, hearing me in discourse with their fellow, came up and saluted me, for each of them had thrown down his piece of meat.

And as I went off with them and told them my whole story, how I had suffered hardships at sea and the fashion of my reaching the valley. But I gave the owner of the meat a number of the stones I had by me, so they all wished me joy of my escape, saying: "By Allah, a new life hath been decreed to thee, for none ever reached yonder valley and came off thence alive before thee, but praised be Allah for thy safety!" We passed the night together in a safe and pleasant place, beyond measure rejoiced at my deliverance from the valley of Serpents and my arrival in an inhabited land. And on the morrow we set out and journeyed over the mighty range of mountains, seeing many serpents in the valley, till we came to a fair great island wherein was a garden of huge champhor trees under each of which a hundred men might take shelter. When the folk have a mind to get camphor, they bore into the upper part of the bole with a long iron, whereupon the liquid camphor, which is the sap of the tree, floweth out and they catch it in vessels, where it concreteth like gum; but after this the tree dieth and becometh firewood.

Moreover, there is in this island a kind of wild beast, called rhinoceros, that pastureth as do steers and buffaloes with us; but it is a huge brute, bigger of body than the camel, and like it feedeth upon the leaves and twigs of trees. It is a remarkable animal with a great and thick horn, ten cubits long, a-middleward its head, wherein, when cleft in twain, is the likeness of a man. Voyagers and pilgrims and travelers declare that this beast called karkadan will carry off a great elephant on its horn and graze about the island and the seacoast therewith and take no heed of it till the elephant dieth and its fat, melting in the sun, runneth down into the rhinoceros's eyes and blindeth him, so that he lieth down on the shore. Then comes the bird roc and carrieth off both the rhinoceros and that which is on its horn, to feed its young withal. Moreover, I saw in this island many kinds of oxen and buffaloes, whose like are not found in our country. Here I sold some of the diamonds which I had by me for gold dinars and silver dirhams and bartered others for the produce of the country, and loading them upon beasts of burden, fared on with the merchants from valley to valley and town to town, buying and selling and viewing foreign countries and the works and creatures of Allah till we came to Bassorah city, where we abode a few days, after which I continued my journey to Baghdad. I arrived at home with great store of diamonds and money and goods, and forgathered with my friends and relations and gave alms and largess and bestowed curious gifts and made presents to all my friends and companions. Then I betook myself to eating well and drinking well and wearing fine clothes and making merry with my fellows, and forgot all my sufferings in the pleasures of return to the solace and delight of life, with light heart and broadened breast. And everyone who heard of my return came and questioned me of my adventures and of foreign countries, and I related to them all that had befallen me, and the much I had suffered, whereat they wondered and gave me joy of my safe return. This, then, is the end of the story of my second voyage, and tomorrow, Inshallah! I will tell you what befell me in my third voyage. The company marveled at his story and supped with him, after which he ordered a hundred dinars of gold to be given to the porter, who took the sum with many thanks and blessings (which he stinted not even when he reached home) and went his way, wondering at what he had heard. Next morning as soon as day came in its sheen and shone, he rose and, praying the dawn prayer, repaired to the house of Sindbad the Seaman, even as he had bidden him, and went in and gave him good morrow. The merchant welcomed him and made him sit with him till the rest of the company arrived, and when they had well eaten and drunken and were merry with joy and jollity, their host began by saying: Hearken, O my brothers, to what I am about to tell you, for it is even more wondrous than what you have already heard. But Allah alone kenneth what things His Omniscience concealed from man! And listen to

The Third Voyage of Sindbad the Seaman

As I told you yesterday, I returned from my second voyage overjoyed at my safety and with great increase of wealth, Allah having requited me all that I had wasted and lost, and I abode awhile in Baghdad city savoring the utmost ease and prosperity and comfort and happiness, till the carnal man was once more seized with longing for travel and diversion and adventure, and yearned after traffic and lucre and emolument, for that the human heart is naturally prone to evil. So, making up my mind, I laid in great plenty of goods suitable for a sea voyage and repairing to Bassorah, went down to the shore and found there a fine ship ready to sail, with a full crew and a numerous company of merchants, men of worth and substance, faith, piety, and consideration. I embarked with them and we set sail on the blessing of Allah Almighty and on His aidance and His favor to bring our voyage to a safe and prosperous issue, and already we congratulated one another on our good fortune and boon voyage.

We fared on from sea to sea and from island to island and city to city, in all delight and contentment, buying and selling wherever we touched, and taking our solace and our pleasure, till one day when as we sailed athwart the dashing sea swollen with clashing billows, behold, the master (who stood on the gunwale examining the ocean in all directions) cried out with a great cry, and buffeted his face and pluckt out his beard and rent his raiment, and bade furl the sail and cast the anchors. So we said to him, "O Rais, what is the matter?" "Know, O my brethren (Allah preserve you!) that the wind hath gotten the better of us and hath driven us out of our course into midocean, and Destiny, for our ill luck, hath brought us to the Mountain of the Zughb, a hairy folk like apes, among whom no man ever fell and came forth alive. And my heart presageth that we all be dead men."

Hardly had the master made an end of his speech when the apes were upon us. They surrounded the ship on all sides, swarming like locusts and crowding the shore. They were the most frightful of wild creatures, covered with black hair like felt, foul of favor and small of stature, being but four spans high, yellow-eyed and black-faced. None knoweth their language nor what they are, and they shun the company of men. We feared to slay them or strike them or drive them away, because of their inconceivable multitude, lest if we hurt one, the rest fall on us and slay us, for numbers prevail over courage. So we let them do their will, albeit we feared they would plunder our goods and gear. They swarmed up the cables and gnawed them asunder, and on like wise they did with all the ropes of the ship, so that if fell off from the wind and stranded upon their mountainous coast. Then they laid hands on all the merchants and crew, and landing us on the island, made off with the ship and its cargo and went their ways, we wot not whither.

We were thus left on the island, eating of its fruits and potherbs and drinking of its streams till one day we espied in its midst what seemed an inhabited house. So we made for it as fast as our feet could carry us and, behold, it was a castle strong and tall, compassed about with a lofty wall, and having a two-leaved gate of ebony wood, both of which leaves open stood. We entered and found within a space wide and bare like a great square, round which stood many high doors open thrown, and at the farther end a long bench of stone and braziers, with cooking gear hanging thereon and about it great Plenty of bones. But we saw no one and marveled thereat with exceeding wonder. Then we sat down in the courtyard a little while, and presently falling asleep, slept from the forenoon till sundown, when lo! the earth trembled under our feet and the air rumbled with a terrible tone.

Then there came down upon us, from the top of the castle, a huge creature in the likeness of a man, black of color, tall and big of bulk, as he were a great date tree, with eyes like coals of fire and eyeteeth like boar's tusks and a vast big gape like the mouth of a well. Moreover, he had long loose lips like camel's hanging down upon his breast, and ears like two jarms falling over his shoulder blades, and the nails of his hands were like the claws of a lion. When we saw this frightful giant, we were like to faint and every moment increased our fear and terror, and we became as dead men for excess of horror and affright. And after trampling upon the earth, he sat awhile on the bench. Then he arose and coming to us, seized me by the arm, choosing me out from among my comrades the merchants. He took me up in his hand and turning me over, felt me as a butcher feeleth a sheep he is about to slaughter, and I but a little mouthful in his hands. But finding me lean and fleshless for stress of toil and trouble and weariness, let me go and took up another, whom in like manner he turned over and felt and let go. Nor did he cease to feel and turn over the rest of us, one after another, till he came to the master of the ship.

Now he was a sturdy, stout, broad-shouldered wight, fat and in full vigor, so he pleased the giant, who seized him as a butcher seizeth a beast, and throwing him down, set his foot on his neck and brake it, after which he fetched a long spit and thrusting it up his backside, brought it forth of the crown of his head. Then, lighting a fierce fire, he set over it the spit with the rais thereon, and turned it over the coals till the flesh was roasted, when he took the spit off the fire and set it like a kobab stick before him. Then he tare the body, limb from limb, as one jointeth a chicken and, rending the fresh with his nails, fell to eating of it and gnawing the bones, till there was nothing left but some of these, which he threw on one side of the wall. This done, he sat for a while, then he lay down on the stone bench and fell asleep, snarking and snoring like the gurgling of a lamb or a cow with its throat cut, nor did he awake till morning, when he rose and fared forth and went his ways.

As soon as we were certified that he was gone, we began to

talk with one another, weeping and bemoaning ourselves for the risk we ran, and saying: "Would Heaven we had been drowned in the sea or that the apes had eaten us! That were better than to be roasted over the coals. By Allah, this is a vile, foul death! But whatso the Lord willeth must come-to pass, and there is no Majesty and there is no Might save in Him, the Glorious, the Great! We shall assuredly perish miserably and none will know of us, as there is no escape for us from this place." Then we arose and roamed about the island, hoping that haply we might find a place to hide us in or a means of flight, for indeed death was a light matter to us, provided we were not roasted over the fire and eaten. However, we could find no hiding place, and the evening overtook us, so, of the excess of our terror, we returned to the castle and sat down awhile.

Presently, the earth trembled under our feet and the black ogre came up to us and turning us over, felt one after other till he found a man to his liking, whom he took and served as he had done the captain, killing and roasting and eating him. After which he lay down on the bench and slept and night, snarling and snoring like a beast with its throat cut, till daybreak, when he arose and went out as before. Then we drew together and conversed and add one to other, "By Allah, we had better throw ourselves into the sea and be drowned than die roasted for this is an abominable death!" Quoth one of us: "Hear ye my words! Let us cast about to kill him, and be at peace from the grief of him and rid the Moslems of his barbarity and tyranny." Then said I: "Hear me, O my brothers. If there is nothing for it but to slay him, let us carry some of this firewood and planks down to the seashore and make us a boat wherein, if we succeed in slaughtering him, we may either embark and let the waters carry us whither Allah willeth, or else abide here till some ship pass, when we will take passage in it. If we fail to kill him, we will embark in the boat and put out to sea. And if we be drowned, we shall at least escape being roasted over a kitchen fire with sliced weasands, whilst if we escape, we escape, and if we be drowned, we die martyrs." "By Allah," said they all, "this rede is a right," and we agreed upon this, and set about carrying it out. So we haled down to the beach the pieces of wood which lay about the bench, and making a boat, moored it to the strand, after which we stowed therein somewhat of victual and returned to the castle.

As soon as evening fell the earth trembled under our feet and in came the blackamoor upon us, snarling like a dog about to bite. He came up to us, and feeling us and turning us over one by one, took one of us and did with him as he had done before and ate him, after which he lay down on the bench and snored and snorted like thunder. As soon as we were assured that he slept, we arose and taking two iron spits of those standing there, heated them in the fiercest of the fire till they were red-hot, like burning coals, when we gripped fast hold of them, and going up to the giant as he lay snoring on the bench, thrust them into his eyes and pressed upon them, all of us, with our united might, so that his eyeballs burst and he became stone-blind. Thereupon he cried with a great cry, whereat our hearts trembled, and springing up from the bench, he fell a-groping after us, blindfold. We fled from him right and left and he saw us not, for his sight was altogether blent, but we were in terrible fear of him and made sure we were dead men despairing of escape. Then he found the door, feeling for it with his hands, and went out roaring aloud, and behold, the earth shook under us for the noise of his roaring, and we quaked for fear. As he quitted the castle we followed him and betook ourselves to the place where we had moored our boat, saying to one another: "If this accursed abide absent till the going down of the sun and come not to the castle, we shall know that he is dead; and if he come back, we will embark in the boat and paddle till we escape, committing our affair to Allah."

But as we spoke, behold, up came the blackamoor with other two as they were Ghuls, fouler and more frightful than he, with eyes like red-hot coals, which when we saw, we hurried into the boat and casting off the moorings, paddled away, and pushed out to sea. As soon as the ogres caught sight of us, they cried out at us, and running down to the seashore, fell a-pelting us with rocks, whereof some fell amongst us and others fell into the sea. We paddled with all our might till we were beyond their reach, but the most part of us were slain by the rock-throwing, and the winds and waves sported with us and carried us into the midst of the dashing sea, swollen with billows clashing. We knew not whither we went, and my fellows died one after another till there remained but three, myself and two others, for as often as one died, we threw him into the sea. We were sore exhausted for stress of hunger, but we took courage and heartened one another and worked for dear life, and paddled with main and might till the winds cast us upon an island, as we were dead men for fatigue and fear and famine.

We landed on the island and walked about it for a while, finding that it abounded in trees and streams and birds, and we ate of the fruits and rejoiced in our escape from the black and our deliverance from the perils of the sea. And thus we did till nightfall, when we lay down and fell asleep for excess of fatigue. But we had hardly closed our eyes before we were aroused by a hissing sound, like the sough of wind, and awakening, saw a serpent like a dragon, a seldseen sight, of monstrous make and belly of enormous bulk, which lay in a circle around us. Presently it reared its head, and seizing one of my companions, swallowed him up to his shoulders. Then it gulped down the rest of him, and we heard his ribs crack in its belly. Presently it went its way, and we abode in sore amazement and grief for our comrade and mortal fear for ourselves, saying: "By Allah, this is a marvelous thing! Each kind of death that threateneth us is more terrible than the last We were rejoicing in our escape from the black ogre and our deliverance from the perils of the sea, but now we have fallen into that which is worse. There is no Majesty and there is no Might save in Allah! By the Almighty, we have escaped from the blackamoor and from drowning, but how shall we escape from this abominable and viperish monster?" Then we walked about the island, eating of its fruits and drinking of its streams till dusk, when we climbed up into a high tree and went to sleep there, I being on the topmost bough.

As soon as it was dark night, up came the serpent, looking right and left, and making for the tree whereon we were, climbed up to my comrade and swallowed him down to his shoulders. Then it coiled about the bole with him, whilst I, who could not take my eyes off the sight, heard his bones crack in its belly, and it swallowed him whole, after which it slid down from the tree. When the day broke and the light showed me that the serpent was gone, I came down, as I were a dead man for stress of fear and anguish, and thought to cast myself into the sea and be at rest from the woes of the world, but could not bring myself to this, for verily life is dear. So I took five pieces of wood, broad and long, and bound one crosswise to the soles of my feet and others in like fashion on my right and left sides and over my breast, and the broadest and largest I bound across my head and made them fast with ropes. Then I lay down on the ground on my back, so that I was completely fenced in by the pieces of wood, which enclosed me like a bier.

So as soon as it was dark, up came the serpent as usual, and made toward me, but could not get at me to swallow me for the wood that fenced me in. So it wriggled round me on every side whilst I looked on like one dead by reason of my terror, and every now and then it would glide away, and come back. But as often as it tried to come at me, it was hindered by the pieces of wood wherewith I had bound myself on every side. It ceased not to beset me thus from sundown till dawn, but when the light of day shone upon the beast it made off, in the utmost fury and extreme disappointment. Then I put out my hand and unbound myself, well-nigh down among the dead men for fear and suffering, and went down to the island shore, whence a ship afar off in the midst of the waves suddenly struck my sight. So I tore off a great branch of a tree and made signs with it to the crew, shouting out the while, which when the ship's company saw they said to one another: "We must stand in and see what this is. Peradventure 'tis a man." So they made for the island and presently heard my cries, whereupon they took me on board and questioned me of my case. I told them all my adventures from first to last, whereat they marveled mightily and covered my shame with some of their clothes. Moreover, they set before me somewhat of food and I ate my fill and I drank cold sweet water and was mightily refreshed, and Allah Almighty quickened me after I was virtually dead. So I praised the Most Highest and thanked Him for His favors and exceeding mercies, and my heart revived in me after utter despair, till meseemed as if all I had suffered were but a dream I had dreamed.

We sailed on with a fair wind the Almighty sent us till we came to an island called Al-Salahitah, which aboundeth in sandalwood, when the captain cast anchor. And when we had cast anchor, the merchants and the sailors landed with their goods to sell and to buy. Then the captain turned to me and said: "Hark'ee, thou art a stranger and a pauper and tellest us that thou hast undergone frightful hardships, wherefore I have a mind to benefit thee with somewhat that may further thee to thy native land, so thou wilt ever bless me and pray for me." "So be it," answered I. "Thou shalt have my prayers." Quoth he: "Know then that there was with us a man, a traveler, whom we lost, and we know not if he be alive or dead, for we had no news of him. So I purpose to commit his bales of goods to thy charge, that thou mayst sell them in this island. A part of the proceeds we will give thee as an equivalent for thy pains and service, and the rest we will keep till we return to Baghdad, where we will inquire for his family and deliver it to them, together with the unsold goods. Say me then, wilt thou undertake the charge and land and sell them as other merchants do?" I replied, "Hearkening and obedience to thee, O my lord, and great is thy kindness to me," and thanked him. Whereupon he bade the sailors and porters bear the bales in question ashore, and commit them to my charge.

The ship's scribe asked him, "O master, what bales are

these, and what merchant's name shall I write upon them?"
and he answered: "Write on them the name of Sindbad the
Seaman, him who was with us in the ship and whom we
lost at the roc's island, and of whom we have no tidings.
For we mean this stranger to sell them, and we will give
him a part of the price for his pains and keep the rest till we
return to Baghdad, where if we find the owner we will
make it over to him, and if not, to his family." And the
clerk said, "Thy words are apposite and thy rede is right."
Now when I heard the captain give orders for the bales to
be inscribed with my name, I said to myself, "By Allah, I
am Sindbad the Seaman!" So I armed myself with courage
and patience and waited till all the merchants had landed
and were gathered together, talking and chattering about
buying and selling. Then I went up to the captain and asked
him, "O my lord, knowest thou what manner of man was
this Sindbad whose goods thou hast committed to me for
sale?" and he answered, "I know of him naught save that he
was a man from Baghdad city, Sindbad hight the Seaman,
who was drowned with many others when we lay anchored
at such an island, and I have heard nothing of him since
then."

At this I cried out with a great cry and said: "O Captain,
whom Allah keep! know that I am that Sindbad the Seaman
and that I was not drowned, but when thou castest anchor at
the island, I landed with the rest of the merchants and crew.
And I sat down in a pleasant place by myself and ate
somewhat of food I had with me and enjoyed myself till I
became drowsy and was drowned in sleep. And when I
awoke, I found no ship, and none near me. These goods are
my goods and these bales are my bales, and all the
merchants who fetch jewels from the Valley of Diamonds

saw me there and will bear me witness that I am the very Sindbad the Seaman; for I related to them everything that had befallen me and told them how you forgot me and left me sleeping on the island, and that betided me which betided me." When the passengers and crew heard my words, they gathered about me and some of them believed me and others disbelieved, but presently, behold, one of the merchants, hearing me mention the Valley of Diamonds, came up to me and said to them: "Hear what I say, good people! When I related to you the most wonderful things in my travels, and I told you that at the time we cast down our slaughtered animals into the Valley of Serpents (I casting with the rest as was my wont), there came up a man hanging to mine, ye believed me not and live me the lie." "Yes," quoth they, "thou didst tell us some such tale, but we had no call to credit thee." He resumed: "Now this is the very man, by token that he gave me diamonds of great value and high price whose like are not to be found, requiting me more than would have come up sticking to my quarter of meat. And I companied with him to Bassorah city, where he took leave of us and went on to his native stead whilst we returned to our own land. This is he, and he told us his name, Sindbad the Seaman, and how the ship left him on the desert island. And know ye that Allah hath sent him hither, so might the truth of my story be made manifest to you. Moreover, these are his goods, for when he first forgathered with us, he told us of them; and the truth of his words is patent."

Hearing the merchant's speech, the captain came up to me and considered me straitly awhile, after which he said, "What was the mark on thy bales?" "Thus and thus," answered I, and reminded him of somewhat that had passed between him and me when I shipped with him from Bassorah. Thereupon he was convinced that I was indeed Sindbad the Seaman and took me round the neck and gave me joy of my safety, saying: "By Allah, O my lord, thy case is indeed wondrous and thy tale marvelous. But lauded be Allah Who hath brought thee and me together again, and Who hath restored to thee thy goods and gear!" Then I disposed of my merchandise to the best of my skill, and profited largely on them, whereat I rejoiced with exceeding joy and congratulated myself on my safety and the recovery of my goods. We ceased not to buy and sell at the several islands till we came to the land of Hind, where we bought cloves and ginger and all manner spices. And thence we fared on to the land of Sind, where also we bought and sold. In these Indian seas I saw wonders without number or count, amongst others a fish like a cow which bringeth forth its young and suckleth them like human beings, and of its skin bucklers are made. There were eke fishes like asses and camels and tortoises twenty cubits wide. And I saw also a bird that cometh out of a sea shell and layeth eggs and hatcheth her chicks on the surface of the water, never coming up from the sea to the land. Then we set sail again with a fair wind and the blessing of Almighty Allah, and after a prosperous voyage, arrived safe and sound at Bassorah. Here I abode a few days, and presently returned to Baghdad, where I went at once to my quarter and my house and saluted my family and familiars and friends. I had gained on this voyage what was beyond count and reckoning, so I gave alms and largess and clad the widow and orphan, by way of thanksgiving for my happy return, and fell to feasting and making merry with my companions and intimates and forgot while eating well and drinking well and dressing well everything that had befallen me and all the perils and hardships I had suffered.

These, then, are the most admirable things I sighted on my third voyage, and tomorrow, an it be the will of Allah, you shall come to me and I will relate the adventures of my fourth voyage, which is still more wonderful than those you have already heard. (Saith he who telleth the tale): Then Sindbad the Seaman bade give Sindbad the Landsman a hundred golden dinars as of wont, and called for food. So they spread the tables and the company ate the night meal and went their ways, marveling at the tale they had heard. The porter after taking his gold passed the night in his own house, also wondering at what his namesake the seaman had told him, and as soon as day broke and the morning showed with its sheen and shone, he rose and praying the dawn prayer, betook himself to Sindbad the Seaman, who returned his salute and received him with an open breast and cheerful favor and made him sit with him till the rest of the company arrived, when he caused set on food and they ate and drank and made merry. Then Sindbad the Seaman bespake them and related to them the narrative of

The Fourth Voyage of Sindbad the Seaman

Know, O my brethren, that after my return from my third voyage and forgathering with my friends, and forgetting all my perils and hardships in the enjoyment of ease and comfort and repose, I was visited one day by a company of merchants who sat down with me and talked of foreign travel and traffic till the old bad man within me yearned to go with them and enjoy the sight of strange countries, and I longed for the society of the various races of mankind and for traffic and profit. So I resolved to travel with them and, buying the necessaries for a long voyage and great store of costly goods, more than ever before, transported them from Baghdad to Bassorah, where I took ship with the merchants in question, who were of the chief of the town. We set out, trusting in the blessing of Almighty Allah, and with a favoring breeze and the best conditions we salled from island to island and sea to sea till one day there arose against us a contrary wind and the captain cast out his anchors and brought the ship to a standstill, fearing lest she should founder in midocean.

Then we all fell to prayer and humbling ourselves before the Most High, but as we were thus engaged there smote us a furious squall which tore the sails to rags and tatters. The anchor cable parted and, the ship foundering, we were cast into the sea, goods and all. I kept myself afloat by swimming half the day till, when I had given myself up for lost, the Almighty threw in my way one of the planks of the ship, whereon I and some others of the merchants scrambled and, mounting it as we would a horse, paddled with our feet in the sea. We abode thus a day and a night, the wind and waves helping us on, and on the second day shortly before the midtime between sunrise and noon the breeze freshened and the sea wrought and the rising waves cast us upon an island, well-nigh dead bodies for weariness and want of sleep, cold and hunger and fear and thirst. We walked about the shore and found abundance of herbs, whereof we ate enough to keep breath in body and to stay our failing spirits, then lay down and slept till morning hard by the sea. And when morning came with its sheen and shone, we arose and walked about the island to the right and left till we came in sight of an inhabited house afar off.

So we made toward it, and ceased not walking till we reached the door thereof when lo! a number of naked men issued from it, and without saluting us or a word said, laid hold of us masterfully and carried us to their King, who signed us to sit. So we sat down and they set food before us such as we knew not and whose like we had never seen in all our lives. My companions ate of it, for stress of hunger, but my stomach revolted from it and I would not eat, and my refraining from it was, by Allah's favor, the cause of my being alive till now. For no sooner had my comrades tasted of it than their reason fled and their condition changed and they began to devour it like madmen possessed of an evil spirit. Then the savages give them to drink of coconut oil and anointed them therewith, and straightway after drinking thereof their eyes turned into their heads and they fell to eating greedily, against their wont.

When I saw this, I was confounded, and concerned for them, nor was I less anxious about myself, for fear of the naked folk. So I watched them narrowly, and it was not long before I discovered them to be a tribe of Magian cannibals whose King was a Ghul. All who came to their country or whoso they caught in their valleys or on their roads they brought to this King and fed them upon that food and anointed them with that oil, whereupon their stomachs dilated that they might eat largely, wilst their reason fled and they lost the power of thought and became idiots. Then they stuffed them with coconut oil and the aforesaid food till they became fat and gross, when they slaughtered them by cutting their throats and roasted them for the King's eating, but as for the savages themselves, they ate human flesh raw. When I saw this, I was sore dismayed for myself and my comrades, who were now become so stupefied that they knew not what was done with them. And the naked folk committed them to one who used every day to lead them out and pasture them on the island like cattle. And they wandered amongst the trees and rested at will, thus waxing very fat.

As for me, I wasted away and became sickly for fear and hunger and my flesh shriveled on my bones, which when the savages saw, they left me alone and took no thought of me and so far forgot me that one day I gave them the slip and walking out of their place, made for the beach, which was distant, and there espied a very old man seated on a high place girt by the waters. I looked at him and knew him for the herdsman who had charge of pasturing my fellows, and with him were many others in like case. As soon as he saw me, he knew me to be in possession of my reason and not afflicted like the rest whom he was pasturing, so signed to me from afar, as who should say, "Turn back and take the right-hand road, for that will lead thee into the King's highway." So I turned back, as he bade me, and followed the right-hand road, now running for fear and then walking leisurely to rest me, till I was out of the old man's sight. By this time the sun had gone down and the darkness set in, so I sat down to rest and would have slept, but sleep came not to me that night for stress of fear and famine and fatigue.

When the night was half spent, I rose and walked on till the day broke in all its beauty and the sun rose over the heads of the lofty hills and athwart the low gravelly plains. Now I was weary and hungry and thirsty, so I ate my fill of herbs and grasses that grew in the island and kept life in body and stayed my stomach, after which I set out again and fared on all that day and the next night, staying my greed with roots and herbs. Nor did I cease walking for seven days and their

74

nights, till the morn of the eighth day, when I caught sight of a faint object in the distance. So I made toward it, though my heart quaked for all I had suffered first and last, and, behold, it was a company of men gathering pepper grains. As soon as they saw me, they hastened up to me and surrounding me on all sides, said to me, "Who art thou, and whence come?" I replied, "Know, O folk, that I am a poor stranger," and acquainted them with my case and all the hardships and perils I had suffered, whereat they marveled and gave me joy of my safety, saying: "By Allah, this is wonderful! But how didst thou escape from these blacks who swarm in the island and devour all who fall in with them, nor is any safe from them, nor can any get out of their clutches?"

And after I had told them the fate of my companions, they made me sit by them till they got quit of their work, and fetched me somewhat of good food, which I ate, for I was hungry, and rested awhile. After which they took ship with me and carrying me to their island home, brought me before their King, who returned my salute and received me honorably and questioned me of my case. I told him all that had befallen me from the day of my leaving Baghdad city, whereupon he wondered with great wonder at my adventures, he and his courtiers, and bade me sit by him. Then he called for food and I ate with him what sufficed me and washed my hands and returned thanks to Almighty Allah for all His favors, praising Him and glorifying Him. Then I left the King and walked for solace about the city, which I found wealthy and populous, abounding in market streets well stocked with food and merchandise and full of buyers and sellers. So I rejoiced at having reached so pleasant a place and took my ease there after my fatigues, and I made friends with the townsfolk, nor was it long before I became more in honor and favor with them and their King than any of the chief men of the realm.

Now I saw that all the citizens, great and small, rode fine horses, high-priced and thoroughbred, without saddles or housings, whereat I wondered and said to the King: "Wherefore, O my lord, dost thou not ride with a saddle? Therein is ease for the rider and increase of power." "What is a saddle?" asked he. "I never saw nor used such a thing in all my life." And I answered, "With thy permission I will make thee a saddle, that thou mayst ride on it and see the comfort thereof." And quoth he, "Do so." So quoth I to him, "Furnish me with some woods." which being brought, I sought me a clever carpenter and sitting by him, showed him how to make the saddletree, portraying for him the fashion thereof in ink on the wood. Then I took wool and teased it and made felt of it, and, covering the saddletree with leather, stuffed it, and polished it, and attached the girth and stirrup leathers. After which I fetched a blacksmith and described to him the fashion of the stirrups and bridle bit. So he forged a fine pair of stirrups and a bit, and filed them smooth and tinned them. Moreover, I made fast to them fringes of silk and fitted bridle leathers to the bit. Then I fetched one of the best of the royal horses and saddling and bridling him, hung the stirrups to the saddle and led him to the King. The thing took his fancy and he thanked me, then he mounted and rejoiced greatly in the saddle and rewarded me handsomely for my work.

When the King's Wazir saw the saddle, he asked of me one like it, and I made it for him. Furthermore, all the grandees and officers of state came for saddles to me, so I fell to making saddles (having taught the craft to the carpenter and blacksmith) and selling them to all who sought, till I amassed great wealth and became in high honor and great favor with the King and his household and grandees. I abode thus till one day, as I was sitting with the King in all respect and contentment, he said to me: "Know thou, O such a one, thou art become one of us, dear as a brother, and we hold thee in such regard and affection that we cannot part with thee nor suffer thee to leave our city. Wherefore I desire of thee obedience in a certain matter, and I will not have thee gainsay me." Answered I: "O King, what is it thou desirest of me? Far be it from me to gainsay thee in aught, for I am indebted to thee for many favors and bounties and much kindness, and (praised be Allah!) I am become one of thy servants." Quoth he: "I have a mind to marry thee to a fair, clever, and agreeable wife who is wealthy as she is beautiful, so thou mayest be naturalized and domiciled with us. I will lodge thee with me in my palace, wherefore oppose me not neither cross me in this." When I heard these words I was ashamed and held my peace nor could make him any answer, by reason of my much bashfulness before him. Asked he, "Why dost thou not reply to me, O my son?" and I answered, saying, "O my master, it is thine to command, O King of the Age!" So he summoned the kazi and the witnesses and married me straightway to a lady of a noble tree and high pedigree, wealthy in moneys and means, the flower of an ancient race, of surpassing beauty and grace, and the owner of farms and estates and many a dwelling place.

Now after the King my master had married me to this choice wife, he also gave me a great and goodly house standing alone, together with slaves and officers, and assigned me pay and allowances. So I became in all ease and contentment and delight and forgot everything which had befallen me of weariness and trouble and hardship. For I loved my wife with fondest love and she loved me no less, and we were as one, and abode in the utmost comfort of life and in its happiness. And I said in myself, "When I return to my native land, I will carry her with me." But whatso is predestined to a man, that needs must be, and none knoweth what shall befall him. We lived thus a great while, till Almighty Allah bereft one of my neighbors of his wife. Now he was a gossip of mine, so hearing the cry of the keeners, I went in to condole him on his loss and found him in very ill plight, full of trouble and weary of soul and mind. I condoled with him and comforted him, saying: "Mourn not for thy wife, who hath now found the mercy of Allah. The Lord will surely give thee a better in her stead, and thy name shall be great and thy life shall be long in the land, Inshallah!"

But he wept bitter tears and replied: "O my friend, how can I marry another wife, and how shall Allah replace her to me with a better than she, whenas I have but one day left to live?" "O my brother," said I, "return to thy senses and announce not glad tidings of thine own death, for thou art well, sound, and in good case." "By thy life, O my friend," rejoined he, "tomorrow thou wilt lose me, and wilt never see me again till the Day of Resurrection." I asked, "How so?" and he answered: "This very day they bury my wife, and they bury me with her in one tomb. For it is the custom with us, if the wife die first, to bury the husband alive with her, and in like manner the wife if the husband die first, so that neither may enjoy life after losing his or her mate." "By Allah," cried I, "this is a most vile, lewd custom, and not to be endured of any!" Meanwhile, behold, the most part of the townsfolk came in and fell to condoling with my gossip for his wife and for himself.

Presently they laid the dead woman out, as was their wont, and setting her on a bier, carried her and her husband without the city till they came to a place in the side of a mountain at the end of the island by the sea. And here they raised a great rock and discovered the mouth of a stone-riveted pit or well, leading down into a vast underground cavern that ran beneath the mountain. Into this pit they threw the corpse, then, tying a rope of palm fibers under the husband's armpits, they let him down into the cavern, and with him a great pitcher of fresh water and seven scones by way of viaticum. When he came to the bottom, he loosed himself from the rope and they drew it up, and stopping the mouth of the pit with the great stone, they returned to the city, leaving my friend in the cavern with his dead wife. When I saw this, I said to myself, "By Allah, this fashion of death is more grievous than the first!" And I went in to the King and said to him, "O my lord, why do ye bury the quick with the dead?" Quoth he: "It hath been the custom, thou must know, of our forebears and our olden kings from time immemorial, if the husband die first, to bury his wife with him, and the like with the wife, so we may not sever them, alive or dead." I asked, "O King of the Age, if the wife of a foreigner like myself die among you, deal ye with him as with yonder man?" and he answered, "Assuredly we do with him even as thou hast seen." When I heard this, my gall bladder was like to burst, for the violence of my dismay and concern for myself. My wit became dazed, I felt as if in a vile dungeon, and hated their society, for I went about in fear lest my wife should die before me and they bury me alive with her. However, after a while I comforted myself, saying, "Haply I shall predecease her, or shall have returned to my own land before she die, for none knoweth which shall go first and which shall go last."

Then I applied myself to diverting my mind from this thought with various occupations, but it was not long before my wife sickened and complained and took to her pillow and fared after a few days to the mercy of Allah. And the King and the rest of the folk came, as was their wont, to condole with me and her family and to console us for her loss, and not less to condole with me for myself. Then the women washed her, and arraying her in her richest raiment and golden ornaments, necklaces, and jewelry, laid her on the bier and bore her to the mountain aforesaid, where they lifted the cover of the pit and cast her in. After which all my intimates and acquaintances and my wife's kith and kin came round me, to farewell me in my lifetime and console me for my own death, whilst I cried out among them, saying: "Almighty Allah never made it lawful to bury the quick with the dead! I am a stranger, not one of your kind, and I cannot abear your custom, and had I known it I never would have wedded among you!" They heard me not and paid no heed to my words, but laying hold of me, bound me by force and let me down. into the cavern, with a large gugglet of sweet water and seven cakes of bread, according to their custom. When I came to the bottom, they called out to me to cast myself loose from the cords, but I refused to do so, so they threw them down on me and, closing the mouth of the pit with the stones aforesaid, went their ways.

I looked about me and found myself in a vast cave full of dead bodies that exhaled a fulsome and loathsome smell, and the air was heavy with the groans of the dying.

Thereupon I fell to blaming myself for what I had done, saying: "By Allah, I deserve all that hath befallen me and all that shall befall me! What curse was upon me to take a wife in this city? There is no Majesty and there is no Might save in Allah, the Glorious, the Great! As often as I say I have escaped from one calamity, I fall into a worse. By Allah, this is an abominable death to die! Would Heaven I had died a decent death and been washed and shrouded like a man and a Moslem. Would I had been drowned at sea, or perished in the mountains! It were better than to die this miserable death!" And on such wise I kept blaming my own folly and greed of gain in that black hole, knowing not night from day, and I ceased not to ban the Foul Fiend and to bless the Almighty Friend. Then I threw myself down on the bones of the dead and lay there, imploring Allah's help, and in the violence of my despair invoking death, which came not to me, till the fire of hunger burned my stomach and thirst set my throat aflame, when I sat up and feeling for the bread, ate a morsel and upon it swallowed a mouthful of water.

After this, the worst night I ever knew, I arose, and exploring the, cavern, found that it extended a long way with hollows in its sides, and its floor was strewn with dead bodies and rotten bones that had lain there from olden time. So I made myself a place in a cavity of the cavern, afar from the corpses lately thrown down, and there slept. I abode thus a long while, till my provision was like to give out, and yet I ate not save once every day or second day, nor did I drink more than an occasional draught, for fear my victual should fail me before my death. And I said to myself: "Eat little and drink little. Belike the Lord shall vouchsafe deliverance to thee!" One day as I sat thus, pondering my case and bethinking me how I should do when my bread and water should be exhausted, behold, the stone that covered the opening was suddenly rolled away and the light streamed down upon me. Quoth I: "I wonder what is the matter. Haply they have brought another corpse." Then I espied folk standing about the mouth of the pit, who presently let down a dead man and a live woman, weeping and bemoaning herself, and with her an ampler supply of bread and water than usual. I saw her and she was a beautiful woman, but she saw me not. And they closed up the opening and went away. Then I took the leg bone of a dead man and, going up to the woman, smote her on the crown of the head, and she cried one cry and fell down in a swoon. I smote her a second and a third time, till she was dead, when I laid hands on her bread and water and found on her great plenty of ornaments and rich apparel, necklaces, jewels and gold trinkets, for it was their custom to bury women in all their finery. I carried the vivers to my sleeping place in the cavern side and ate and drank of them sparingly, no more than sufficed to keep the life in me, lest the provaunt come speedily to an end and I perish of hunger and thirst.

Yet did I never wholly lose hope in Almighty Allah. I abode thus a great while, killing all the live folk they let down into the cavern and taking their provisions of meat and drink, till one day, as I slept, I was awakened by something scratching and burrowing among the bodies in a corner of the cave and said, "What can this be?" fearing wolves or hyenas. So I sprang up, and seizing the leg bone aforesaid, made for the noise. As soon as the thing was ware of me, it fled from me into the inward of the cavern, and lo! it was a wild beast. However, I followed it to the further end, till I saw afar off a point of light not bigger than a star, now appearing and then disappearing. So I made for it, and as I drew near, it grew larger and brighter, till I was certified that it was a crevice in the rock, leading to the open country, and I said to myself: "There must be some reason for this opening. Either it is the mouth of a second pit such as that by which they let me down, or else it is a natural fissure in the stonery." So I bethought me awhile, and nearing the light, found that it came from a breach in the back side of the mountain, which the wild beasts had enlarged by burrowing, that they might enter and devour the dead and freely go to and from. When I saw this, my spirits revived and hope came back to me and I made sure of life, after having died a death. So I went on, as in a dream, and making shift to scramble through the breach, found myself on the slope of a high mountain overlooking the salt sea and cutting off all access thereto from the island, so that none could come at that part of the beach from the city. I praised my Lord and thanked Him, rejoicing greatly and heartening myself with the prospect of deliverance.

Then I returned through the crack to the cavern and brought out all the food and water I had saved up, and donned some of the dead folk's clothes over my own. After which I gathered together all the collars and necklaces of pearls and jewels and trinkets of gold and silver set with precious stones and other ornaments and valuables I could find upon the corpses, and making them into bundles with the graveclothes and raiment of the dead, carried them out to the back of the mountain facing the seashore, where I established myself, purposing to wait there till it should please Almighty Allah to send me relief by means of some passing ship. I visited the cavern daily, and as often as I found folk buried alive there, I killed them all indifferently, men and women, and took their victual and valuables and transported them to my seat on the seashore.

Thus I abode a long while till one day I caught sight of a ship passing in the midst of the clashing sea swollen with dashing billows. So I took a piece of a white shroud I had with me, and tying it to a staff, ran along the seashore making signals therewith and calling to the people in the ship, till they espied me, and hearing my shouts, sent a boat to fetch me off. When it drew near, the crew called out to me, saying, "Who art thou, and how camest thou to be on this mountain, whereon never saw we any in our born days?" I answered: "I am a gentleman and a merchant who hath been wrecked and saved myself on one of the planks of the ship, with some of my goods. And by the blessing of the Almighty and the decrees of Destiny and my own strength and skill, after much toil and moil I have landed with my gear in this place, where I awaited some passing ship to take me off." So they took me in their boat, together with the bundles I had made of the jewels and valuables from the cavern, tied up in clothes and shrouds, and rowed back with me to the ship, where the captain said to me: "How camest thou, O man, to yonder place on yonder mountain behind which lieth a great city? All my life I have sailed these seas and passed to and fro hard by these heights, yet never saw I here any living thing save wild beasts and birds." I repeated to him the story I had told the sailors, but acquainted him with nothing of that which had befallen me in the city and the cavern, lest there should be any of the islandry in the ship.

Then I took out some of the best pearls I had with me and offered them to the captain, saying: "O my lord, thou hast been the means of saving me off this mountain. I have no ready money, but take this from me in requital of thy kindness and good offices.-But he refused to accept it of me, saying: "When we find a shipwrecked man on the seashore or on an island, we take him up and give him meat and drink, and if he be naked we clothe him, nor take we aught from him- nay, when we reach a port of safety, we set him ashore with a present of our own money and entreat him kindly and charitably, for the love of Allah the Most High." So I prayed that his life be long in the land and rejoiced in my escape, trusting to be delivered from my stress and to forget my past mishaps, for every time I remembered being let down into the cave with my dead wife I shuddered in horror.

Then we pursued our voyage and sailed from island to island and sea to sea till we arrived at the Island of the Bell which containeth a city two days' journey in extent, whence after a six days' ran we reached the Island Kala, hard by the land of Hind. This place is govemed by a potent and puissant King, and it produceth excellent camphor and an abundance of the Indian rattan. Here also is a lead mine. At last by the decree of Allah we arrived in safety at Bassorah town, where I tarried a few days, then went on to Baghdad city, and finding my quarter, entered my house with lively pleasure. There I forgathered with my family and friends, who rejoiced in my happy return and give me joy of my safety. I laid up in my storehouses all the goods I had brought with me, and gave alms and largess to fakirs and beggars and clothed the widow and the orphan. Then I gave myself up to pleasure and enjoyment, returning to my old merry mode of rife.

Such, then, be the most marvelous adventures of my fourth

voyage, but tomorrow, if you will kindly come to me, I will tell you that which befell me in my fifth voyage, which was yet rarer and more marvelous than those which forewent it. And thou, O my brother Sindbad the Landsman, shalt sup with me as thou art wont. (Saith he who telleth the tale): When Sindbad the Seaman had made an end of his story, he called for supper, so they spread the table and the guests ate the evening meal, after which he gave the porter a hundred dinars as usual, and he and the rest of the company went their ways, glad at heart and marveling at the tales they had heard, for that each story was more extraordinary than that which forewent it. The porter Sindbad passed the night in his own house, in all joy and cheer and wonderment, and as soon as morning came with its sheen and shone, he prayed the dawn prayer and repaired to the house of Sindbad the Seaman, who welcomed him and bade him sit with him till the rest of the company arrived, when they ate and drank and made merry and the talk went round amongst them. Presently, their host began the narrative of

The Fifth Voyage of Sindbad the Seaman

Know, O my brothers, that when I had been awhile on shore after my fourth voyage, and when, in my comfort and pleasures and merrymakings and in my rejoicing over my large gains and profits, I had forgotten all I had endured of perils and sufferings, the carnal man was again seized with the longing to travel and to see foreign countries and islands. Accordingly I bought costly merchandise suited to my purpose and, making it up into bales, repaired to Bassorah, where I walked about the river quay till I found a fine tall ship, newly builded, with gear unused and fitted ready for sea. She pleased me, so I bought her and, embarking my goods in her, hired a master and crew, over whom I set certain of my slaves and servants as inspectors. A number of merchants also brought their outfits and paid me freight and passage money. Then, after reciting the fatihah, we set sail over Allah's pool in all joy and cheer, promising ourselves a prosperous voyage and much profit.

We sailed from city to city and from island to island and from sea to sea viewing the cities and countries by which we passed, and selling and buying in not a few, till one day we came to a great uninhabited island, deserted and desolate, whereon was a white dome of biggest bulk half buried in the sands. The merchants landed to examine this dome, leaving me in the ship, and when they drew near, behold, it was a huge roc's egg. They fell a-beating it with stones, knowing not what it was, and presently broke it open, whereupon much water ran out of it and the young roc appeared within. So they pulled it forth of the shell and cut its throat and took of it great store of meat. Now I was in the ship and knew not what they did, but presently one of the passengers came up to me and said, "O my lord, come and look at the egg that we thought to be a dome." So I looked, and seeing the merchants beating it with stones, called out to them: "Stop, stop! Do not meddle with that egg, or the bird roc will come out and break our ship and destroy us." But they paid no heed to me and gave not over smiting upon the egg, when behold, the day grew dark and dun and the sun was hidden from us, as if some great cloud had passed over the firmament. So we raised our eyes and saw that what we took for a cloud was the roc poised between us and the sun, and it was his wings that darkened the day. When he came and saw his egg broken, he cried a loud cry, whereupon his mate came flying up and they both began circling about the ship, crying out at us with voices louder than thunder. I called to the rais and crew, "Put out to sea and seek safety in flight, before we be all destroyed!" So the merchants came on board and we cast off and made haste from the island to gain the open sea.

When the rocs saw this, they flew off, and we crowded all sail on the ship, thinking to get out of their country, but presently the two reappeared and flew after us and stood over us, each carrying in its claws a huge boulder which it had brought from the mountains. As soon as the he-roc came up with us, he let fall upon us the rock he held in his pounces, but the master put about ship, so that the rock missed her by some small matter and plunged into the waves with such violence that the ship pitched high and then sank into the trough of the sea, and the bottom the ocean appeared to us. Then the she-roc let fall her rock, which was bigger than that of her mate, and as Destiny had decreed, it fell on the poop of the ship and crushed it, the rudder flying into twenty pieces. Whereupon the vessel foundered and all and everything on board were cast into the main. As for me, I struggled for sweet life till Almighty Allah threw in my way one of the planks of the ship, to which I clung and bestriding it, fell a-paddling with my feet. Now the ship had gone down hard by an island in the midst of the main, and the winds and waves bore me on till, by permission of the Most High, they cast me up on the shore of the island, at the last gasp for toil and distress and half-dead with hunger and thirst. So I landed more like a corpse than a live man, and throwing myself down on the beach, lay there awhile till I began to revive and recover spirits, when I walked about the island, and found it as it were one of the garths and gardens of Paradise. Its trees, in abundance dight, bore ripe-yellow fruit for freight, its streams ran clear and bright, its flowers were fair to scent and to sight, and its birds warbled with delight the praises of Him to whom belong Permanence and All-might. So I ate my fill of the fruits and slaked my thirst with the water of the streams till I could no more, and I returned thanks to the Most High and glorified Him, after which I sat till nightfall hearing no voice and seeing none inhabitant. Then I lay down, well-nigh dead for travail and trouble and terror, and slept without surcease till morning, when I arose and walked about under the trees till I came to the channel of a draw well fed by a spring of running water, by which well sat an old man of venerable aspect, girt about with a waistcloth made of the fiber of palm fronds. Quoth I to myself. "Haply this Sheikh is of those who were wrecked in the ship and hath made his way to this island."

So I drew near to him and saluted him, and he returned my salaam by signs, but spoke not, and I said to him, "O nuncle mine, what causeth thee to sit here?" He shook his head and moaned and signed to me with his hand as who should say, "Take me on thy shoulders and carry me to the other side of the well channel." And quoth I in my mind: "I will deal kindly with him and do what he desireth. It may be I shall win me a reward in Heaven, for he may be a paralytic." So I took him on my back, and carrying him to the place whereat he pointed, said to him, "Dismount at thy leisure." But he would not get off my back, and wound his legs about my neck. I looked at them, and seeing that they were like a buffalo's hide for blackness and roughness, was affrighted and would have cast him off, but he clung to me and gripped my neck with his legs till I was well-nigh choked, the world grew black in my sight and I fell senseless to the ground like one dead. But he still kept his seat and raising his legs, drummed with his heels and beat harder than palm rods my back and shoulders, till he forced me to rise for excess of pain. Then he signed to me with his hand to carry him hither and thither among the trees which bore the best fruits, and if ever I refused to do his bidding or loitered or took my leisure, he beat me with his feet more grievously than if I had been beaten with whips. He ceased not to signal with his hand wherever he was minded to go, so I carried him about the island, like a captive slave, and he dismounted not night or day. And whenas he wished to sleep, he wound his legs about my neck and leaned back and slept awhile, then arose and beat me, whereupon I sprang up in haste, unable to gainsay him because of the pain he inflicted on me. And indeed I blamed myself and sore repented me of having taken compassion on him, and continued in this condition, suffering fatigue not to be described, till I said to myself: "I wrought him a weal and he requited me with my ill. By Allah, never more will I do any man a service so long as I live!" And again and again I besought the Most High that I might die, for stress of weariness and misery.

And thus I abode a long while till one day I came with him to a place wherein was abundance of gourds, many of them dry. So I took a great dry gourd and cutting open the head, scooped out the inside and cleaned it, after which I gathered grapes from a vine which grew hard by and squeezed them into the gourd till it was full of the juice. Then I stopped up the mouth and set it in the sun, where I left it for some days until it became strong wine, and every day I used to drink of it, to comfort and sustain me under my fatigues with that froward and obstinate fiend. And as often as I drank myself drunk, I forgot my troubles and took new heart. One day he saw me and signed to me with his hand, as who should say, "What is that?" Quoth I, "It is an excellent cordial, which cheereth the heart and reviveth the spirits." Then, being heated with wine, I ran and danced with him among the trees, clapping my hands and singing and making merry, and I staggered under him by design.

When he saw this, he signed to me to give him the gourd that he might drink, and I feared him and gave it him. So he took it, and draining it to the dregs, cast it on the ground, whereupon he grew frolicsome and began to clap hands and jig to and fro on my shoulders, and he made water upon me so copiously that all my dress was drenched. But presently, the fumes of the wine rising to his head, he became helplessly drunk and his side muscles and limbs relaxed and he swayed to and fro on my back. When I saw that he had lost his senses for drunkenness, I put my hand to his legs and, loosing them from my neck, stooped down well-nigh to the ground and threw him at full length. Then I took up a great stone from among the trees and coming up to him, smote him therewith on the head with all my might and crushed in his skull as he lay dead-drunk. Thereupon his flesh and fat and blood being in a pulp, he died and went to his deserts, The Fire, no mercy of Allah be upon him!

I then returned, with a heart at ease, to my former station on the seashore, and abode in that island many days, eating of its fruits and drinking of its waters and keeping a lookout for passing ships, till one day, as I sat on the beach recalling all that had befallen me and saying, "I wonder if Allah will save me alive and restore me to my home and family and friends!" behold, a ship was making for the island through the dashing sea and clashing waves. Presently it cast anchor and the passengers landed, so I made for them, and when they saw me all hastened up to me and gathering round me, questioned me of my case and how I came thither. I told them all that had betided me, whereat they marveled with exceeding marvel and said: "He who rode on thy shoulder is called the Sheikh-al-Bahr or Old Man of the Sea, and none ever felt his legs on neck and came off alive but thou, and those who die under him he eateth. So praised be Allah for thy safety!" Then they set somewhat of food before me, whereof I ate my fill, and gave me somewhat of clothes, wherewith I clad myself anew and covered my nakedness. After which they took me up into the ship and we sailed days and nights till Fate brought us to a place called the City of Apes, builded with lofty houses, all of which gave upon the sea, and it had a single gate studded and strengthened with iron nails.

Now every night as soon as it is dusk the dwellers in this city used to come forth of the gates and, putting out to sea in boats and ships, pass the night upon the waters in their fear lest the apes should come down on them from the mountains. Hearing this, I was sore troubled, remembering what I had before suffered from the ape kind. Presently I landed to solace myself in the city, but meanwhile the ship set sail without me, and I repented of having gone ashore, and calling to mind my companions and what had befallen me with the apes, first and after, sat down and fell aweeping and lamenting. Presently one of the townsfolk accosted me and said to me, "O my lord, meseemeth thou art a stranger to these parts?" "Yes," answered I, "I am indeed a stranger and a poor one, who came hither in a ship which cast anchor here, and I landed to visit the town. But when I would have gone on board again, I found they had sailed without me." Quoth he, "Come and embark with us, for if thou lie the night in the city, the apes will destroy thee." "Hearkening and obedience," replied I, and rising, straightway embarked with him in one of the boats, whereupon they pushed off from shore, and anchoring a mile or so from the land, there passed the night. At daybreak they rowed back to the city, and landing, went each about his business. Thus they did every night, for if any tarried in the town by night the apes came down on him and slew him. As soon as it was day, the apes left the place and ate of the fruits of the gardens, then went back to the mountains and slept there till nightfall, when they again came down upon the city.

Now this place was in the farthest part of the country of the blacks, and one of the strangest things that befell me during my sojourn in the city was on this wise. One of the company with whom I passed the night in the boat asked me: "O my lord, thou art apparently a stranger in these parts. Hast thou any craft whereat thou canst work?" and I answered: "By Allah, O my brother, I have no trade nor know I any handicraft, for I was a merchant and a man of money and substance and had a ship of my own, laden with great store of goods and merchandise. But it foundered at sea and all were drowned excepting me, who saved myself on a piece of plank which Allah vouchsafed to me of His favor."

Upon this he brought me a cotton bag and giving it to me, said: "Take this bag and fill it with pebbles from the beach and go forth with a company of the townsfolk to whom I will give a charge respecting thee. Do as they do and belike thou shalt gain what may further thy return voyage to thy native land." Then he carried me to the beach, where I filled my bag with pebbles large and small, and presently we saw a company of folk issue from the town, each bearing a bag like mine, filled with pebbles. To these he committed me, commending me to their care, and saying: "This man is a stranger, so take him with you and teach him how to gather, that he may get his daily bread, and you will earn your reward and recompense in Heaven." "On our head and eyes be it!" answered they, and bidding me welcome, fared on with me till we came to a spacious wady, full of lofty trees with trunks so smooth that none might climb them.

Now sleeping under these trees were many apes, which when they saw us rose and fled from us and swarmed up among the branches, whereupon my companions began to pelt them with what they had in their bags, and the apes fell to plucking of the fruit of the trees and casting them at the folk. I looked at the fruits they cast at us and found them to be Indian or coconuts, so I chose out a great tree full of apes, and going up to it, began to pelt them with stones, and they in return pelted me with nuts, which I collected, as did the rest. So that even before I had made an end of my bagful of pebbles, I had gotten great plenty of nuts. And as soon as my companions had in like manner gotten as many nuts as they could carry, we returned to the city, where we arrived at the fag end of day. Then I went in to the kindly man who had brought me in company with the nut-gatherers and gave him all I had gotten, thanking him for his kindness, but he would not accept them, saying, "Sell them and make profit by the price," and presently he added (giving me the key of a closet in his house): "Store thy nuts in this safe place and go thou forth every morning and gather them as thou hast done today, and choose out the worst for sale and supplying thyself; but lay up the rest here, so haply thou mayst collect enough to serve thee for thy return home." "Allah requite thee!" answered I, and did as he advised me, going out daily with the coconut gatherers, who commended me to one another and showed me the best-stocked trees. Thus did I for some time, till I had laid up great store of excellent nuts, besides a large sum of money, the price of those I had sold. I became thus at my ease and bought all I saw and had a mind to, and passed my time pleasantly, greatly enjoying my stay in the city, till as I stood on the beach one day a great ship steering through the heart of the sea presently cast anchor by the shore and landed a company of merchants, who proceeded to sell and buy and barter their goods for coconuts and other commodities.

Then I went to my friend and told him of the coming of the ship and how I had a mind to return to my own country, and he said, " 'Tis for thee to decide." So I thanked him for his bounties and took leave of him. Then, going to the captain of the ship, I agreed with him for my passage and embarked my coconuts and what else I possessed. We weighed anchor the same day and sailed from island to island and sea to sea, and whenever we stopped, I sold and traded with my coconuts, and the Lord requited me more than I erst had and lost.

Amongst other places, we came to an island abounding in cloves and cinnamon and pepper, and the country people told me that by the side of each pepper bunch groweth a great leaf which shadeth it from the sun and casteth the water off it in the wet season; but when the rain ceaseth, the leaf turneth over and droopeth down by the side of the bunch. Here I took in great store of pepper and cloves and cinnamon, in exchange for coconuts, and we passed thence to the Island of Al-Usirat, whence cometh the Comorin aloes wood, and thence to another island, five days' journey in length, where grows the Chinese lign aloes, which is better than the Comorin. But the people of this island are fouler of condition and religion than those of the other, for that they love fornication and wine bibbing, and know not prayer nor call to prayer.

Thence we came to the pearl fisheries, and I gave the divers some of my coconuts and said to them, "Dive for my luck and lot!" They did so and brought up from the deep bright great store of large and priceless pearls, and they said to me, "By Allah, O my master, thy luck is a lucky!" Then we sailed on, with the blessing of Allah (Whose name be exalted!), and ceased not sailing till we arrived safely at Bassorah. There I abode a little and then went on to Baghdad, where I entered my quarter and found my house and forgathered with my family and saluted my friends, who gave me joy of my safe return, and I laid up all my goods and valuables in my storehouses. Then I distributed alms and largess and clothed the widow and the orphan and made presents to my relations and comrades, for the Lord had requited me fourfold that I had lost. After which I returned to my old merry way of life and forgot all I had suffered in the great profit and gain I had made.

Such, then, is the history of my fifth voyage and its wonderments, and now to supper, and tomorrow, come again and I will tell you what befell me in my sixth voyage, for it was still more wonderful than this. (Saith he who telleth the tale): Then he called for food, and the servants spread the table, and when they had eaten the evening meal, he bade give Sindbad the Porter a hundred golden dinars and the landsman returned home and lay him down to sleep, much marveling at all he had heard. Next morning, as soon as it was light, he prayed the dawn prayer, and, after blessing Mohammed the Cream of all creatures, betook himself to the house of Sindbad the Seaman and wished him a good day. The merchant bade him sit, and talked with him till the rest of the company arrived. Then the servants spread the table, and when they had well eaten and drunken and were mirthful and merry, Sindbad the Seaman began in these words the narrative of

The Sixth Voyage of Sindbad the Seaman

Know, O my brothers and friends and companions all, that I abode some time, after my return from my fifth voyage, in great solace and satisfaction and mirth and merriment, joyance and enjoyment, and I forgot what I had suffered, seeing the great gain and profit I had made, till one day as I sat making merry and enjoying myself with my friends, there came in to me a company of merchants whose case told tales of travel, and talked with me of voyage and adventure and greatness of pelf and lucre. Hereupon I remembered the days of my return abroad, and my joy at once more seeing my native land and forgathering with my family and friends, and my soul yearned for travel and traffic. So, compelled by Fate and Fortune, I resolved to undertake another voyage, and, buying me fine and costly merchandise meet for foreign trade, made it up into bales, with which I journeyed from Baghdad to Bassorah. Here I found a great ship ready for sea and full of merchants and notables, who had with them goods of price, so I embarked my bales therein. And we left Bassorah in safety and good spirits under the safeguard of the King, the Preserver, and continued our voyage from place to place and from city to city, buying and selling and profiting and diverting ourselves with the sight of countries where strange folk dwell. And Fortune and the voyage smiled upon us till one day, as we went along, behold, the captain suddenly cried with a great cry and cast his turban on the deck. Then he buffeted his face like a woman and plucked out his beard and fell down in the waist of the ship well-nigh fainting for stress of grief and rage, and crying, "Oh, and alas for the ruin of my house and the orphanship of my poor children!" So all the merchants and sailors came round about him and asked him, "O master, what is the matter?" For the light had become night before, their sight. And he answered, saying: "Know, O folk, that we have wandered from our course and left the sea whose ways we wot, and come into a sea whose ways I know not, and unless Allah vouchsafe us a means of escape, we are all dead men. Wherefore pray ye to the Most High that He deliver us from this strait. Haply amongst you is one righteous whose prayers the Lord will accept." Then he arose and clomb the mast to see an there were any escape from that strait. And he would have loosed the sails, but the wind redoubled upon the ship and whirled her round thrice and drave her backward, whereupon her rudder brake and she fell off toward a high mountain.

With this the captain came down from the mast, saying: "There is no Majesty and there is no Might save in Allah, the Glorious, the Great, nor can man prevent that which is foreordained of Fate! By Allah, we are fallen on a place of sure destruction, and there is no way of escape for us, nor can any of us be saved!" Then we all fill a-weeping over ourselves and bidding one another farewell for that our days were come to an end, and we had lost an hopes of life. Presently the ship struck the mountain and broke up, and all and everything on board of her were plunged into the sea. Some of the merchants were drowned and others made shift to reach the shore and save themselves upon the mountain, I amongst the number. And when we got ashore, we found a great island, or rather peninsula, whose base was strewn with wreckage and crafts and goods and gear cast up by the sea from broken ships whose passengers had been drowned, and the quantity confounded count and calculation. So I climbed the cliffs into the inward of the isle and walked on inland till I came to a stream of sweet water that welled up at the nearest foot of the mountains and disappeared in the earth under the range of hills on the opposite side. But all the other passengers went over the mountains to the inner tracts, and, dispersing hither and thither, were confounded at what they saw and became like madmen at the sight of the wealth and treasures wherewith the shores were strewn. As for me, I looked into the bed of the stream aforesaid and saw therein great plenty of rubies, and great royal pearls and all kinds of jewels and precious stones, which were as gravel in the bed of the rivulets that ran through the fields, and the sands sparkled and glittered with gems and precious ores. Moreover, we found in the island abundance of the finest lign aloes, both Chinese and Comorin. And there also is a spring of crude ambergris, which floweth like wax or gum over the stream banks, for the great heat of the sun, and runneth down to the seashore, where the monsters of the deep come up and, swallowing it, return into the sea.

But it burneth in their bellies, so they cast it up again and it congealeth on the surface of the water, whereby its color and quantities are changed, and at last the waves cast it ashore, and the travelers and merchants who know it collect it and sell it. But as to the raw ambergris which is not swallowed, it floweth over the channel and congealeth on the banks, and when the sun shineth on it, it melteth and scenteth the whole valley with a musk-like fragrance. Then when the sun ceaseth from it, it congealeth again. But none can get to this place where is the crude ambergris, because of the mountains which enclose the island on all sides and which foot of man cannot ascend.

We continued thus to explore the island, marveling at the wonderful works of Allah and the riches we found there, but sore troubled for our own case, and dismayed at our prospects. Now we had picked up on the beach some small matter of victual from the wreck and husbanded it carefully eating but once every day or two, in our fear lest it should fail us and we die miserably of famine and affright. Moreover, we were weak for colic brought on by seasickness and low diet, and my companions deceased, one after other, till there was but a small company of us left. Each that died we washed and shrouded in some of the clothes and linen cast ashore by the tides, and after a little, the rest of my fellows perished one by one, till I had buried the last of the party and abode alone on the island, with but a little provision left, I who was wont to have so much. And I wept over myself, saying: "Would Heaven I had died before my companions and they had washed me and buried me! It had been better than I should perish and none wash me and shroud me and bury me. But there is no Majesty and there is no Might save in Allah, the glorious, the

Great!" Now after I had buried the last of my party and abode alone on the island, I arose and dug me a deep grave on the seashore, saying to myself: "Whenas I grow weak and know that death cometh to me, I will cast myself into the grave and die there, so the wind may drift the sand over me and cover me and I be buried therein."

Then I fell to reproaching myself for my little wit in leaving my native land and betaking me again to travel after all I had suffered during my first five voyages, and when I had not made a single one without suffering more horrible perils and more terrible hardships than in its forerunners, and having no hope of escape from my present stress. And I repented me of my folly and bemoaned myself, especially as I had no need of money, seeing that I had enough and could not spend what I had- no, nor a half of it in all my life. However, after a while Allah sent me a thought, and I said to myself: "By God, needs must this stream have an end as well as a beginning, ergo an issue somewhere, and belike its course may lead to some inhabited place. So my best plan is to make me a little boat big enough to sit in, and carry it and, launching it on the river, embark therein and drop down the stream. If I escape, I escape, by God's leave, and if I perish, better die in the river than here." Then, sighing for myself, I set to work collecting a number of pieces of Chinese and Comorin aloes wood and I bound them together with ropes from the wreckage. Then I chose out from the broken-up ships straight planks of even size and fixed them firmly upon the aloes wood, making me a boat raft a little narrower than the channel of the stream, and I tied it tightly and firmly as though it were nailed. Then I loaded it with the goods, precious ores and jewels, and the union pearls which were like gravel, and the best of the ambergris crude and pure, together with what I had collected on the island and what was left me of victual and wild herbs. Lastly I lashed a piece of wood on either side, to serve me as oars, and launched it, and embarking, did according to the saying of the poet:

Fly, fly with life whenas evils threat,
Leave the house to tell of its builder's fate!
Land after land shalt thou seek and find,
But no other life on thy wish shall wait.
Fret not thy soul in thy thoughts o' night,
All woes shall end or sooner or late.
Whoso is born in one land to die,
There and only there shall gang his pit.
Nor trust great things to another wight,
Soul hath only soul for confederate.

My boat raft drifted with the stream, I pondering the issue of my affair, and the drifting ceased not till I came to the place where it disappeared beneath the mountain. I rowed my conveyance into the place, which was intensely dark, and the current carried the raft with it down the underground channel. The thin stream bore me on through a narrow tunnel where the raft touched either side and my head rubbed against the roof, return therefrom being impossible. Then I blamed myself for having thus risked my life, and said, "If this passage grow any straiter, the raft will hardly pass, and I cannot turn back, so I shall inevitably perish miserably in this place." And I threw myself down upon my face on the raft, by reason of the narrowness of the channel, whilst the stream ceased not to carry me along, knowing not night from day for the excess of the gloom which encompassed me about and my terror and concern for myself lest I should perish. And in such condition my course continued down the channel, which now grew wider and then straiter. Sore a-weary by reason of the darkness which could be felt, I feel asleep as I lay prone on the craft, and I slept knowing not an the time were long or short.

When I awoke at last, I found myself in the light of Heaven and opening my eyes, I saw myself in a broad of the stream and the raft moored to an island in the midst of a number of Indians and Abyssinians. As soon as these blackamoors saw that I was awake, they came up to me and bespoke me in their speech. But I understood not what they said and thought that this was a dream and a vision which had betided me for stress of concern and chagrin. But I was delighted at my escape from the river. When they saw I understood them not and made them no answer, one of them came forward and said to me in Arabic: "Peace be with thee, O my brother! Who art thou, and whence faredst thou hither? How camest thou into this river, and what manner of land lies behind yonder mountains, for never knew we anyone make his way thence to us?" Quoth I: "And upon thee be peace and the ruth of Allah and His blessing! Who are ye, and what country is this?" "O my brother," answered he, "we are husbandmen and tillers of the soil, who came out to water our fields and plantations, and finding thee asleep on this raft, laid hold of it and made it fast by us, against thou shouldst awake at thy leisure. So tell us how thou camest hither." I answered, "For Allah's sake, O my lord, ere I speak give me somewhat to eat, for I am starving, and after ask me what thou wilt."

So he hastened to fetch me food and I ate my fill, till I was refreshed and my fear was calmed by a good bellyful and my life returned to me. Then I rendered thanks to the Most High for mercies great and small, glad to be out of the river and rejoicing to be amongst them, and I told them all my adventures from first to last, especially my troubles in the narrow channel. They consulted among themselves and said to one another, "There is no help for it but we carry him with us and present him to our King, that he may acquaint him with his adventures." So they took me, together with raft boat and its lading of moneys and merchandise, jewels, minerals, and golden gear, and brought me to their King, who was King of Sarandib, telling him what had happened. Whereupon he saluted me and bade me welcome. Then he questioned me of my condition and adventures through the man who had spoken Arabic, and I repeated to him my story from beginning to end, whereat he marveled exceedingly and gave me joy of my deliverance. After which I arose and fetched from the raft great store of precious ores and jewels and ambergris and lip aloes and presented them to the King, who accepted them and entreated me with the utmost honor, appointing me a lodging in his own palace. So I consorted with the chief of the islanders, and they paid me the utmost respect. And I quitted not the royal palace.

Now the Island Sarandib lieth under the equinoctial line, its night and day both numbering twelve hours. It measureth eighty leagues long by a breadth of thirty and its width is bounded by a lofty mountain and a deep valley. The mountain is conspicuous from a distance of three days, and it containeth many kinds of, rubies and other minerals, and spice trees of all sorts. The surface is covered with emery, wherewith gems are cut and fashioned; diamonds are in its rivers and pearls are in its valleys. I ascended that mountain and solaced myself with a view of its marvels, which are indescribable, and afterward I returned to the King. Thereupon all the travelers and merchants who came to the place questioned me of the affairs of my native land and of the Caliph Harun al-Rashid and his rule, and I told them of him and of that wherefor he was renowned, and they praised him because of this, whilst I in turn questioned them of the manners and customs of their own countries and got the knowledge I desired.

One day the King himself asked me of the fashions and form of government of my country, and I acquainted him with the circumstance of the Caliph's sway in the city of Baghdad and the justice of his rule. The King marveled at my account of his appointments and said: "By Allah, the Caliph's ordinances are indeed wise and his fashions of praiseworthy guise, and thou hast made me love him by what thou tellest me. Wherefore I have a mind to make him a present and send it by thee." Quoth I: "Hearkening and obedience, O my lord. I will bear thy gift to him and inform him that thou art his sincere lover and true friend." Then I abode with the King in great honor and regard and consideration for a long while till one day, as I sat in his palace, I heard news of a company of merchants that were fitting out ship for Bassorah, and said to myself, "I cannot do better than voyage with these men." So I rose without stay or delay and kissed the King's hand and acquainted him with my longing to set out with the merchants, for that I pined after my people and mine own land. Quoth he, "Thou art thine own master, yet if it be thy will to abide with us, on our head and eyes be it, for thou gladdenest us with thy company." "By Allah, O my lord," answered I, "thou hast indeed overwhelmed me with thy favors and well-doings, but I weary for a sight of my friends and family and native country."

When he heard this, he summoned the merchants in question and commended me to their care, paying my freight and passage money. Then he bestowed on me great riches from his treasuries and charged me with a magnificent present for the Caliph Harun al-Rashid. Moreover, he gave me a sealed letter, saying, "Carry this with thine own hand to the Commander of the Faithful, and give him many salutations from us!" "Hearing and obedience," I replied. The missive was written on the skin of the khawi (which is finer than lamb parchment and of yellow color), with ink of ultramarine, and the contents were as follows: "Peace be with thee from the King of Al-Hind, before whom are a thousand elephants and upon whose palace crenelles are a thousand jewels. But after (laud to the Lord and praises to His Prophet!) we send thee a trifling gift, which be thou pleased to accept. Thou art to us a brother and a sincere friend, and great is the love we bear for thee in heart. Favor us therefore with a reply. The gift besitteth not thy dignity, but we beg of thee, O our brother, graciously to accept it, and peace be with thee." And the present was a cup of ruby a span high, the inside of which was adorned with precious pearls; and a bed covered with the skin of the serpent which swalloweth the elephant, which skin hath spots each like a dinar and whoso sitteth upon it never sickeneth; and a hundred thousand miskals of Indian lign aloes and a slave girl like a shining moon.

Then I took leave of him and of all my intimates and acquaintances in the island, and embarked with the merchants aforesaid. We sailed with a fair wind,

committing ourselves to the care of Allah (be He extolled
and exalted!), and by His permission arrived at Bassorah,
where I passed a few days and nights equipping myself and
packing up my bales. Then I went on to Baghdad city, the
House of Peace, where I sought an audience of the Caliph
and laid the King's presents before him. He asked me
whence they came, and I said to him, "By Allah, O
Commander of the Faithful, I know not the name of the city
nor the way thither!" He then asked me, "O Sindbad, is this
true which the King writeth?" and I answered, after kissing
the ground: "O my lord, I saw in his kingdom much more
than he hath written in his letter. For state processions a
throne is set for him upon a huge elephant eleven cubits
high, and upon this he sitteth having his great lords and
officers and guests standing in two ranks, on his right hand
and on his left. At his head is a man hending in hand a
golden javelin and behind him another with a great mace of
gold whose head is an emerald a span long and as thick as a
man's thumb. And when he mounteth horse there mount
with him a thousand horsemen clad in gold brocade and
silk, and as the King proceedeth a man precedeth him,
crying, 'This is the King of great dignity, of high authority!'
And he continueth to repeat his praises in words I
remember not, saying at the end of his panegyric, 'This is
the King owning the crown whose like nor Solomon nor the
Mihraj ever possessed.' Then he is silent and one behind
him proclaimeth, saying, 'He will die! Again I say he will
die!' and the other addeth, 'Extolled be the perfection of the
Living who dieth not!' Moreover, by reason of his justice
and ordinance and intelligence, there is no kazi in his city,
and all his lieges distinguish between truth and falsehood."
Quoth the Caliph: "How great is this King! His letter hath

shown me this, and as for the mightiness of his dominion thou hast told us what thou hast eyewitnessed. By Allah, he hath been endowed with wisdom, as with wide rule."

Then I related to the Commander of the Faithful all that had befallen me in my last voyage, at which he wondered exceedingly and bade his historians record my story and store it up in his treasuries, for the edification of all who might see it. Then he conferred on me exceeding great favors, and I repaired to my quarter and entered my home, where I warehoused all my goods and possessions. Presently my friends came to me and I distributed presents among my family and gave alms and largess, after which I yielded myself to joyance and enjoyment, mirth and merrymaking, and forgot all that I had suffered.

Such, then, O my brothers, is the history of what befell me in my sixth voyage, and tomorrow, Inshallah! I will tell you the story of my seventh and last voyage, which is still more wondrous and marvelous than that of the first six. (Saith he who telleth the tale): Then be bade lay the table, and the company supped with him, after which he gave the porter a hundred dinars, as of wont, and they all went their ways, marveling beyond measure at that which they had heard. Sindbad the Landsman went home and slept as of wont. Next day he rose and prayed the dawn prayer and repaired to his namesake's house, where, after the company was all assembled, the host began to relate

The Seventh Voyage of Sindbad the Seaman

Know, O company, that after my return from my sixth voyage, which brought me abundant profit, I resumed my former life in all possible joyance and enjoyment and mirth

108

and making merry day and night. And I tarried sometime in this solace and satisfaction, till my soul began once more to long to sail the seas and see foreign countries and company with merchants and hear new things. So, having made up my mind, I packed up in bales a quantity of precious stuffs suited for sea trade and repaired with them from Baghdad city to Bassorah town, where I found a ship ready for sea, and in her a company of considerable merchants. I shipped with them and, becoming friends, we set forth on our venture in health and safety, and sailed with a wind till we came to a city called Madinat-al-Sin.

But after we had left it, as we fared on in all cheer and confidence, devising of traffic and travel, behold, there sprang up a violent head wind and a tempest of rain fell on us and drenched us and our goods. So we covered the bales with our cloaks and garments and drugget and canvas, lest they be spoiled by the rain, and betook ourselves to prayer and supplication to Almighty Allah, and humbled ourselves before Him for deliverance from the peril that was upon us. But the captain arose and, tightening his girdle, tucked up his skirts, and after taking refuge with Allah from Satan the Stoned, clomb to the masthead, whence he looked out right and left, and gazing at the passengers and crew, fell to buffeting his face and plucking out his beard. So we cried to him, "O Rais, what is the matter?" and he replied, saying: "Seek ye deliverance of the Most High from the strait into which we have fallen, and bemoan yourselves and take leave of one another. For know that the wind hath gotten the mastery of us, and hath driven us into the uttermost of the seas world." Then he came down from the masthead and opening his sea chest, pulled but a bag of blue cotton, from which he took a powder like ashes. This he set in a saucer wetted with a little water, and after waiting a short time, smelt and tasted it. And then he took out of the chest a booklet, wherein he read awhile, and said, weeping:

"Know, O ye passengers, that in this book is a marvelous matter, denoting that whoso cometh hither shall surely die, without hope of escape. For that this ocean is called the Sea of the Clime of the King, wherein is the sepulcher of our lord Solomon, son of David (on both be peace!), and therein are serpents of vast bulk and fearsome aspect. And what ship soever cometh to these climes, there riseth to her a great fish out of the sea and swalloweth her up with all and everything on board her." Hearing these words from the captain, great was our wonder, but hardly had he made an end of speaking when the ship was lifted out of the water and let fall again, and we applied to praying the death prayer and committing our souls to Allah.

Presently we heard a terrible great cry like the loud-pealing thunder whereat we were terror-struck and became as dead men, giving ourselves up for lost. Then, behold, there came up to us a huge fish, as big as a tall mountain, at whose sight we became wild for affright and, weeping sore, made ready for death, marveling at its vast size and gruesome semblance. When lo! a second fish made its appearance, than which we had seen naught more monstrous. So we bemoaned ourselves of our lives and farewelled one another. But suddenly up came a third fish bigger than the two first, whereupon we lost the power of thought and reason and were stupefied for the excess of our fear and horror. Then the three fish began circling round about the ship and the third and biggest opened his mouth to swallow it, and we looked into its mouth and, behold, it was wider than the gate of a city and its throat was like a long valley.

So we besought the Almighty and called for succor upon His Apostle (on whom be blessing and peace!), when suddenly a violent squall of wind arose and smote the ship, which rose out of the water and settled upon a great reef, the haunt of sea monsters, where it broke up and fell asunder into planks, and all and everything on board were plunged into the sea.

As for me, I tore off all my clothes but my gown, and swam a little way, till I happened upon one of the ship's planks, whereto I clung and bestrode it like a horse, whilst the winds and the waters sported with me and the waves carried me up and cast me down. And I was in most piteous plight for fear and distress and hunger and thirst. Then I reproached myself for what I had done and my soul was weary after a life of ease and comfort, and I said to myself: "O Sindbad, O Seaman, thou repentest not and yet thou art ever suffering hardships and travails, yet wilt thou not renounce sea travel, or an thou say, 'I renounce,' thou liest in thy renouncement. Endure then with patience that which thou sufferest, for verily thou deservest all that betideth thee!" And I ceased not to humble myself before Almighty Allah and weep and bewail myself, recalling my former estate of solace and satisfaction and mirth and merriment and joyance. And thus I abode two days, at the end of which time I came to a great island abounding in trees and streams. There I landed and ate of the fruits of the island and drank of its waters, till I was refreshed and my life returned to me and my strength and spirits were restored and I recited:

"Oft when thy case shows knotty and tangled skein,
    Fate downs from Heaven and straightens every ply.
In patience keep thy soul till clear thy lot,

For He who ties the knot can eke untie."

Then I walked about till I found on the further side a great river of sweet water, running with a strong current, whereupon I called to mind the boat raft I had made aforetime and said to myself: "Needs must I make another. Haply I may free me from this strait. If I escape, I have my desire and I vow to Allah Almighty to foreswear travel. And if I perish, I shall be at peace and shall rest from toil and moil." So I rose up and gathered together great store of pieces of wood from the trees (which were all of the finest sandalwood, whose like is not albe' I knew it not), and made shift to twist creepers and tree twigs into a kind of rope, with which I bound the billets together and so contrived a raft. Then saying, "An I be saved, 'tis of God's grace," I embarked thereon and committed myself to the current, and it bore me on for the first day and the second and the third after leaving the island whilst I lay in the raft, eating not and drinking, when I was athirst, of the water of the river, till I was weak and giddy as a chicken for stress of fatigue and famine and fear.

At the end of this time I came to a high mountain, whereunder ran the river, which when I saw, I feared for my life by reason of the straitness I had suffered in my former journey, and I would fain have stayed the raft and landed on the mountainside. But the current overpowered me and drew it into the subterranean passage like an archway, whereupon I gave myself up for lost and said, "There is no Majesty and there is no Might save in Allah, the Glorious, the Great!" However, after a little the raft glided into open air and I saw before me a wide valley, whereinto the river fell with a noise like the rolling of thunder and a swiftness as the rushing of the wind. I held onto the raft, for fear of falling off it, whilst the waves tossed me right and left, and the craft continued to descend with the current, nor could I avail to stop it nor turn it shoreward till it stopped me at a great and goodly city, grandly edified and containing much people. And when the townsfolk saw me on the raft, dropping down with the current, they threw me out ropes, which I had not strength enough to hold. Then they tossed a net over the craft and drew it ashore with me, whereupon I fell to the ground amidst them, as I were a dead man, for stress of fear and hunger and lack of sleep.

After a while, there came up to me out of the crowd an old man of reverend aspect, well stricken in years, who welcomed me and threw over me abundance of handsome clothes, wherewith I covered my nakedness. Then he carried me to the hammam bath and brought me cordial sherbets and delicious perfumes. Moreover, when I came out, he bore me to his house, where his people made much of me and, seating me in a pleasant place, set rich food before me, whereof I ate my fill and returned thanks to God the Most High for my deliverance. Thereupon his pages fetched me hot water, and I washed my hands, and his handmaids brought me silken napkins, with which I dried them and wiped my mouth. Also the Sheikh set apart for me an apartment in a part of his house, and charged his pages and slave girls to wait upon me and do my will and supply my wants. They were assiduous in my service, and I abode with him in the guest chamber three days, taking my ease of good eating and good drinking and good scents till life returned to me and my terrors subsided and my heart was calmed and my mind was eased.

On the fourth day the Sheikh, my host, came in to me and

said: "Thou cheerest us with thy company, O my son, and praised be Allah for thy safety! Say, wilt thou now come down with me to the beach and the bazaar and sell thy goods and take their price? Belike thou mayest buy thee wherewithal to traffic. I have ordered my servants to remove thy stock in trade from the sea, and they have piled it on the shore." I was silent awhile and said to myself, "What mean these words, and what goods have I?" Then said he: "O my son, be not troubled nor careful, but come with me to the market, and if any offer for thy goods what price contenteth thee, take it. But an thou be not satisfied, I lay em up for thee in my warehouse, against a fitting occasion for sale." So I bethought me of my case and said to myself, "Do his bidding and see what are these goods!" and I said to him: "O my nuncle the Sheikh I hear and obey. I may not gainsay thee in aught, for Allah's blessing is on all thou dost."

Accordingly he guided me to the market street, where I found that he had taken in pieces the raft which carried me and which was of sandalwood, and I heard the broker crying it for sale. Then the merchants came and opened the gate of bidding for the wood and bid against one another till its price reached a thousand dinars, when they left bidding and my host said to me: "Hear, O my son, this is the current price of thy goods in hard times like these. Wilt thou sell them for this, or shall I lay them up for thee in my storehouses till such time as prices rise?" "O my lord," answered I, "the business is in thy hands. Do as thou wilt." Then asked he: "Wilt thou sell the wood to me, O my son, for a hundred gold pieces over and above what the merchants have bidden for it?" and I answered, "Yes, I have sold it to thee for monies received." So he bade his servants transport the wood to his storehouses, and, carrying me back to his house, seated me, and counted out to me the purchase money. After which he laid it in bags and, setting them in a privy place, locked them up with an iron padlock and gave me its key.

Some days after this the Sheikh said to me, "O my son, I have somewhat to propose to thee, wherein I trust thou wilt do my bidding." Quoth I, "What is it?" Quoth he: "I am a very old man, and have no son, but I have a daughter who is young in years and fair of favor and endowed with abounding wealth and beauty. Now I have a mind to marry her to thee, that thou mayest abide with her in this our country. And I will make, thee master of all I have in hand, for I am an old man and thou shalt stand in my stead." I was silent for shame and made him no answer, whereupon he continued: "Do my desire in this, O my son, for I wish but thy weal. And if thou wilt but as I say, thou shalt have her at once and be as my son, and all that is under my hand or that cometh to me shall be thine. If thou have a mind to traffic and travel to thy native land, none shall hinder thee, and thy property will be at thy sole disposal. So do as thou wilt." "By Allah, O my uncle," replied I, "thou art become to me even as my father, and I am a stranger and have undergone many hardships, while for stress of that which I have suffered naught of judgment or knowledge is left to me. It is for thee, therefore, to decide what I shall do."

Hereupon he sent his servants for the kazi and the witnesses and married me to his daughter, making for us a noble marriage feast and high festival. When I went in to her, I found her perfect in beauty and loveliness and symmetry and grace, clad in rich raiment and covered with a profusion of ornaments and necklaces and other trinkets of gold and silver and precious stones, worth a mint of money, a price none could pay. She pleased me, and we loved each other, and I abode with her in all solace and delight of life till her father was taken to the mercy of Allah Almighty. So we shrouded him and buried him, and I laid hands on the whole of his property and all his servants and slaves became mine. Moreover, the merchants installed me in his office, for he was their sheikh and their chief, and none of them purchased aught but with his knowledge and by his leave. And now his rank passed on to me.

When I became acquainted with the townsfolk, I found that at the beginning of each month they were transformed, in that their faces changed and they became like unto birds and they put forth wings wherewith they flew unto the upper regions of the firmament; and none remained in the city save the women and children. And I said in my mind, "When the first of the month cometh, I will ask one of them to carry me with them, whither they go." So when the time came and their complexion changed and their forms altered, I went in to one of the townsfolk and said to him: "Allah upon thee! Carry me with thee, that I might divert myself with the rest and return with you." "This may not be," answered he. But I ceased not to solicit him, and I importuned him till he consented. Then I went out in his company, without telling any of my family or servants or friends, and he took me on his back and flew up with me so high in air that I heard the angels glorifying God in the heavenly dome, whereat I wondered and exclaimed: "Praised be Allah! Extolled be the perfection of Allah!"

Hardly had I made an end of pronouncing the tasbih-praised be Allah!- when there came out a fire from Heaven and all but consumed the company. Whereupon they fied from it and descended with curses upon me and, casting me down on a high mountain, went away exceeding wroth with me, and left me there alone. As I found myself in this plight, I repented of what I had done and reproached myself for having undertaken that for which I was unable, saying: "There is no Majesty and there is no Might save in Allah, the Glorious, the Great! No sooner am I delivered from one affliction than I fall into a worse." And I continued in this case, knowing not whither I should go, when lo! there came up two young men, as they were moons, each using as a staff a rod of red gold. So I approached them and saluted them; and when they returned my salaam, I said to them: Allah upon you twain. Who are ye, and what are ye?" Quoth they, "We are of the servants of the Most High Allah, abiding in this mountain," and giving me a rod of red gold they had with them, went their ways and left me.

I walked on along the mountain ridge, staying my steps with the staff and pondering the case of the two youths, when behold, a serpent came forth from under the mountain, with a man in her jaws whom she had swallowed even to below his navel, and he was crying out and saying, "Whoso delivereth me, Allah will deliver him from all adversity!" So I went up to the the serpent and smote her on the head with the golden staff, whereupon she cast the man forth of her mouth. Then I smote her a second time, and she turned and fled, whereupon he came up to me and said, "Since my deliverance from yonder serpent hath been at thy hands I will never leave thee, and thou shalt be my comrade on this mountain." "And welcome," answered I. So we fared on along the mountain till we fell in with a company of folk, and I looked and saw amongst them the very man who had carried me and cast me down there. I went up to him and spake him fair, excusing to him and saying, "O my comrade, it is not thus that friend should deal with friend." Quoth he, "It was thou who well-nigh destroyed us by thy tasbih and thy glorifying God on my back." Quoth I, "Pardon me, for I had no knowledge of this matter, but if thou wilt take me with thee, I swear not to say a word."

So he relented and consented to carry me with him, but he made an express condition that so long as I abode on his back, I should abstain from pronouncing the tasbih or otherwise glorifying God. Then I gave the wand of gold to him whom I had delivered from the serpent and bade him farewell, and my friend took me on his back and flew with me as before, till he brought me to the city and set me down in my own house. My wife came to meet me and, saluting me, gave me joy of my safety and then said: "Beware of going forth hereafter with yonder folk, neither consort with them, for they are brethren of the devils, and know not how to mention the name of Allah Almighty, neither worship they Him." "And how did thy father with them?" asked I, and she answered: "My father was not of them, neither did he as they. And as now he is dead, methinks thou hadst better sell all we have and with the price buy merchandise and journey to thine own country and people, and I with thee; for I care not to tarry in this city, my father and my mother being dead." So I sold all the Sheikh's property piecemeal, and looked for one who should be journeying thence to Bassorah that I might join myself to him.

And while thus doing I heard of a company of townsfolk who had a mind to make the voyage but could not find them a ship, so they bought wood and built them a great ship, wherein I took passage with them, and paid them all the hire. Then we embarked, I and my wife, with all our movables, leaving our houses and domains and so forth, and set sail, and ceased not sailing from island to island and from sea to sea, with a fair wind and a favoring, till we arrived at Bassorah safe and sound. I made no stay there, but freighted another vessel and, transferring my goods to her, set out forthright for Baghdad city, where I arrived in safety, and entering my quarter and repairing to my house, forgathered with my family and friends and familiars and laid up my goods in my warehouses.

When my people, who, reckoning the period of my absence on this my seventh voyage, had found it to be seven and twenty years and had given up all hope of me, heard of my return, they came to welcome me and to give me joy of my safety. And I related to them all that had befallen me, whereat they marveled with exceeding marvel. Then I foreswore travel and vowed to Allah the Most High I would venture no more by land or sea, for that this seventh and last voyage had surfeited me of travel and adventure, and I thanked the Lord (be He praised and glorified!), and blessed Him for having restored me to my kith and kin and country and home. "Consider, therefore, O Sindbad, O Landsman," continued Sindbad the Seaman, "what sufferings I have undergone and what perils and hardships I have endured before coming to my present state." "Allah upon thee, O my Lord!" answered Sindbad the, Landsman. "Pardon me the wrong I did thee." And they ceased not from friendship and fellowship, abiding in all cheer and pleasures and solace of life till there came to them the Destroyer of delights and the Sunderer of Societies, and the Shatterer of palaces and the Caterer for Cemeteries; to wit, the Cup of Death, and glory be to the Living One who dieth not!

III.   Aladdin, or The Wonderful Lamp

It hath reached me, O King of the Age, that there dwelt in a city of the cities of China a man which was a tailor, withal a pauper, and he had one son, Aladdin hight. Now this boy had been from his babyhood a ne'er-do-well, a scapegrace. And when he reached his tenth year, his father inclined to teach him his own trade, and, for that he was overindigent to expend money upon his learning other work or craft or apprenticeship, he took the lad into his shop that he might be taught tailoring. But, as Aladdin was a scapegrace and a ne'er-do-well and wont to play at all times with the gutter boys of the quarter, he would not sit in the shop for a single day. Nay, he would await his father's leaving it for some purpose, such as to meet a creditor, when he would run off at once and fare forth to the gardens with the other scapegraces and low companions, his fellows. Such was his case- counsel and castigation were of no avail, nor would he obey either parent in aught or learn any trade. And presently, for his sadness and, sorrowing because of his son's vicious indolence, the tailor sickened and died.

Aladdin continued in his former ill courses, and when his mother saw that her spouse had deceased and that her son was a scapegrace and good for nothing at all, she sold the shop and whatso was to be found therein and fell to spinning cotton yarn. By this toilsome industry she fed herself and found food for her son Aladdin the scapegrace, who, seeing himself freed from bearing the severities of his sire, increased in idleness and low habits. Nor would he ever stay at home save at meal hours while his miserable wretched mother lived only by what her hands could spin until the youth had reached his fifteenth year. It befell one day of the days that as he was sitting about the quarter at play with the vagabond boys, behold, a dervish from the Maghrib, the Land of the Setting Sun, came up and stood gazing for solace upon the lads. And he looked hard at Aladdin and carefully considered his semblance, scarcely noticing his companions the while. Now this dervish was a Moorman from Inner Morocco, and he was a magician who could upheap by his magic hill upon hill, and he was also an adept in astrology. So after narrowly considering Aladdin, he said in himself, "Verily, this is the lad I need and to find whom I have left my natal land." Presently he led one of the children apart and questioned him anent the scapegrace saying, "Whose son is he?" And he sought all information concerning his condition and whatso related to him.

After this he walked up to Aladdin, and drawing him aside, asked, "O my son, haply thou art the child of Such-a-one the tailor?" and the lad answered, "Yes, O my lord, but 'tis long since he died." The Maghrabi, the magician, hearing these words, threw himself upon Aladdin and wound his arms around his neck and fell to bussing him, weeping the while with tears trickling a-down his cheeks. But when the lad saw the Moorman's case, he was seized with surprise thereat and questioned him, saying, "What causeth thee weep, O my lord, and how camest thou to know my father?" "How canst thou, O my son," replied the Moorman, in a soft voice saddened by emotion, "question me with such query after informing me that thy father and my brother is deceased? For that he was my brother german, and now I come from my adopted country and after long exile I rejoiced with exceeding joy in the hope of looking upon him once more and condoling with him over the past. And now thou hast announced to me his demise. But blood hideth not from blood, and it hath revealed to me that thou art my nephew, son of my brother, and I knew thee amongst all the lads, albeit thy father, when I parted from him, was yet unmarried."

Then he again clasped Aladdin to his bosom, crying: "O my son, I have none to condole with now save thyself. And thou standest in stead of thy sire, thou being his issue and representative and 'whoso leaveth issue dieth not,' O my child!" So saying, the magician put hand to purse, and pulling out ten gold pieces, gave them to the lad, asking, "O my son, where is your house and where dwelleth she, thy mother and my brother's widow?" Presently Aladdin arose with him and showed him the way to their home, and meanwhile quoth the wizard: "O my son, take these moneys and give them to thy mother, greeting her from me, and let her know that thine uncle, thy father's brother, hath reappeared from his exile and that Inshallah- God willing- on the morrow I will visit her to salute her with the salaam and see the house wherein my brother was homed and look upon the place where he lieth buried." Thereupon Aladdin kissed the Maghrabi's hand, and after running in his joy at fullest speed to his mother's dwelling entered to her clean contrariwise to his custom, inasmuch as he never came near her save at mealtimes only. And when he found her, the lad exclaimed in his delight: "O my mother, I give thee glad tidings of mine uncle who hath returned from his exile, and who now sendeth me to salute thee." "O my son," she replied, "meseemeth thou mockest me! Who is this uncle, and how canst thou have an uncle in the bonds of life?" He rejoined: "How sayest thou, O my mother, that I have no living uncles nor kinsmen, when this man is my father's own brother? Indeed he embraced me and bussed me, shedding tears the while, and bade me acquaint thee herewith." She retorted, "O my son, well I wot thou haddest an uncle, but he is now dead, nor am I ware that thou hast other eme."

The Moroccan magician fared forth next morning and fell to finding out Aladdin, for his heart no longer permitted him to part from the lad. And as he was to-ing and fro-ing about the city highways, he came face to face with him disporting himself, as was his wont, amongst the vagabonds and the scapegraces. So he drew near to him, and taking his hand, embraced him and bussed him. Then pulled out of his poke two dinars and said: "Hie thee to thy mother and give her these couple of ducats and tell her that thine uncle would eat the evening meal with you. So do thou take these two gold pieces and prepare for us a succulent supper. But before all things, show me once more the way to your home." "On my head and mine eyes be it, O my uncle," replied the lad and forewent him, pointing out the street leading to the house. Then the Moorman left him and went his ways and Aladdin ran home and, giving the news and the two sequins to his parent, said, "My uncle would sup with us."

So she arose straightway and, going to the market street, bought all she required. Then, returning to her dwelling, she borrowed from the neighbors whatever was needed of pans and platters, and so forth, and when the meal was cooked and suppertime came she said to Aladdin: "O my child, the meat is ready, but peradventure thine uncle wotteth not the way to our dwelling. So do thou fare forth and meet him on the road." He replied, "To hear is to obey," and before the twain ended talking a knock was heard at the door. Aladdin went out and opened, when, behold, the Maghrabi, the magician, together with a eunuch carrying the wine and the dessert fruits. So the lad led them in and the slave went about his business. The Moorman on entering saluted his sister-in-law with the salaam, then began to shed tears and to question her, saying, "Where be the place whereon my brother went to sit?" She showed it to him, whereat he went up to it and prostrated himself in prayer and kissed the floor, crying: how scant is my satisfaction and how luckless is my lot, for that I have lost thee, O my brother, O vein of my eye!" And after such fashion he continued weeping and wailing till he swooned away for excess of sobbing and lamentation, wherefor Aladdin's mother was certified of his soothfastness. So, coming up to him, she raised him from the floor and said, "What gain is there in slaying thyself?"

As soon as he was seated at his ease, and before the food trays were served up, he fell to talking with her and saying: "O wife of my brother, it must be a wonder to thee how in all thy days thou never sawest me nor learnst thou aught of me during the lifetime of my brother who hath found mercy. Now the reason is that forty years ago I left this town and exiled myself from my birthplace and wandered forth over all the lands of Al-Hind and Al-Sind and entered Egypt and settled for a long time in its magnificent city, which is one of the world wonders, till at last I fared to the regions of the setting sun and abode for a space of thirty years in the Moroccan interior. Now one day of the days, O wife of my brother, as I was sitting alone at home, I fell to thinking of mine own country and of my birthplace and of my brother (who hath found mercy). And my yearning to see him waxed excessive and I bewept and bewailed my strangerhood and distance from him. And at last my longings drave me homeward until I resolved upon traveling to the region which was the falling place of my head and my homestead, to the end that I might again see my brother. Then quoth I to myself: 'O man, how long wilt thou wander like a wild Arab from thy place of birth and native stead? Moreover, thou hast one brother and no more, so up with thee and travel and look upon him ere thou die, for who wotteth the woes of the world and the changes of the days? 'Twould be saddest regret an thou lie down to die without beholding thy brother. And Allah (laud be to the Lord!) hath vouchsafed thee ample wealth, and belike he may be straitened and in poor case, when thou wilt aid thy brother as well as see him.'

"So I arose at once and equipped me for wayfare and recited the fatihah. Then, whenas Friday prayers ended, I mounted and traveled to this town, after suffering manifold toils and travails which I patiently endured whilst the Lord (to Whom be honor and glory!) veiled me with the veil of His protection. So I entered, and whilst wandering about the streets the day before yesterday I beheld my brother's son Aladdin disporting himself with the boys and, by God the Great, O wife of my brother, the moment I saw him this heart of mine went forth to him (for blood yearneth unto blood!), and my soul felt and informed me that he was my very nephew. So I forgot all my travails and troubles at once on sighting him, and I was like to fly for joy. But when he told me of the dear one's departure to the ruth of

Allah Almighty, I fainted for stress of distress and disappointment. Perchance, however, my nephew hath informed thee of the pains which prevailed upon me. But after a fashion I am consoled by the sight of Aladdin, the legacy bequeathed to us by him who hath found mercy for that 'whoso leaveth issue is not wholly dead.'" And when he looked at his sister-in-law, she wept at these his words, so he turned to the lad, that he might cause her to forget the mention of her mate, as a means of comforting her and also of completing his deceit, and asked him, saying: "O my son Aladdin, what hast thou learned in the way of work, and what is thy business? Say me, hast thou mastered any craft whereby to earn a livelihood for thyself and for thy mother?" The lad was abashed and put to shame and he hung down his head and bowed his brow groundward. But his parent spake out: "How, forsooth? By Allah, he knoweth nothing at all, a child so ungracious as this I never yet saw- no, never! All the day long he idleth away his time with the sons of the quarter, vagabonds like himself, and his father (O regret of me!) died not save of dolor for him. And I also am now in piteous plight. I spin cotton and toil at my distant night and day, that I may earn me a couple of scones of bread which we eat together. This is his condition, O my brother-in-law, and, by the life of thee, he cometh not near me save at mealtimes, and none other. Indeed, I am thinking to lock the house door, nor ever open to him again, but leave him to go and seek a livelihood whereby he can live, for that I am now grown a woman in years and have no longer strength to toil and go about for a maintenance after this fashion. O Allah, I am compelled to provide him with daily bread when I require to be provided!"

Hereat the Moorman turned to Aladdin and said: "Why is

this, O son of my brother, thou goest about in such ungraciousness? 'Tis a disgrace to thee and unsuitable for men like thyself. Thou art a youth of sense, O my son, and the child of honest folk, so 'tis for thee a shame that thy mother, a woman in years, should struggle to support thee. And now that thou hast grown to man's estate, it becometh thee to devise thee some device whereby thou canst live, O my child. Look around thee and Alhamdolillah- praise be to Allah- in this our town are many teachers of all manner of crafts, and nowhere are they more numerous. So choose thee some calling which may please thee to the end that I stablish thee therein, and when thou growest up, O my son, thou shalt have some business whereby to live. Haply thy father's industry may not be to thy liking, and if so it be, choose thee some other handicraft which suiteth thy fancy. Then let me know and I will aid thee with all I can, O my son." But when the Maghrabi saw that Aladdin kept silence and made him no reply, he knew that the lad wanted none other occupation than a scapegrace life, so he said to him: "O son of my brother, let not my words seem hard and harsh to thee, for if despite all I say thou still dislike to learn a craft, I will open thee a merchant's store furnished with costliest stuffs and thou shalt become famous amongst the folk and take and give and buy and sell and be well known in the city."

Now when Aladdin heard the words of his uncle the Moorman, and the design of making him a khwajah- merchant and gentleman- he joyed exceedingly, knowing that such folk dress handsomely and fare delicately. So he looked at the Maghrabi smiling and drooping his head groundward and saying with the tongue of the case that he was content. The Maghrabi the magician, looked at Aladdin

127

and saw him smiling whereby he understood that the lad was satisfied to become a trader. So he said to him: "Since thou art content that I open thee a merchant's store and make thee a gentleman, do thou, O son of my brother, prove thyself a man and Inshallah- God willing- tomorrow I will take thee to the bazaar in the first place have a fine suit of clothes cut out for thee, such gear as merchants wear; and secondly, I will look after a store for thee and keep my word."

Now Aladdin's mother had somewhat doubted the Moroccan being her brother-in-law, but as soon as she heard his promise of opening a merchant's store for her son and setting him up with stuffs and capital and so forth, the woman decided and determined in her mind that this Maghrabi was in very sooth her husband's brother, seeing that no stranger man would do such goodly deed by her son. So she began directing the lad to the right road and teaching him to cast ignorance from out his head and to prove himself a man. Moreover, she bade him ever obey his excellent uncle as though he were his son, and to make up for the time he had wasted in frowardnes with his fellows. After this she arose and spread the table, then served up supper, so all sat down and fell to eating and drinking while the Maghrabi conversed with Aladdin upon matters of business and the like, rejoicing him to such degree that he enjoyed no sleep that night. But when the Moorman saw that the dark hours were passing by, and the wine was drunken, he arose and sped to his own stead. But ere going he agreed to return next morning and take Aladdin and look to his suit of merchant's clothes being cut out for him.

And as soon as it was dawn, behold, the Maghrabi rapped at the door, which was opened by Aladdin's mother. The

Moorman, however, would not enter, but asked to take the lad with him to the market street. Accordingly Aladdin went forth to his uncle and, wishing him good morning, kissed his hand, and the Moroccan took him by the hand and fared with him to the bazaar. There he entered a clothier's shop containing all kinds of clothes, and called for a suit of the most sumptuous, whereat the merchant brought him out his need, all wholly fashioned and ready sewn, and the Moorman said to the lad, "Choose, O my child, whatso pleaseth thee." Aladdin rejoiced exceedingly, seeing that his uncle had given him his choice, so he picked out the suit most to his own liking and the Moroccan paid to the merchant the price thereof in ready money. Presently he led the lad to the hammam baths, where they bathed. Then they came out and drank sherbets, after which Aladdin arose and, donning his new dress in huge joy and delight, went up to his uncle and kissed his hand and thanked him for his favors.

The Maghrabi, the magician, after leaving the hammam with Aladdin, took him and trudged with him to the merchants' bazaar, and having diverted him by showing the market and its sellings and buyings, and to him: "O my son, it besitteth thee to become familiar with the folk, especially with the merchants, so thou mayest learn of them merchant craft, seeing that the same hath now become thy calling." Then he led him forth and showed him the city and its cathedral mosques, together with all the pleasant sights therein, and lastly made him enter a cook's shop. Here dinner was served to them on platters of silver and they dined well and ate and drank their sufficiency, after which they went their ways. Presently the Moorman pointed out to Aladdin the pleasaunces and noble buildings, and went in with him to the Sultan's palace and diverted him with displaying all the apartments, which were mighty fine and grand, and led him finally to the khan of stranger merchants, where he himself had his abode. Then the Moroccan invited sundry traders which were in the caravanserai, and they came and sat down to supper, when he notified to them that the youth was his nephew, Aladdin by name. And after they had eaten and drunken and night had fallen, he rose up, and taking the lad with him, led him back to his mother, who no sooner saw her boy as he were one of the merchants than her wits took flight and she waxed sad for very gladness.

Then she fell to thanking her false connection, the Moorman, for all his benefits and said to him: "O my brother-in-law, I can never say enough though I expressed my gratitude to thee during the rest of thy days and praised thee for the good deeds thou hast done by this my child." Thereupon quoth the Moroccan: "O wife of my brother, deem this not mere kindness of me, for that the lad is mine own son, and 'tis incumbent on me to stand in the stead of my brother, his sire. So be thou fully satisfied!" And quoth she: "I pray Allah by the honor of the Hallows, the ancients and the moderns, that He preserve thee and cause thee continue, O my brother-in-law, and prolong for me thy life. So shalt thou be a wing overshadowing this orphan lad, and he shall ever be obedient to thine orders, nor shall he do aught save whatso thou biddest him thereunto." The Maghrabi replied: "O wife of my brother, Aladdin is now a man of sense and the son of goodly folk, and I hope to Allah that he will follow in the footsteps of his sire and cool thine eyes. But I regret that, tomorrow being Friday, I shall not be able to open his shop, as 'tis meeting day when all the merchants, after congregational prayer, go forth to the gardens and pleasaunces. On the Sabbath, however, Inshallah!- an it please the Creator- we will do our business. Meanwhile tomorrow I will come to thee betimes and take Aladdin for a pleasant stroll to the gardens and pleasaunces without the city, which haply he may hitherto not have beheld. There also he shall see the merchants and notables who go forth to amuse themselves, so shall he become acquainted with them and they with him."

The Maghrabi went away and lay that night in his quarters, and early next morning he came to the tailor's house and rapped at the door. Now Aladdin (for stress of his delight in the new dress he had donned and for the past day's enjoyment in the hammam and in eating and drinking and gazing at the folk, expecting futhermore his uncle to come at dawn and carry him off on pleasuring to the gardens) had not slept a wink that night, nor-closed his eyelids, and would hardly believe it when day broke. But hearing the knock at the door, he went out at once in hot haste, like a spark of fire, and opened and saw his uncle, the magician, who embraced him and kissed him. Then, taking his hand, the Moorman said to him as they fared forth together, "O son of my brother, this day will I show thee a sight thou never sawest in all thy life," and he began to make the lad laugh and cheer him with pleasant talk. So doing, they left the city gate, and the Moroccan took to promenading with Aladdin amongst the gardens and to pointing out for his pleasure the mighty fine pleasaunces and the marvelous high-built pavilions. And whenever they stood to stare at a garth or a mansion or a palace, the Maghrabi would say to his companion, "Doth this please thee, O son of my brother?"

Aladdin was nigh to fly with delight at seeing sights he had never seen in all his born days, and they ceased not to stroll about and solace themselves until they waxed a-weary, then they entered a mighty grand garden which was near-hand, a place that the heart delighted and the sight belighted, for that its swift-running rills flowed amidst the flowers and the waters jetted from the jaws of lions molded in yellow brass like unto gold. So they took seat over against a lakelet and rested a little while, and Aladdin enjoyed himself with joy exceeding and fell to jesting with his uncle and making merry with him as though the magician were really his father's brother.

Presently the Maghrabi arose, and loosing his girdle, drew forth from thereunder a bag full of victual, dried fruits and so forth, saying to Aladdin: "O my nephew, haply thou art become a-hungered, so come forward and eat what thou needest." Accordingly the lad fell upon the food and the Moorman ate with him, and they were gladdened and cheered by rest and good cheer. Then quoth the magician: "Arise, O son of my brother, an thou be reposed, and let us stroll onward a little and reach the end of our walk." Thereupon Aladdin arose and the Moroccan paced with him from garden to garden until they left all behind them and reached the base of a high and naked hill, when the lad, who during all his days had never issued from the city gate and never in his life had walked such a walk as this, said to the Maghrabi: "O uncle mine, whither are we wending? We have left the gardens behind us one and all and have reached the barren hill country. And if the way be still long, I have no strength left for walking. Indeed I am ready to fall with fatigue. There are no gardens before us, so let us hark back and return to town." Said the magician: "No, O my son. This is right road, nor are the gardens ended, for we are going to look at one which hath ne'er its like amongst those of the kings, and all thou hast beheld are naught in comparison therewith. Then gird thy courage to walk. Thou art now a man, Alhamdolillah- praise be to Allah!"

Then the Maghrabi fell to soothing Aladdin with soft words and telling him wondrous tales, lies as well as truth, until they reached the site intended by the African magician, who had traveled from the sunset land to the regions of China for the sake thereof. And when they made the place, the Moorman said to Aladdin: "O son of my brother, sit thee down and take thy rest, for this is the spot we are now seeking and, Inshallah, soon will I divert thee by displaying marvel matters whose like not one in the world ever saw, nor hath any solaced himself with gazing upon that which thou art about to behold. But when thou art rested, arise and seek some wood chips and fuel sticks which be small and dry, wherewith we may kindle a fire. Then will I show thee, O son of my brother, matters beyond the range of matter." Now when the lad heard these words, he longed to look upon what his uncle was about to do and, forgetting his fatigue, he rose forthright and fell to gathering small wood chips and dry sticks, and continued until the Moorman cried to him, "Enough, O son of my brother!"

Presently the magician brought out from his breast pocker a casket, which he opened, and drew from it all he needed of incense. Then he fumigated and conjured and adjured, muttering words none might understand. And the ground straightway clave asunder after thick gloom and quake of earth and bellowings of thunder. Hereat Aladdin was startled and so affrighted that he tried to fly, but when the African magician saw his design, he waxed wroth with exceeding wrath, for that without the lad his work would profit him naught, the hidden hoard which he sought to open being not to be opened save by means of Aladdin. So, noting this attempt to run away, the magician arose, and raising his hand, smote Aladdin on the head a buffet so sore that well-nigh his back teeth were knocked out, and he fell swooning to the ground. But after a time he revived by the magic of the magician, and cried, weeping the while: "O my uncle, what have I done that deserveth from thee such a blow as this?" Hereat the Maghrabi fell to soothing him, and said: "O my son, 'tis my intent to make thee a man. Therefore do thou not gainsay me, for that I am thine uncle and like unto thy father. Obey me, therefore, in all I bid thee, and shortly thou shalt forget all this travail and toil whenas thou shalt look upon the marvel matters I am about to show thee."

And soon after the ground had cloven asunder before the Moroccan, it displayed a marble slab wherein was fixed a copper ring. The Maghrabi, striking a geomantic table, turned to Aladdin and said to him: "An thou do all I shall bid thee, indeed thou shalt become wealthier than any of the kings. And for this reason, O my son, I struck thee, because here lieth a hoard which is stored in thy name, and yet thou designedst to leave it and to levant. But now collect thy thoughts, and behold how I opened earth by my spells and adjurations. Under yon stone wherein the ring is set lieth the treasure wherewith I acquainted thee. So set thy hand upon the ring and raise the slab, for that none other amongst the folk, thyself excepted, hath power to open it, nor may any of mortal birth save thyself set foot within this enchanted treasury which hath been kept for thee. But 'tis needful that thou learn of me all wherewith I would charge thee, nor gainsay e'en a single syllable of my words. All this, O my child, is for thy good, the hoard being of immense value, whose like the kings of the world never accumulated, and do thou remember that 'tis for thee and me."

So poor Aladdin forgot his fatigue and buffet and tear-shedding, and he was dumbed and dazed at the Maghrabi's words and rejoiced that he was fated to become rich in such measure that not even the sultans would be richer than himself. Accordingly he cried: "O my uncle, bid me do all thou pleasest, for I will be obedient unto thy bidding." The Maghrabi replied: "O my nephew, thou art to me as my own child and even dearer, for being my brother's son and for my having none other kith and kin except thyself. And thou, O my child, art my heir and successor." So saying, he went up to Aladdin and kissed him and said: "For whom do I intend these my labors? Indeed, each and every are for thy sake, O my son, to the end that I may leave thee a rich man and one of the very greatest. So gainsay me not in all I shall say to thee, and now go up to yonder ring and uplift it as I bade thee." Aladdin answered: "O uncle mine, this ring is overheavy for me. I cannot raise it single-handed, so do thou also come forward and lend me strength and aidance toward uplifting it, for indeed I am young in years." The Moorman replied: "O son of my brother, we shall find it impossible to do aught if I assist thee, and all our efforts would be in vain. But do thou set thy hand upon the ring and pull it up, and thou shalt raise the slab forthright, and in very sooth I told thee that none can touch it save thyself. But whilst haling at it cease not to pronounce thy name and the names of thy father and mother, so 'twill rise at once to thee, nor shalt thou feel its weight."

Thereupon the lad mustered up strength and girt the loins of resolution and did as the Moroccan had bidden him, and hove up the slab with all ease when he pronounced his name and the names of his parents, even as the magician had bidden him. And as soon as the stone was raised he threw it aside, and there appeared before him a sardab, a souterrain, whereunto led a case of some twelve stairs, and the Maghrabi said: "O Aladdin, collect thy thoughts and do whatso I bid thee to the minutest detail, nor fail in aught thereof. Go down with all care into yonder vault until thou reach the bottom, and there shalt thou find a space divided into four halls, and in each of these thou shalt see four golden jars and others of virgin or and silver. Beware, however, lest thou take aught therefrom or touch them, nor allow thy gown or its skirts even to brush the jars or the walls. Leave them and fare forward until thou reach the fourth hall, without lingering for a single moment on the way. And if thou do aught contrary thereto, thou wilt at once be transformed and become a black stone. When reaching the fourth hall, thou wilt find therein a door, which do thou open, and pronouncing the names thou spakest over the slab, enter therethrough into a garden adorned everywhere with fruit-bearing trees. This thou must traverse by a path thou wilt see in front of thee measuring some fifty cubits long beyond which thou wilt come upon an open saloon, and herein a ladder of some thirty rungs. Thou shalt there find a lamp hanging from its ceiling, so mount the ladder and take that lamp and place it in thy breast pocket after pouring out its contents. Nor fear evil from it for thy clothes, because its contents are not common oil. And on return thou art allowed to pluck from the trees whoso thou pleasest, for all is thine so long as the lamp is in thy hand."

Now when the Moorman ended his charge to Aladdin, he drew off a seal ring and put it upon the lad's forefinger, saying: "O my son, verily this signet shall free thee from all hurt and fear which may threaten thee, but only on condition that thou bear in mind all I have told thee. So arise straightway and go down the stairs, strengthening thy purpose and girding the loins of resolution. Moreover, fear not, for thou art now a man and no longer a child. And in shortest time, O my son, thou shalt will thee immense riches and thou shalt become the wealthiest of the world."

Accordingly, Aladdin arose and descended into the souterrain, where he found the four jars, each containing four jars of gold, and these he passed by as the Moroccan had bidden him, with the utmost care and caution. Thence he fared into the garden and walked along its length until he entered the saloon, where he mounted the ladder and took the lamp, which he extinguished, pouring out the oil which was therein, and placed it in his breast pocket. Presently, descending the ladder, he returned to the garden, where he fell to gazing at the trees, whereupon sat birds glorifying with loud voices their Great Creator. Now he had not observed them as he went in, but all these trees bare for fruitage costly gems. Moreover, each had its own kind of growth and jewels of its peculiar sort and these were of every color, green and white, yellow, red, and other such brilliant hues, and the radiance flashing from these gems paled the rays of the sun in forenoon sheen. Furthermore the size of each stone so far surpassed description that no King of the Kings of the World owned a single gem equal to the larger sort, nor could boast of even one half the size of the smaller kind of them. Aladdin walked amongst the trees and gazed upon them and other things which surprised the sight and bewildered the wits, and as he considered them, he saw that in lieu of common fruits the produce was of mighty fine jewels and precious stones, such as emeralds and diamonds, rubies, spinels, and balases, pearls and similar gems, astounding the mental vision of man.

And forasmuch as the lad had never beheld things like these during his born days, nor had reached those years of discretion which would teach him the worth of such valuables (he being still but a little lad), he fancied that all these jewels were of glass or crystal. So he collected them until he had filled his breast pockets, and began to certify himself if they were or were not common fruits, such as grapes, figs, and suchlike edibles. But seeing them of glassy substance, he, in his ignorance of precious stones and their prices, gathered into his breast pockets every kind of growth the trees afforded, and having failed of his purpose in finding them food, he said in his mind, "I will collect a portion of these glass fruits for playthings at home." So he fell to plucking them in quantities and cramming them in his pokes and breast pockets till these were stuffed full. After which he picked others which he placed in his waist shawl and then, girding himself therewith, carried off all he availed to, purposing to place them in the house by way of ornaments and, as hath been mentioned, never imagining that they were other than glass. Then he hurried his pace in fear of his uncle, the Maghrabi, until he had passed through the four halls and lastly on his return reached the souterrain, where he cast not a look at the jars of gold, albeit he was able and allowed to take of the contents on his way back. But when he came to the souterrain stairs and clomb the steps till naught remained but the last, and finding this higher than an the others, he was unable alone and unassisted, burthened moreover as he was, to mount it. So he said to the Maghrabi, "O my uncle, lend me thy hand and aid me to climb." But the Moorman answered: "O my son, give me the lamp and lighten thy load. Belike 'tis that weighteth thee down." The lad rejoined: "O my uncle, 'tis not the lamp downweigheth me at all, but do thou lend me a hand, and as soon as I reached ground I will give it to thee." Hereat the Moroccan, the magician, whose only object was the lamp and none other, began to insist upon Aladdin giving it to him at once. But the lad (forasmuch as he had placed it at the bottom of his breast pocket and his other pouches, being full of gems, bulged outward) could not reach it with his fingers to hand it over, so the wizard after much vain persistency in requiring what his nephew was unable to give fell to raging with furious rage and to demanding the lamp, whilst Aladdin could not get at it. Yet had the lad promised truthfully that he would give it up as soon as he might reach ground, without lying thought or ill intent. But when the Moorman saw that he would not hand it over, he waxed wroth with wrath exceeding and cut off all his hopes of winning it. So he conjured and adjured and cast incense a-middlemost the fire, when forthright the slab made a cover of itself, and by the might of magic lidded the entrance. The earth buried the stone as it was aforetime, and Aladdin, unable to issue forth, remained underground.

Now the sorcerer was a stranger and, as we have mentioned, no uncle of Aladdin's, and he had misrepresented himself and preferred a lying claim, to the end that he might obtain the lamp by means of the lad for whom this hoard had been upstored. So the accursed heaped the earth over him and left him to die of hunger. For this Maghrabi was an African of Afrikiyah proper, born in the inner Sunset Land, and from his earliest age upward he had been addicted to witchcraft and had studied and practiced every manner of occult science, for which unholy lore the city of Africa is notorious. And he ceased not to read and hear lectures until he had become a past master in all such knowledge. And of the abounding skill in spells and conjurations which he had acquired by the perusing and the lessoning of forty years, one day of the days he discovered by devilish inspiration that there lay in an extreme city of the cities of China, named Al-Kal'as, an immense hoard, the like whereof none of the kings in this world had ever accumulated. Moreover, that the most marvelous article in this enchanted treasure was a wonderful lamp, which whoso possessed could not possibly be surpassed by any man upon earth, either in high degree or in wealth and opulence, nor could the mightiest monarch of the universe attain to the all-sufficiency of this lamp with its might of magical means. When the Maghrabi assured himself by his science and saw that this hoard could be opened only by the presence of a lad named Aladdin, of pauper family and abiding in that very city, and learnt how taking it would be easy and without hardships, he straightway and without stay or delay equipped himself for a voyage to China (as we have already told), and be did what he did with Aladdin fancying that he would become Lord of the Lamp. But his attempt and his hopes were baffled and his work was clean wasted. Whereupon, determining to do the lad die, he heaped up the earth over him by gramarye to the end that the unfortunate might perish, reflecting that "The live man hath no murtherer." Secondly, he did so with the design that, as Aladdin could not come forth from underground, he would also be impotent to bring out the lamp from the souterrain. So presently he wended his ways and retired to his own land, Africa, a sadder man and disappointed of all his expectations.

Such was the case with the wizard, but as regards Aladdin, when the earth was heaped over him, he began shouting to the Moorman, whom he believed to be his uncle, and praying him to lend a hand that he might issue from the souterrain and return to earth's surface. But however loudly he cried, none was found to reply. At that moment he comprehended the sleight which the Moroccan had played upon him, and that the man was no uncle, but a liar and a wizard. Then the unhappy despaired of life, and learned to his sorrow that there was no escape for him, so he fell to beweeping with sore weeping the calamity had befallen him. And after a little while he stood up and descended the stairs to see if Allah Almighty had lightened his grief load by leaving a door of issue. So he turned him to the right and to the left, but he saw naught save darkness and four walls closed upon him, for that the magician had by his magic locked all the doors and had shut up even the garden wherethrough the lad erst had passed, lest it offer him the means of issuing out upon earth's surface, and that he might surely die. Then Aladdin's weeping waxed sorer and his wailing louder whenas he found all the doors fast shut, for he had thought to solace himself awhile in the garden. But when he felt that all were locked, he fell to shedding tears and lamenting like unto one who hath lost his every hope, and he returned to sit upon the stairs of the flight whereby he had entered the souterrain.

But it is a light matter for Allah (be He exalted and extolled!) whenas He designeth aught to say, "Be," and it becometh, for that He createth joy in the midst of annoy. And on this wise it was with Aladdin. Whilst the Maghrabi, the magician, was sending him down into the souterrain, he set upon his finger by way of gift a seal ring and said: "Verily this signet shall save thee from every strait an thou fall into calamity and ill shifts of time, and it shall remove from thee all hurt and harm, and aid thee with a strong arm whereso thou mayest be set." Now this was by Destiny of God the Great, that it might be the means of Aladdin's escape. For whilst he sat wailing and weeping over his case and cast away all hope of life, and utter misery overwhelmed him, he rubbed his hands together for excess of sorrow, as is the wont of the woeful. Then, raising them in supplication to Allah, he cried, "I testify that there is no God save Thou alone, the Most Great, the Omnipotent, the All-conquering, Quickener of the dead, Creator of man's need and Granter thereof, Resolver of his difficulties and duress and Bringer of joy, not of annoy. Thou art my sufficiency and Thou art the Truest of Trustees. And I bear my witness that Mohammed is Thy servant and Thine Apostle, and I supplicate Thee, O my God, by his favor with Thee to free me from this my foul plight."

And whilst implored the Lord and was chafing his hands in the soreness of his sorrow for that had befallen him of calamity, his fingers chanced to rub the ring, when, lo and behold! forthright its familiar rose upright before him and cried: "Adsum! Thy slave between thy hands is come! Ask whatso thou wantest, for that I am the thrall of him on whose hand is the ring, the signet of my lord and master." Hereat the lad looked at him and saw standing before him a Marid like unto an Ifrit of our lord Solomon's Jinns. He trembled at the terrible sight, but, hearing the Slave of the

Ring say, "Ask whatso thou wantest. Verily, I am thy thrall seeing that the signet of my lord be upon thy finger," he recovered his spirits and remembered the Moorman's saying when giving him the ring. So he rejoiced exceedingly and became brave and cried, "Ho, thou slave of the Lord of the Ring, I desire thee to set me upon the face of the earth." And hardly had he spoken this speech when suddenly the ground clave asunder and he found himself at the door of the hoard and outside it in full view of the world. Now for three whole days he had been sitting in the darkness of the treasury underground, and when the sheen of day and the shine of sun smote his face he found himself unable to keep his eyes open; so he began to unclose the lids a little and to close them a little until his eyeballs regained force and got used to the light and were purged of the noisome murk. Withal he was astounded at finding himself without the hoard door whereby he had passed in when it was opened by the Maghrabi, the magician, especially as the adit had been lidded and the ground had been smoothed, showing no sign whatever of entrance.

Thereat his surprise increased until he fancied himself in another place, nor was his mind convinced that the stead was the same until he saw the spot whereupon they had kindled the fire of wood chips and dried sticks, and where the African wizard had conjured over the incense. Then he turned him rightward and leftward and sighted the gardens from afar and his eyes recognized the road whereby he had come. So he returned thanks to Allah Almighty, Who had restored him to the face of earth and had freed him from death after he had cut off all hopes of life. Presently he arose and walked along the way to the town, which now he knew well, until he entered the streets and passed on to his own home. Then he went in to his mother, and on seeing her, of the overwhelming stress of joy at his escape and the memory of past affright and the hardships he had borne and the pangs of hunger, he fell to the ground before his parent in a fainting fit. Now his mother had been passing sad since the time of his leaving her, and he found her moaning and crying about him. However, on sighting him enter the house she joyed with exceeding joy, but soon was overwhelmed with woe when he sank upon the ground swooning before her eyes. Still, she did not neglect the matter or treat it lightly, but at once hastened to sprinkle water upon his face, and after she asked of the neighbors some scents which she made him snuff up. And when he came round a little, he prayed her to bring him somewhat of food saying, "O my mother, 'tis now three days since I ate anything at all." Thereupon she arose and brought him what she had by her, then, setting it before him, said: "Come forward, O my son. Eat and be cheered, and when thou shalt have rested, tell me what hath betided and affected thee, O my child. At this present I will not question thee, for thou art aweary in very deed." Aladdin ate and drank and was cheered, and after he had rested and had recovered spirits he cried: "Ah, O my mother, I have a sore grievance against thee for leaving me to that accursed wight who strave to compass my destruction and designed to take my life. Know thou that I beheld death with mine own eyes at the hand of this damned wretch, whom thou didst to be my uncle, and had not Almighty Allah rescued me from him, I and thou, O my mother, had been cozened by the excess of this accursed's promises to work my welfare, and by the great show of affection which he manifested to us. Learn, O my mother, that this fellow is a sorcerer, a Moorman, an accursed, a liar, a traitor, a hypocrite, nor deem I that the devils under the earth are damnable as he. Allah abase him in his every book! Hear then, O my mother, what this abominable one did, and all that I shall tell thee will be soothfast and certain. See how the damned villain brake every promise he made, certifying that he would soon work all good with me. And do thou consider the fondness which he displayed to me and the deeds which he did by me, and all this only to win his wish, for his design was to destroy me. And Alhamdolillah- laud to the Lord- for my deliverance. Listen and learn, O my mother, how this accursed entreated me."

Then Aladdin informed his mother of all that had befallen him, weeping the for stress of gladness- how the Maghrabi had led him to a hill wherein was hidden the hoard and how he had conjured and fumigated, adding: "After which, O my mother, mighty fear gat hold of me when the hill split and the earth gaped before me by his wizardry. And I trembled with terror at the rolling of thunder in mine ears and the murk which fell upon us when he fumigated and muttered spells. Seeing these horrors, I in mine affright desiped to fly, but when he understood mine intent, he reviled me and smote me a buffet so sore that it caused me swoon. However, inasmuch as the treasury was to be opened only by means of me, O my mother, he could not descend therein himself, it being in my name and not in his. And for that he is an ill-omened magician, he understood that I was necessary to him and this was his need of me."

Aladdin acquainted his mother with all that had befallen him from the Maghrabi, the magician, and said: "After he had buffeted me, he judged it advisable to soothe me in order that he might send me down into the enchanted treasury, and first he drew from his finger a ring, which he placed upon mine. So I descended and found four halls all full of gold and silver, which counted as naught, and the accursed had charged me not to touch aught thereof. Then I entered a mighty fine flower garden everywhere bedecked with tall trees whose foilage and fruitage bewildered the wits, for all, O my mother, were of varicolored glass, and lastly I reached the hall wherein hung this lamp. So I took it straightway and put it out and poured forth its contents." And so saying, Aladdin drew the lamp from his breast pocket and showed it to his mother, together with the gems and jewels which he had brought from the garden. And there were two large bag pockets full of precious stones, whereof not one was to be found amongst the kings of the world. But the lad knew naught anent their worth, deeming them glass or crystal. And presently he resumed:

"After this, O mother mine, I reached the hoard door carrying the lamp and shouted to the accursed sorcerer which called himself my uncle to lend me a hand and hale me up, I being unable to mount of myself the last step for the overweight of my burthen. But he would not and said only, 'First hand me the lamp!' As, however, I had placed it at the bottom of my breast pocket and the other pouches bulged out beyond it, I was unable to get at it and said, 'O my uncle, I cannot reach thee the lamp, but I will give it to thee when outside the treasury.' His only need was the lamp, and he designed, O my mother, to snatch it from me and after that slay me, as indeed he did his best to do by heaping the earth over my head. Such then is what befell me from this foul sorcerer." Hereupon Aladdin fell to abusing the magician in hot wrath and with a burning heart, and crying: "Wellaway! I take refuge from this damned wight, the forswearer the wrongdoer, the forswearer, the lost to all humanity, the archtraitor, the hyprocrite, the annihilator of ruth and mercy." When Aladdin's mother heard his words and what had befallen him from the Maghrabi, the magician, she said: "Yea, verily, O my son, he is a miscreant, a hypocrite who murthereth the folk by his magic. But 'twas the grace of Allah Almighty, O my child, that saved thee from the tricks and the treachery of this accursed sorcerer whom I deemed to be truly thine uncle."

Then, as the lad had not slept a wink for three days and found himself nodding, he sought his natural rest, his mother doing on like wise, nor did he awake till about noon on the second day. As soon as he shook off slumber he called for somewhat of food, being sore a-hungered, but said his mother: "O my son, I have no victual for thee, inasmuch as yesterday thou atest all that was in the house. But wait patiently a while. I have spun a trifle of yarn which I will carry to the market street and sell it and buy with what it may be worth some victual for thee." "O my mother," said he, "keep your yarn and sell it not, but fetch me the lamp I brought hither that I may go vend it, and with its price purchase provaunt, for that I deem 'twill bring more money than the spinnings." So Aladdin's mother arose and fetched the lamp for her son, but while so doing she saw that it was dirty exceedingly, so that said: "O my son, here is the lamp, but 'tis very foul. After we shall have washed it and polished it 'twill sell better." Then, taking a handful of sand, she began to rub therewith, but she had only begun when appeared to her one of the Jann, whose favor was frightful and whose bulk was horrible big, and he was gigantic as one of the Jababirah. And forthright he cried to her: "Say whatso thou wantest of me. Here am I, thy slave and slave to whoso holdeth the lamp, and not I alone, but all the Slaves of the Wonderful Lamp which thou hendest in hand."

She quaked and terror was sore upon her when she looked at that frightful form, and her tongue being tied, she could not return aught reply, never having been accustomed to espy similar semblances. Now her son was standing afar off, and he had already seen the Jinni of the ring which he had rubbed within the treasury, so when he heard the slave speaking to his parent, he hastened forward, and snatching the lamp from her hand, said: "O Slave of the Lamp, I am a-hungered, and 'tis my desire that thou fetch me somewhat to eat, and let it be something toothsome beyond our means." The Jinni disappeared for an eye twinkle and returned with a mighty fine tray and precious of price, for that 'twas all in virginal silver, and upon it stood twelve golden platters of meats manifold and dainties delicate, with bread snowier than snow; also two silvern cups and as many black jacks full of wine clear-strained and long-stored. And after setting all these before Aladdin, he vanished from vision.

Thereupon the lad went and sprinkled rose-water upon his mother's face and caused her snuff up perfumes pure and pungent, and said to her when she revived: "Rise, O mother mine, and let us eat of these meats wherewith Almighty Allah hath eased our poverty." But when she saw that mighty fine silvern tray she fell to marveling at the matter, and quoth she: "O my son, who be this generous, this beneficent one who hath abated our hunger pains and our penury? We are indeed under obligation to him, and meseemeth 'tis the Sultan who, hearing of our mean condition and our misery, hath sent us this food tray." Quoth he: "O my mother, this be no time for questioning. Arouse thee and let us eat, for we are both a-famished." Accordingly they sat down to the tray and fell to feeding, when Aladdin's mother tasted meats whose like in all her time she had never touched. So they devoured them with sharpened appetites and all the capacity engendered by stress of hunger. And secondly, the food was such that marked the tables of the kings. But neither of them knew whether the tray was or was not valuable, for never in their born days had they looked upon aught like it.

As soon as they had finished the meal (withal leaving victual enough for supper and eke for the next day), they arose and washed their hands and sat at chat, when the mother turned to her son and said: "Tell me, O my child, what befell thee from the slave, the Jinni, now that Alhamdolillah- laud to the Lord!- we have eaten our full of the good things wherewith He hath favored us and thou hast no pretext for saying to me, 'I am a-hungered.'" So Aladdin related to her all that took place between him and the slave what while she had sunk upon the ground a-swoon for sore terror, and at this she, being seized with mighty great surprise, said: "'Tis true, for the Jinns do present themselves before the sons of Adam, but I, O my son, never saw them in all my life, and meseemeth that this be the same who saved thee when thou wast within the enchanted hoard." "This is not he, O my mother. This who appeared before thee is the Slave of the Lamp!" "Who may this be, O my son?" "This be a slave of sort and shape other than he. That was the familiar of the ring, and this his fellow thou sawest was the Slave of the Lamp thou hendest in hand." And when his parent heard these words she cried: "There! there! So this accursed, who showed himself to me and went nigh unto killing me with affright, is attached to the lamp." "Yes," he replied, and she rejoined: "Now I conjure thee, O my son, by the milk wherewith I suckled thee, to throw away from thee this lamp and this ring, because they can cause us only extreme terror, and I especially can never a-bear a second glance at them. Moreover, all intercourse with them is unlawful, for that the Prophet (whom Allah save and assain!) warned us against them with threats."

He replied: "Thy commands, O my mother, be upon my head and mine eyes, but as regards this saying thou saidest, 'tis impossible that I part or with lamp or with ring. Thou thyself hast seen what good the slave wrought us whenas we were famishing, and know, O my mother, that the Maghrabi, the liar, the magician, when sending me down into the hoard, sought nor the silver nor the gold wherewith the four halls were fulfilled, but charged me to bring him only the lamp (naught else), because in very deed he had learned its priceless value. And had he not been certified of it, he had never endured such toil and trouble, nor had he traveled from his own land to our land in search thereof, neither had he shut me up in the treasury when he despaired of the lamp which I would not hand to him. Therefore it besitteth us, O my mother, to keep this lamp and take all care thereof, nor disclose its mysteries to any, for this is now our means of livelihood and this it is shall enrich us. And likewise as regards the ring, I will never withdraw it from my finger, inasmuch as but for this thou hadst nevermore seen me on life- nay, I should have died within the hoard underground. How then can I possibly remove it

150

from my finger? And who wotteth that which may betide me by the lapse of time, what trippings or calamities or injurious mishaps wherefrom this ring may deliver me? However, for regard to thy feelings I will stow away the lamp, nor ever suffer it to be seen of thee hereafter." Now when his mother heard his words and pondered them, she knew they were true and said to him: "Do, O my son, whatso thou willest. For my part, I wish never to see them nor ever sight that frightful spectacle I erst saw."

Aladdin and his mother continued eating of the meats brought them by the Jinni for two full told days till they were finished. But when he learned that nothing of food remained for them, he arose and took a platter of the platters which the slave had brought upon the tray. Now they were all of the finest gold, but the lad knew naught thereof, so he bore it to the bazaar and there, seeing a man which was a Jew, a viler than the Satans, offered it to him for sale. When the Jew espied it, he took the lad aside that none might see him, and he looked at the platter and considered it till he was certified that it was of gold refined. But he knew not whether Aladdin was acquainted with its value or he was in such matters a raw laddie, so he asked him, "For how much, O my lord, this platter?" and the other answered, "Thou wottest what be its worth." The Jew debated with himself as to how much he should offer, because Aladdin had returned him a craftsmanlike reply, and he thought of the smallest valuation. At the same time he feared lest the lad, haply knowing its worth, should expect a considerable sum. So he said in his mind, "Belike the fellow is an ignoramus in such matters, nor is ware of the price of the platter." Whereupon he pulled out of his pocket a dinar, and Aladdin eyed the gold piece lying in his palm and, hastily taking it, went his way, whereby the Jew was certified of his customer's innocence of all such knowledge, and repented with entire repentance that he had given him a golden dinar in lieu of a copper carat, a bright-polished groat.

However, Aladdin made no delay, but went at once to the baker's, where he bought him bread and changed the ducat. Then, going to his mother, he gave her the scones and the remaining small coin and said, "O my mother, hie thee and buy thee all we require." So she arose and walked to the bazaar and laid in the necessary stock, after which they ate and were cheered. And whenever the price of the platter was expended, Aladdin would take another and carry it to the accursed Jew, who brought each and every at a pitiful price; and even this he would have minished but, seeing how he had paid a dinar for the first, he feared to offer a lesser sum, lest the lad go and sell to some rival in trade and thus he lose his usurious gains. Now when all the golden platters were sold, there remained only the silver tray whereupon they stood, and for that it was large and weighty, Aladdin brought the Jew to his house and produced the article when the buyer, seeing its size, gave him ten dinars, and these being accepted, went his ways.

Aladdin and his mother lived upon the sequins until they were spent, then he brought out the lamp and rubbed it, and straightway appeared the slave who had shown himself aforetime. And said the lad: "I desire that thou bring me a tray of food like unto that thou broughtest me erewhiles, for indeed I am famisht." Accordingly, in the glance of an eye the slave produced a similar tray supporting twelve platters of the most sumptuous, furnished with requisite cates, and thereon stood clean bread and sundry glass bottles of strained wine. Now Aladdin's mother had gone out when she knew he was about to rub the lamp, that she might not again look upon the Jinni; but after a while she returned, and when she sighted the tray covered with silvern platters and smelt the savor of the rich meats diffused over the house, she marveled and rejoiced. Thereupon quoth he: "Look, O my mother! Thou badest me throw away the lamp. See now its virtues," and quoth she, "O my son, Allah increase his weal, but I would not look upon him." Then the lad sat down with his parent to the tray and they ate and drank until they were satisfied, after which they removed what remained for use on the morrow.

As soon as the meats had been consumed, Aladdin arose and stowed away under his clothes a platter of the platters and went forth to find the Jew, purposing to sell it to him, but by fiat of Fate he passed by the shop of an ancient jeweler, an honest man and a pious who feared Allah. When the Sheikh saw the lad, he asked him, saying: "O my son, what dost thou want? For that times manifold have I seen thee passing hereby and having dealings with a Jewish man, and I have espied thee handing over to him sundry articles. Now also I fancy thou hast somewhat for sale and thou seekest him as a buyer thereof. But thou wottest not, O my child, that the Jews ever hold lawful to them the good of Moslems, the confessors of Allah Almighty's unity, and always defraud them, especially this accursed Jew with whom thou hast relations and into whose hands thou hast fallen. If then, O my son, thou have aught thou wouldest sell, show the same to me and never fear, for I will give thee its full price, by the truth of Almighty Allah."

Thereupon Aladdin brought out the platter, which when the ancient goldsmith saw, he took and weighed it in his scales and asked the lad, saying, "Was it the fellow of this thou soldest to the Jew?" "Yes, its fellow and its brother," he answered, and quoth the old man, "What price did he pay thee?" Quoth the lad, "One dinar." The ancient goldsmith, hearing from Aladdin how the Jew used to give only one dinar as the price of the platter, cried, "Ah! I take refuge from this accursed who cozeneth the servants of Allah Almighty!" Then, looking at the lad, he exclaimed: "O my son, verily yon tricksy Jew hath cheated thee and laughed at thee, this platter being pure silver and virginal. I have weighed it and found it worth seventy dinars, and, if thou please to take its value,-take it." Thereupon the Sheikh counted out to him seventy gold pieces, which he accepted, and presently thanked him for his kindness in exposing the Jew's rascality.

And after this, whenever the price of a platter was expended, he would bring another, and on such wise he and his mother were soon in better circumstances. Yet they ceased not to live after their olden fashion as middle-class folk, without spending on diet overmuch or squandering money. But Aladdin had now thrown off the ungraciousness of his boyhood. He shunned the society of scapegraces and he began to frequent good men and true, repairing daily to the market street of the merchants and there companying with the great and small of them, asking about matters of merchandise and learning the price of investments and so forth. He likewise frequented the bazaars of the goldsmiths and the jewelers, where he would sit and divert himself by inspecting their precious stones and by noting how jewels were sold and bought therein. Accordingly, he presently became ware that the tree truits wherewith he had filled his pockets what time he entered the enchanged treasury were neither glass nor crystal, but gems rich and rare, and he understood that he had acquired immense wealth such as the kings never can possess. He then considered all the precious stones which were in the jewelers' quarter, but found that their biggest was not worth his smallest.

On this wise he ceased not every day repairing to the bazaar and making himself familiar with the folk and winning their loving will, and inquiring anent selling and buying, giving and taking, the dear and the cheap, until one day of the days when, after rising at dawn and donning his dress he went forth, as was his wont, to the jewelers' bazaar and as he passed along it he heard the crier crying as follows: "By command of our magnificent master, the King of the Time and the Lord of the Age and the Tide, let all the folk lock up their shops and stores and retire within their houses, for that the Lady Badr al-Budur, daughter of the Sultan, designeth to visit the hammam. And whoso gainsayeth the order shall be punished with death penalty, and be his blood upon his own neck!" But when Aladdin heard the proclamation, he longed to look upon the King's daughter and said in his mind, "Indeed all the lieges talk of her beauty and loveliness, and the end of my desires is to see her." Then Aladdin fell to contriving some means whereby he might look upon the Princess Badr al-Budur, and at last judged best to take his station behind the hammam door, whence he might see her face as she entered. Accordingly, without stay or delay he repaired to the baths before she was expected and stood a-rear of the entrance, a place whereat none of the folk happened to be looking.

Now when the Sultan's daughter had gone the rounds of the city and its main streets and had solaced herself by sight-seeing, she finally reached the hammam, and whilst entering she raised her veil and Aladdin saw her favor, he said: "In very truth her fashion magnifieth her Almighty Fashioner, and glory be to Him Who created her and adorned her with this beauty and loveliness." His strength was struck down from the moment he saw her and his thoughts were distraught. His gaze was dazed, the love of her gat hold of the whole of his heart, and when he returned home to his mother, he was as one in ecstasy. His parent addressed him, but he neither replied nor denied, and, when she set before him the morning meal he continued in like case, so quoth she: "O my son, what is't may have befallen thee? Say me, doth aught ail thee? Let me know what ill hath betided thee, for, unlike thy custom, thou speakest not when I bespeak thee." Thereupon Aladdin (who used to think that all women resembled his mother and who, albeit he had heard of the charms of Badr al-Budur, daughter of the Sultan, yet knew not what "beauty" and "loveliness" might signify) turned to his parent and exclaimed, "Let me be!" However, she persisted in praying him to come forward and eat, so he did her bidding, but hardly touched food. After which he lay at full length on his bed all the night through in cogitation deep until morning morrowed.

The same was his condition during the next day, when his mother was perplexed for the case of her son and unable to learn what had happened to him. So, thinking that belike he might be ailing, she drew near him and asked him, saying: "O my son, an thou sense aught of pain or suchlike, let me know, that I may fare forth and fetch thee the physician. And today there be in this our city a leech from the land of the Arabs whom the Sultan hath sent to summon, and the bruit abroad reporteth him to be skillful exceedingly. So, an be thou ill, let me go and bring him to thee." Aladdin, hearing his parent's offer to summon the mediciner, said: "O my mother, I am well in body and on no wise ill. But I ever thought that all women resembled thee until yesterday, when I beheld the Lady Badr al-Budur, daughter of the Sultan, as she was faring for the baths." Then he related to her all and everything that had happened to him, adding: "Haply thou also hast heard the crier a-crying: 'Let no man open shop or stand in street that the Lady Badr al-Budur may repair to the hammam without eye seeing her.' But I have looked upon her even as she is, for she raised her veil at the door, and when I viewed her favor and beheld that noble work of the Creator, a sore fit of ecstasy, O my mother, fell upon me for love of her, and firm resolve to win her hath opened its way into every limb of me, nor is repose possible for me except I win her. Wherefor I purpose asking her to wife from the Sultan, her sire, in lawful wedlock." When Aladdin's mother heard her son's words, she belittled his wits and cried: "O my child, the name of Allah upon thee! Meseemeth thou hast lost thy senses. But be thou rightly guided, O my son, nor be thou as the men Jinn-maddened!" He replied: "Nay, O mother of mine, I am not out of my mind, nor am I of the maniacs, nor shall this thy saying alter one jot of what is in my thoughts. For rest is impossible to me until I shall have won the dearling of my heart's core, the beautiful Lady Badr al-Budur. And now I am resolved to ask her of her sire the Sultan."

She rejoined: "O my son, by my life upon thee, speak not such speech, lest any overhear thee and say thou be insane. So cast away from thee such nonsense! Who shall undertake a matter like this, or make such request to the

King? Indeed, I know not how, supposing thy speech to be soothfast, thou shalt manage to crave such grace of the Sultan, or through whom thou desirest to propose it." He retorted: "Through whom shall I ask it, O my mother, when thou art present? And who is there fonder and more faithful to me than thyself? So my design is that thou thyself shalt proffer this my petition." Quoth she: "O my son, Allah remove me far therefrom! What! Have I lost my wits, like thyself? Cast the thought away, and a long way, from thy heart. Remember whose son thou art, O my child, the orphan boy of a tailor, the poorest and meanest of the tailors toiling in this city; and I, thy mother, am also come of pauper folk and indigent. How then durst thou ask to wife the daughter of the Sultan, whose sire would not deign marry her with the sons of the kings and the sovereigns, except they were his peers in honor and grandeur and majesty, and were they but one degree lower, he would refuse his daughter to them." Aladdin took patience until his parent had said her say, when quoth he: "O my mother, everything thou hast called to mind is known to me. Moreover, 'tis thoroughly well known to me that I am the child of pauper parents, withal do not these words of thee divert me from my design at all, at all. Nor the less do I hope of thee, an I be thy son and thou truly love me, that thou grant me this favor. Otherwise thou wilt destroy me, and present death hovereth over my head except I win my will of heart's dearling. And I, O my mother, am in every case thy child."

Hearing these words, his parent wept of her sorrow for him and said: "O my child! Yes, in very deed I am thy mother, nor have I any son or life's blood of my liver except thyself, and the end of my wishes is to give thee a wife and rejoice in thee. But suppose that I would seek a bride of our likes and equals, her people will at once ask an thou have any land or garden, merchandise or handicraft, wherewith thou canst support her, and what is the reply I can return? Then, if I cannot possibly answer the poor like ourselves, how shall I be bold enough, O my son, to ask for the daughter of the Sultan of China land, who hath no peer or behind or before him? Therefore do thou weigh this matter in thy mind. Also who shall ask her to wife for the son of a snip? Well indeed I wot that my saying aught of this kind will but increase our misfortunes, for that it may be the cause of our incurring mortal danger from the Sultan- peradventure even death for thee and me.

"And, as concerneth myself, how shall I venture upon such rash deed and perilous, O my son? And in what way shall I ask the Sultan for his daughter to be thy wife, and indeed how ever shall I even get access to him? And should I succeed therein, what is to be my answer an they ask me touching thy means? Haply the King will hold me to be a madwoman. And lastly, suppose that I obtain audience of the Sultan, what offering is there I can submit to the King's majesty? 'Tis true, O my child, that the Sultan is mild and merciful, never rejecting any who approach him to require justice or ruth or protection, nor any who pray him for a present, for he is liberal and lavisheth favor upon near and far. But he dealeth his boons to those deserving them, to men who have done some derring-do in battle under his eyes or have rendered as civilians great service to his estate. But thou! Do thou tell me what feat thou hast performed in his presence or before the public that thou meritest from him such grace? And secondly, this boon thou ambitionest is not for one of our condition, nor is it possible that the

King grant to thee the bourne of thine aspiration. For whoso goeth to the Sultan and craveth of him a favor, him it besitteth to take in hand somewhat that suiteth the royal majesty, as indeed I warned thee aforetime. How, then, shalt thou risk thyself to stand before the Sultan and ask his daughter in marriage when thou hast with thee naught to offer him of that which beseemeth his exalted station?"

Hereto Aladdin replied: "O my mother, thou speakest to the point and hast reminded me aright, and 'tis meet that I revolve in mind the whole of thy remindings. But, O my mother, the love of Princess Badr al-Budur hath entered into the core of my heart, nor can I rest without I win her. However, thou hast also recalled to me a matter which I forgot, and 'tis this emboldeneth me to ask his daughter of the King. Albeit thou, O my mother, declarest that I have no gift which I can submit to the Sultan, as is the wont of the world, yet in very sooth I have an offering and a present whose equal, O my mother, I hold none of the kings to possess- no, even aught like it. Because verily that which I deemed glass or crystal was nothing but precious stones, and I hold that all the kings of the world have never possessed anything like one of the smallest thereof. For by frequenting the jeweler folk I have learned that they are the costliest gems, and these are what I brought in my pockets from the hoard, whereupon, an thou please, compose thy mind.

"We have in our house a bowl of China porcelain, so arise thou and fetch it, that I may fill it with these jewels, which thou shalt carry as a gift to the King, and thou shalt stand in his presence and solicit him for my requirement. I am certified that by such means the matter will become easy to thee, and if thou be unwilling, O my mother, to strive for the winning of my wish as regards the Lady Badr al-Budur, know thou that surely I shall die. Nor do thou imagine that this gift is of aught save the costliest of stones, and be assured, O my mother, that in my many visits to the jewelers' bazaar I have observed the merchants selling for sums man's judgment may not determine jewels whose beauty is not worth one quarter-carat of what we possess, seeing which I was certified that ours are beyond all price. So arise, O my mother, as I bade thee, and bring me the porcelain bowl aforesaid, that I may arrange therein some of these gems, and we will see what semblance they show."

So she brought him the china bowl, saying in herself, "I shall know what to do when I find out if the words of my child concerning these jewels be soothfast or not." And she set it before her son, who pulled the stones out of his pockets and disposed them in the bowl, and ceased not arranging therein gems of sorts till such time as he had filled it. And when it was brimful, she could not fix her eyes firmly upon it; on the contrary, she winked and blinked for the dazzle of the stones and their radiance and excess of lightninglike glance, and her wits were bewildered thereat. Only she was not certified of their value being really of the enormous extent she had been told. Withal she reflected that possibly her son might have spoken aright when he declared that their like was not to be found with the kings. Then Aladdin turned to her and said: "Thou hast-seen, O my mother, that this present intended for the Sultan is magnificent, and I am certified that it will procure for thee high honor with him, and that he will receive thee with all respect. And now, O my mother, thou hast no excuse, so compose thy thoughts and arise. Take thou this bowl, and away with it to the palace."

His mother rejoined: "O my son, 'tis true that the present is highpriced exceedingly and the costliest of the costly, also that according to thy word none owneth its like. But who would have the boldness to go and ask the Sultan for his daughter, the Lady Badr al-Budur? I indeed dare not say to him, 'I want thy daughter!' when he shall ask me, 'What is thy want?' For know thou, O my son, that my tongue will be tied. And granting that Allah assist me and I embolden myself to say to him, 'My wish is to become a connection of thine through the marriage of thy daughter the Lady Badr al-Budur, to my son Aladdin,' they will surely decide at once that I am demented and will thrust me forth in disgrace and despised. I will not tell thee that I shall thereby fall into danger of death, for 'twill not be I only, but thou likewise. However, O my son, of my regard for thine inclination I needs must embolden myself and hie thither. Yet, O my. child, if the King receive me and honor me on account of the gift and inquire of me what thou desirest, and in reply I ask of him that which thou desirest in the matter of thy marriage with his daughter, how shall I answer him and he ask me, as is man's wont, 'What estates hast thou, and what income?' And perchance, O my son, he will question me of this before questioning me of thee."

Aladdin replied: "Tis not possible that the Sultan should make such demand what time he considereth the jewels and their magnificence, nor is it meet to think of such things as these, which may never occur. Now do thou but arise and set before him this present of precious stones and ask of him his daughter for me, and sit not yonder making much of the difficulty in thy fancy. Ere this thou hast learned, O mother mine, that the lamp which we possess hath become to us a stable income, and that whatso I want of it the same

162

is supplied to me. And my hope is that by means thereof I shall learn how to answer the Sultan should he ask me of that thou sayest." Then Aladdin and his mother fell to talking over the subject all that night long, and when morning morrowed, the dame arose and heartened her heart, especially as her son had expounded to her some little of the powers of the lamp and the virtues thereof; to wit, that it would supply all they required of it. Aladdin, however, seeing his parent take courage when he explained to her the workings of the lamp, feared lest she might tattle to the folk thereof, so he said to her: "O my mother, beware how thou talk to any of the properties of the lamp and its profit, as this is our one great good. Guard thy thoughts lest thou speak overmuch concerning it before others, whoso they be. Haply we shall lose it and lose the boon fortune we possess and the benefits we expect, for that 'tis of him." His mother replied, "Fear not therefor, O my son," and she arose and took the bowl full of jewels, which she wrapped up in a fine kerchief, and went forth betimes that she might reach the Divan ere it became crowded.

When she passed into the palace, the levee not being fully attended, she saw the wazirs and sundry of the lords of the land going into the presence room, and after a short time, when the Divan was made complete by the Ministers and high officials and chieftains and emirs and grandees, the Sultan appeared, and the wazirs made their obeisance and likewise did the nobles and the notables. The King seated himself upon the throne of his kingship, and all present at the levee stood before him with crossed arms awaiting his commandment to sit, and when they received it, each took his place according to his degree. Then the claimants came before the Sultan, who delivered sentence, after his wonted way, until the Divan was ended, when the King arose and withdrew into the palace and the others all went their ways. And when Aladdin's mother saw the throne empty and the King passing into his harem, she also wended her ways and returned home. But as soon as her son espied her, bowl in hand, he thought that haply something untoward had befallen her, but he would not ask of aught until such time as she had set down the bowl, when she acquainted him with that had occurred and ended by adding: "Alhamdolillah- laud to the Lord!- O my child, that I found courage enough and secured for myself standing place in the levee this day. And, albe' I dreaded to bespeak the King yet (Inshallah!) on the morrow I will address him. Even today were many who, like myself, could not get audience of the Sultan. But be of good cheer, O my son, and tomorrow needs must I bespeak him for thy sake, and what happened not may happen." When Aladdin heard his parent's words, he joyed with excessive joy, and, although he expected the matter to be managed hour by hour, for excess of his love and longing to the Lady Badr al-Budur, yet he possessed his soul in patience.

They slept well that night, and betimes next morning the mother of Aladdin arose and went with her bowl to the King's Court, which she found closed. So she asked the people and they told her that the Sultan did not hold a levee every day, but only thrice in the sennight, wherefor she determined to return home. And after this, whenever she saw the Court open she would stand before the King until the reception ended, and when it was shut she would go to make sure thereof, and this was the case for the whole month. The Sultan was wont to remark her presence at every levee, but on the last day when she took her station, as was her wont, before the Council, she allowed it to close, and lacked boldness to come forward and speak even a syllable. Now as the King, having risen, was making for his harem accompanied by the Grand Wazir, he turned to him and said: "O Wazir, during the last six or seven levee days I see yonder old woman present herself at every reception, and I also note that she always carrieth a something under her mantilla. Say me, hast thou, O Wazir, any knowledge of her and her intention?" "O my lord the Sultan," said the other, "verily women be weakly of wits, and haply this goodwife cometh hither to complain before thee against her goodman or some of her people." But this reply was far from satisfying the Sultan- nay, he bade the Wazir, in case she should come again, set her before him, and forthright the Minister placed hand on head and exclaimed, "To hear is to obey, O our lord the Sultan!"

Now one day of the days, when she did according to her custom, the Sultan cast his eyes upon her as she stood before him and said to his Grand Wazir: "This be the very woman whereof I spake to thee yesterday, so do thou straightway bring her before me, that I may see what be her suit and fulfill her need." Accordingly the Minister at once introduced her, and when in the presence she saluted the King by kissing her finger tips and raising them to her brow, and, praying for the Sultan's glory and continuance and the permanence of his prosperity, bussed ground before him. Thereupon quoth he: "O woman, for sundry days I have seen thee attend the levee sans a word said, so tell me an thou have any requirement I may grant." She kissed ground a second time and after blessing him, answered: "Yea, verily, as thy head liveth, O King of the Age, I have a want. But first of all do thou deign grant me a promise of safety, that I may prefer my suit to the ears of our lord the Sultan, for haply thy Highness may find it a singular." The King, wishing to know her need, and being a man of unusual mildness and clemency, gave his word for her immunity and bade forthwith dismiss all about him, remaining without other but the Grand Wazir. Then he turned toward his suppliant and said: "Inform me of thy suit. Thou hast the safeguard of Allah Almighty." "O King of the Age," replied she, "I also require of thee pardon," and quoth he, "Allah pardon thee even as I do."

Then quoth she: "O our lord the Sultan, I have a son, Aladdin hight, and he, one day of the days, having heard the crier commanding all men to shut shop and shun the streets for that the Lady Badr al-Budur, daughter of the Sultan, was going to the hammam, felt an uncontrollable longing to look upon her, and hid himself in a stead whence he could sight her right well, and that place was behind the door of the baths. When she entered, he beheld her and considered her as he wished, and but too well, for since the time he looked upon her, O King of the Age, unto this hour, life hath not been pleasant to him. And he hath required of me that I ask her to wife for him from thy Highness, nor could I drive this fancy from his mind, because love of her hath mastered his vitals and to such degree that he said to me, 'Know thou, O mother mine, that an I win not my wish surely I shall die.' Accordingly I hope that thy Highness will deign be mild and merciful and pardon this boldness on the part of me and my child and refrain to punish us therefor."

When the Sultan heard her tale, he regarded her with kindness and, laughing aloud, asked her, "What may be that thou carriest, and what be in yonder kerchief?" And she, seeing the Sultan laugh in lieu of waxing wroth at her words, forthright opened the wrapper and set before him the bowl of jewels, whereby the audience hall was illumined as it were by lusters and candelabra. And he was dazed and amazed at the radiance of the rare gems, and he fell to marveling at their size and beauty and excellence and cried: "Never at all until this day saw I anything like these jewels for size and beauty and excellence, nor deem I that there be found in my Treasury a single one like them." Then he turned to his Minister and asked: "What sayest thou, O Wazir? Tell me, hast thou seen in thy time such mighty fine jewels as these?" The other answered: "Never saw I such, O our lord the Sultan, nor do I think that there be in the treasures of my lord the Sultan the fellow of the least thereof." The King resumed: "Now indeed whoso hath presented to me such jewels meriteth to become bridegroom to my daughter, Badr al-Budur, because, as far as I see, none is more deserving of her than he." When the Wazir heard the Sultan's words, he was tongue-tied with concern, and he grieved with sore grief, for the King had promised to give the Princess in marriage to his son. So after a little while he said: "O King of the Age, thy Highness deigned promise me that the Lady Badr al-Budur should be spouse to my son, so 'tis but right that thine Exalted Highness vouchsafe us a delay of three months, during which time, Inshallah! my child may obtain and present an offering yet costlier than this." Accordingly the King, albeit he knew that such a thing could not be done, or by the Wazir or by the greatest of his grandees, yet of his grace and kindness granted him the required delay.

Then he turned to the old woman, Aladdin's mother, and said: "Go to thy son and tell him I have pledged my word that my daughter shall be in his name. Only 'tis needful that I make the requisite preparations of nuptial furniture for her use, and 'tis only meet that he take patience for the next three months." Receiving this reply, Aladdin's mother thanked the Sultan and blessed him, then, going forth in hottest haste, as one flying for joy, she went home. And when her son saw her entering with a smiling face, he was gladdened at the sip of good news, especially because she had returned without delay, as on the past days, and had not brought back the bowl. Presently he asked her saying: "Inshallah, thou bearest me, O my mother, glad tidings, and peradventure the jewels and their value have wrought their work, and belike thou hast been kindly received by the King and he hath shown thee grace and hath given ear to thy request?" So she told him the whole tale, how the Sultan had entreated her well and had marveled at the extraordinary size of the gems and their surpassing water, as did also the Wazir, adding: "And he promised that his daughter should be thine. Only, O my child, the Wazir spake of a secret contract made with him by the Sultan before he pledged himself to me and, after speaking privily, the King put me off to the end of three months. Therefore I have become fearful lest the Wazir be evilly disposed to thee, and perchance he may attempt to change the Sultan's mind."

When Aladdin heard his mother's words and how the Sultan had promised him his daughter, deferring, however, the wedding until after the third month, his mind was gladdened and he rejoiced exceedingly and said: Inasmuch as the King hath given his word after three months (well, it is a long time!), at all events my gladness is mighty great." Then he thanked his parent, showing her how her good work had exceeded her toil and travail, and said to her: "By Allah, O my mother, hitherto I was as 'twere in my grave and therefrom thou hast withdrawn me. And I praise Allah Almighty because I am at this moment certified that no man in the world is happier than I, or more fortunate." Then he took patience until two of the three months had gone by.

Now one day of the days his mother fared forth about sundown to the bazaar that she might buy somewhat of oil, and she found all the market shops fast shut and the whole city decorated, and the folk placing waxen tapers and flowers at their casements. And she beheld the soldiers and household troops and agas riding in procession, and flambeaux and lusters flaming and flaring, and she wondered at the marvelous sight and the glamour of the scene. So she went in to an ouman's store which stood open still and bought her need of him and said: "By thy life, O uncle, tell me what be the tidings in town this day, that people have made all these decorations and every house and market street are adorned and the troops all stand on guard?" The oilman asked her, "O woman, I suppose thou art a stranger, and not one of this city?" and she answered, "Nay, I am thy townswoman." He rejoined: "Thou a townswoman, and yet wottest not that this very night the son of the Grand Wazir goeth in to the Lady Badr al-Budur, daughter of the Sultan! He is now in the hammam, and all this power of soldiery is on guard and standing under arms to await his coming forth, when they will bear him in bridal procession to the palace, where the Princess expecteth him."

As the mother of Aladdin heard these words, she grieved and was distraught in thought and perplexed how to inform her son of this sorrowful event, well knowing that the poor youth was looking, hour by hour, to the end of the three months. But she returned straightway home to him, and when she entered she said, "O my son, I would give thee certain tidings, yet hard to me will be the sorrow they shall occasion thee." He cried, "Let me know what be thy news," and she replied: "Verily the Sultan hath broken his promise to thee in the matter of the Lady Badr al-Budur, and this very night the Grand Wazir's son goeth in to her. And for some time, O my son, I have suspected that the Minister would change the King's mind, even as I told thee how he had spoken privily to him before me." Aladdin asked: "How learnedst thou that the Wazir's son is this night to pay his first visit to the Princess?" So she told him the whole tale, how when going to buy oil she had found the city decorated and the eunuch officials and lords of the land with the troops under arms awaiting the bridegroom from the baths, and that the first visit was appointed for that very night.

Hearing this, Aladdin was seized with a fever of jealousy brought on by his grief. However, after a short while he remembered the lamp and, recovering his spirits, said: "By thy life, O my mother, do thou believe that the Wazir's son will not enjoy her as thou thinkest. But now leave we this discourse, and arise thou and serve up supper, and after eating let me retire to my own chamber and all will be well and happy." After he had supped Aladdin retired to his chamber and, locking the door, brought out the lamp and rubbed it, whenas forthright appeared to him its familiar, who said: "Ask whatso thou wantest, for I am thy slave and slave to him who holdeth the lamp in hand, I and all the Slaves of the Lamp." He replied: "Hear me! I prayed the Sultan for his daughter to wife and he plighted her to me after three months, but he hath not kept his word- nay, he hath given her to the son of the Wazir, and this very night the bridegroom will go in to her. Therefore I command thee (an thou be a trusty servitor to the lamp), when thou shalt see bride and bridegroom bedded together this night, at once take them up and bear them hither abed. And this be what I want of thee." The Marid replied, "Hearing and obeying, and if thou have other service but this, do thou demand of me all thou desirest." Aladdin rejoined, "At the present time I require naught save that I bade thee do."

Hereupon the slave disappeared and Aladdin returned to pass the rest of the evening with his mother. But at the hour when he knew that the servitor would be coming, he arose and retired to his chamber, and after a little while, behold, the Marid came, bring to him the newly wedded couple upon their bridal bed. Aladdin rejoiced to see them with exceeding joy, then he cried to the slave, "Carry yonder gallowsbird hence and lay him at full length in the privy." His bidding was done straightway, but before leaving him, the slave blew upon the bridegroom a blast so cold that it shriveled him, and the plight of the Wazir's son became piteous. Then the servitor, returning to Aladdin, said to him, "An thou require aught else, inform me thereof," and said the other, "Return a-morn, that thou mayest restore them to their stead," whereto, "I hear and obey," quoth the Marid, and evanished.

Presently Aladdin arose, hardly believing that the affair had been such a success for him, but whenas he looked upon the Lady Badr al-Budur lying under his own roof, albeit he had long burned with her love, yet he preserved respect for her and said: "O Princess of fair ones, think not that I brought thee hither to minish thy honor. Heaven forfend!

171

Nay, 'twas only to prevent the wrong man enjoying thee, for that thy sire, the Sultan, promised thee to me. So do thou rest in peace." When the Lady Badr al-Budur, daughter of the Sultan, saw herself in that mean and darksome lodging, and heard Aladdin's words, she was seized with fear and trembling and waxed clean distraught, nor could she return aught of reply. Presently the youth arose, and stripping off his outer dress, placed a scimitar between them and lay upon the bed beside the Princess. And he did no villain deed, for it sufficed him to prevent the consummation of her nuptials with the Wazir's son. On the other hand, the Lady Badr al-Budur passed a night the evilest of all nights, nor in her born days had she seen a worse. And the same was the case with the Minister's son, who lay in the chapel of ease and who dared not stir for the fear of the Jinni which overwhelmed him.

As soon as it was morning the slave appeared before Aladdin without the lamp being rubbed, and said to him: "O my lord, an thou require aught, command me therefor, that I may do it upon my head and mine eyes." Said the other: "Go, take up and carry the bride and bridegroom to their own apartment." So the servitor did his bidding in an eye glance and bore away the pair and placed them in the palace as whilom they were and without their seeing anyone. But both died of affright when they found themselves being transported from stead to stead. And the Marid had barely time to set them down and wend his ways ere the Sultan came on a visit of congratulation to his daughter. And when the Wazir's son heard the doors thrown open, he sprang straightway from his couch and donned his dress, for he knew that none save the King could enter at that hour. Yet it was exceedingly hard for him to leave his bed, wherein he wished to warm himself a trifle after his cold night in the watercloset which he had lately left. The Sultan went in to his daughter, Badr al-Budur, and, kissing her between the eyes, gave her good morning and asked her of her bridegroom and whether she was pleased and satisfied with him. But she returned no reply whatever and looked at him with the eye of anger, and although he repeated his words again and again, she held her peace, nor bespake him with a single syllable.

So the King quitted her and, going to the Queen, informed her of what had taken place, between him and his daughter, and the mother, unwilling to leave the Sultan angered with their child, said to him: "O King of the Age, this be the custom of most newly married couples, at least during their first days of marriage, for that they are bashful and somewhat coy. So deign thou excuse her, and after a little while she will again become herself and speak with the folk as before, whereas now her shame, O King of the Age, keepeth her silent.

However, 'tis my wish to fare forth and see her." Thereupon the Queen arose and donned her dress, then, going to her daughter, wished her good morning and kissed her between the eyes. Yet would the Princess make no answer at all, whereat quoth the Queen to herself: "Doubtless some strange matter hath occurred to trouble her with such trouble as this." So she asked her, saying: "O my daughter, what hath caused this thy case? Let me know what hath betided thee that when I come and give thee good morniing, thou hast not a word to say to me." Thereat the Lady Badr al-Budur raised her head and said: "Pardon me, O my mother, 'twas my duty to meet thee with all respect and worship, seeing that thou hast honored me by this visit.

However, I pray thee to hear the cause of this my condition and see how the night I have just spent hath been to me the evilest of the nights. Hardly had we lain down, O my mother, than one whose form I wot not uplifted our bed and transported it to a darksome place, fulsome and mean."

Then the Princess related to the Queen Mother all that had befallen her that night- how they had taken away her bridegroom, leaving her lone and lonesome, and how after a while came another youth who lay beside her in lieu of her bridegroom, after placing his scimitar between her and himself. "And in the morning," she continued, "he who carried us off returned and bore us straight back to our own stead. But at once when he arrived hither he left us, and suddenly my sire, the Sultan, entered at the hour and moment of our coming and I had nor heart nor tongue to speak him withal, for the stress of the terror and trembling which came upon me. Haply such lack of duty may have proved sore to him, so I hope, O my mother, that thou wilt acquaint him with the cause of this my condition, and pardon me for not answering him and blame me not, accept my excuses."

When the Queen heard these words of Princess Badr al-Budur, she said to her: "O my child, compose thy thoughts. An thou tell such tale before any, haply shall he say, 'Verily, the Sultan's daughter hath lost her wits.' And thou hast done right well in not choosing to recount thine adventure to thy father, and beware, and again I say beware, O my daughter, lest thou inform him thereof." The Princess replied: "O my mother, I have spoken to thee like one sound in senses, nor have I lost my wits. This be what befell me, and if thou believe it not because coming from me, ask my bridegroom." To which the Queen replied: "Rise up straightway, O my daughter, and banish from thy thoughts such fancies as these. And robe thyself and come forth to glance at the bridal feasts and festivities they are making in the city for the sake of thee and thy nuptials, and listen to the drumming and the singing and look at the decorations all intended to honor thy marriage, O my daughter."

So saying, the Queen at once summoned the tirewoman, who dressed and prepared the Lady Badr al-Budur, and presently she went in to the Sultan and assured him that their daughter had suffered during all her wedding night from swevens and nightmare, and said to him, "Be not severe with her for not answering thee." Then the Queen sent privily for the Wazir's son and asked of the matter, saying, "Tell me, are these words of the Lady Badr al-Budur soothfast or not?" But he, in his fear of losing his bride out of hand, answered, "O my lady, I have no knowledge of that whereof thou speakest." Accordingly the mother made sure that her daughter had seen visions and dreams. The marriage feasts lasted throughout that day with almes and singers and the smiting of all manner instruments of mirth and merriment, while the Queen and the Wazir and his son strave right strenuously to enhance the festivities that the Princess might enjoy herself. And that day they left nothing of what exciteth to pleasure unrepresented in her presence, to the end that she might forget what was in her thoughts and derive increase of joyance.

Yet did naught of this take any effect upon her- nay, she sat in silence, sad of thought, sore perplexed at what had befallen her during the last night. It is true that the Wazir's son had suffered even more he had passed his sleeping hours lying in the watercloset. He, however had falsed the story and had cast out remembrance of the night, in the first place for his fear of losing his bride and with her the honor of a connection which brought him such excess of consideration and for which men envied him so much, and secondly, on account of the wondrous loveliness of the Lady Badr al-Budur and her marvelous beauty.

Aladdin also went forth that day and looked at the merrymakings, which extended throughout the city as well as the palace, and he fell a-laughing, especially when he heard the folk prating of the high honor which had accrued to the son of the Wazir and the prosperity of his fortunes in having become son-in-law to the Sultan, and the high consideration shown by the wedding fetes. And he said in his mind: "Indeed ye wot not, O ye miserables, what befell him last night, that ye envy him!" But after darkness fell and it was time for sleep, Aladdin arose and, retiring to his chamber, rubbed the lamp, whereupon the slave incontinently appeared and was bidden to bring him the Sultan's daughter, together with her bridegroom, as on the past night, ere the Wazir's son could abate her maidenhead. So the Marid without stay or delay evanished for a little while until the appointed time, when he returned carrying the bed whereon lay the Lady Badr al-Budur and the Wazir's son. And he did with the bridegroom as he had done before; to wit, he took him and laid him at full length in the jakes and there left him dried-up for excess of fear and trembling. Then Aladdin arose and, placing the scimitar between himself and the Princess, lay down beside her, and when day broke the slave restored the pair to their own place, leaving Aladdin filled with delight at the state of the Minister's son.

Now when the Sultan woke up a-morn, he resolved to visit his daughter and see if she would treat him as on the past day. So, shaking off his sleep, he sprang up and arrayed himself in his raiment, and going to the apartment of the Princess, bade open the door. Thereat the son of the Wazir arose forthright and came down from his bed and began donning his dress whilst his ribs were wrung with cold. For when the King entered the slave had but just brought him back. The Sultan, raising the arras, drew near his daughter as she lay abed and gave her good morning. Then, kissing her between the eyes, he asked her of her case. But he saw her looking sour and sad, and she answered him not at all only glowering at him as one in anger, and her plight was pitiable. Hereat the Sultan waxed wroth with her for that she would not reply, and he suspected that something evil had befallen her, whereupon he bared his blade and cried to her, brand in hand, saying: "What be this hath betided thee? Either acquaint me with what happened or this very moment I will take thy life! Is such conduct the token of honor and respect I expect of thee, that I address thee and thou answerest me not a word?"

When the Lady Badr al-Budur saw her sire in high dudgeon and the naked glaive in his grip, she was freed from her fear of the past, so she raised her head and said to him: "O my beloved father, be not wroth with me, nor be hasty in thy hot passion, for I am excusable in what thou shalt see of my case. So do thou lend an ear to what occurred to me, and well I wot that after hearing my account of what befell to me during these two last nights, thou wilt pardon me, and thy Highness will be softened to pitying me even as I claim of thee affection for thy child." Then the Princess informed her father of all that had betided her, adding: "O my sire, an thou believe me not, ask my bridegroom and he will recount to thy Highness the whole adventure. Nor did I know either what they would do with him when they bore him away from my side or where they would place him." When the Sultan heard his daughter's words, he was saddened and his eyes brimmed with tears, then he sheathed his saber and kissed her, saying: "O my daughter, wherefore didst thou not tell me what happened on the past night, that I might have guarded thee from this torture and terror which visited thee a second time? But now 'tis no matter. Rise and cast out all such care, and tonight I will set a watch to ward thee, nor shall any mishap again make thee miserable."

Then the Sultan returned to his palace and straightway bade summon the Grand Wazir and asked him as he stood before him in his service: "O Wazir, how dost thou look upon this matter? Haply thy son hath informed thee of what occurred to him and to my daughter." The Minister replied, "O King of the Age, I have not seen my son or yesterday or today." Hereat the Sultan told him all that had afflicted the Princess, adding: "'Tis my desire that thou at once seek tidings of thy son concerning the facts of the case. Peradventure of her fear my daughter may not be fully aware of what really befell her, withal I hold all her words to be truthful." So the Grand Wazir arose, and going forth, bade summon his son and asked him anent all his lord had told him whether it be true or untrue. The youth replied: "O my father the Wazir, Heaven forbid that the Lady Badr al-Budur speak falsely. Indeed all she said was sooth, and these two nights proved to us the evilest of our nights instead of being nights of pleasure and marriage joys. But what befell me was the greater evil, because instead of sleeping abed with my bride, I lay in the wardrobe, a black hole, frightful, noisome of stench, truly damnable, and my ribs were bursten with cold." In fine, the young man told his father the whole tale, adding as he ended it: "O dear father mine, I implore thee to speak with the Sultan that he may set me free from this marriage. Yes, indeed 'tis a high honor for me to be the Sultan's son-in-law, and especially the love of the Princess hath gotten hold of my vitals, but I have no strength left to endure a single night like unto these two last."

The Wazir, hearing the words of his son, was saddened and sorrowful exceedingly, for it was his desire to advance and promote his child by making him son-in-law to the Sultan. So he became thoughtful and perplexed about the affair and the device whereby to manage it, and it was sore grievous for him to break off the marriage, it having been a rare enjoyment to him that he had fallen upon such high good fortune. Accordingly he said: "Take patience, O my son, until we see what may happen this night, when we will set watchmen to ward you. Nor do thou give up the exalted distinction which hath fallen to none save to thyself." Then the Wazir left him and, returning to the sovereign, reported that all told to him by the Lady Badr al-Budur was a true tale. Whereupon quoth the Sultan, "Since the affair is on this wise, we require no delay," and he at once ordered all the rejoicings to cease and the marriage to be broken off. This caused the folk and the citizens to marvel at the matter, especially when they saw the Grand Wazir and his son leaving the palace in pitiable plight for grief and stress of passion, and the people fell to asking, "What hath happened, and what is the cause of the wedding being made null and void?"

Nor did any know aught of the truth save Aladdin, the lover who claimed the Princess's hand, and he laughed in his sleeve. But even after the marriage was dissolved, the

Sultan forgot nor even recalled to mind his promise made to Aladdin's mother, and the same was the case with the Grand Wazir, while neither had any inkling of whence befell them that which had befallen. So Aladdin patiently awaited the lapse of the three months after which the Sultan had pledged himself to give him to wife his daughter. But soon as ever the term came, he sent his mother to the Sultan for the purpose of requiring him to keep his covenant. So she went to the palace, and when the King appeared in the Divan and saw the old woman standing before him, he remembered his promise to her concerning the marriage after a term of three months, and he turned to the Minister and said: "O Wazir, this be the ancient dame who presented me with the jewels and to whom we pledged our word that when the three months had elapsed we would summon her to our presence before all others." So the Minister went forth and fetched her, and when she went in to the Sultan's presence she saluted him and prayed for his glory and permanence of prosperity. Hereat the King asked her if she needed aught, and she answered: "O King of the Age, the three months' term thou assignedst to me is finished, and this is thy time to my son Aladdin with thy daughter, the Lady Badr al-Budur."

The Sultan was distraught at this demand, especially when he saw the old woman's pauper condition, one of the meanest of her kind, and yet the offering she had brought to him was of the most magnificent, far beyond his power to pay the price. Accordingly he turned to the Grand Wazir and said: "What device is there with thee? In very sooth I did pass my word, yet meseemeth that they be pauper folk, and not persons of high condition." The Grand Wazir, who was dying of envy and who was especially saddened by what had befallen his son, said to himself, "How shall one like this wed the King's daughter and my son lose this highmost honor?" Accordingly he answered his sovereign, speaking privily: "O my lord, 'tis an easy matter to keep off a poor devil such as this, for he is not worthy that thy Highness give his daughter to a fellow whom none knoweth what he may be." "By what means," inquired the Sultan, "shall we put off the man when I pledged my promise, and the word of the kings is their bond?" Replied the Wazir: "O my lord, my rede is that thou demand of him forty platters made of pure sand gold and full of gems (such as the woman brought thee aforetime), with forty white slave girls to carry the platters and forty black eunuch slaves." The King rejoined: "By Allah, O Wazir, thou hast spoken to the purpose, seeing that such thing is not possible, and by this way we shall be freed."

Then quoth he to Aladdin's mother: "Do thou go and tell thy son that I am a man of my word even as I plighted it to him, but on condition that he have power to pay the dower of my daughter. And that which I require of him is a settlement consisting of twoscore platters of virgin gold, all brimming with gems the like of those thou broughtest to me, and as many white handmaids to carry them and twoscore black eunuch slaves to serve and escort the bearers. An thy son avail hereto, I will marry him with my daughter." Thereupon she returned home wagging her head and saying in her mind: "Whence can my poor boy procure these platters and such jewels? And granted that he return to the enchanted treasury and pluck them from the trees- which, however, I hold impossible- yet given that he bring them, whence shall he come by the girls and the blacks?" Nor did she leave communing with herself till she reached her home, where she found Aladdin awaiting her, and she lost no time in saying: "O my son, did I not tell thee never to fancy that thy power would extend to the Lady Badr al-Budur, and that such a matter is not possible to folk like ourselves?" "Recount to me the news," quoth he, so quoth she: "O my child, verily the Sultan received me with all honor according to his custom, and meseemeth his intentions toward us be friendly. But thine enemy is that accursed Wazir, for after I addressed the King in thy name as thou badest me say, 'In very sooth the promised term is past,' adding, "Twere well an thy Highness would deign issue commandment for the espousals of thy daughter the Lady Badr al-Budur to my son Aladdin,' he turned to and addressed the Minister, who answered privily, after which the Sultan gave me his reply." Then she enumerated the King's demand and said: "O my son, he indeed expecteth of thee an instant reply, but I fancy that we have no answer for him." When Aladdin heard these words, he laughed and said: "O my mother, thou affirmest that we have no answer and thou deemest the case difficult exceedingly, but compose thy thoughts and arise and bring me somewhat we may eat. And after we have dined, an the Compassionate be willing, thou shalt see my reply. Also the Sultan thinketh like thyself that he hath demanded a prodigious dower in order to divert me from his daughter, whereas the fact is that he hath required of me a matter far less than I expected. But do thou fare forth at once and purchase the provision and leave me to procure thee a reply."

So she went out to fetch her needful from the bazaar and Aladdin retired to his chamber and, taking the lamp, rubbed it, when forthright appeared to him its slave and said, "Ask, O my lord, whatso thou wantest." The other replied: "I have demanded of the Sultan his daughter to wife, and he hath required of me forty bowls of purest gold each weighing ten pounds and all to be filled with gems such as we find in the gardens of the hoard; furthermore, that they be borne on the heads of as many white handmaids, each attended by her black eunuch slave, also forty in full rate. So I desire that thou bring all these into my presence." "Hearkening and obeying, O my lord," quoth the slave and, disappearing for the space of an hour or so, presently returned bringing the platters and jewels, handmaids and eunuchs. Then, setting them before him, the Marid cried: "This be what thou demandest of me. Declare now an thou want any matter or service other than this." Aladdin rejoined: "I have need of naught else, but an I do, I will summon thee and let thee know."

The slave now disappeared, and after a little while, Aladdin's mother returned home, and on entering the house, saw the blacks and the handmaids. Hereat she wondered and exclaimed, "All this proceedeth from the lamp which Allah perpetuate to my son!" But ere she doffed her mantilla Aladdin said to her: "O my mother, this be thy time. Before the Sultan enter his seraglio palace do thou carry to him what he required, and wend thou with it at once, so may he know that I avail to supply all he wanteth and yet more. Also that he is beguiled by his Grand wazir, and the twain imagined vainly that they would baffle me." Then he arose forthright and opened the house door, when the handmaids and blackamoors paced forth in pairs, each girl with her eunuch besider her, until they crowded the quarter, Aladdin's mother foregoing them. And when the folk of that ward sighted such mighty fine sight and marvelous spectacle, all stood at gaze and they considered the forms and figures of the handmaids, marveling at their beauty and loveliness, for each and every wore robes inwrought with gold and studded with jewels, no dress being worth less than a thousand dinars. They stared as intently at the bowls, and albeit these were covered with pieces of brocade, also orfrayed and dubbed with precious stones, yet the sheen outshot from them dulled the shine of sun.

Then Aladdin's mother walked forward and all the handmaids and eunuchs paced behind her in the best of ordinance and disposition, and the citizens gathered to gaze at the beauty of the damsels, glorifying God the Most Great, until the train reached the palace and entered it accompanied by the tailor's widow. Now when the agas and chamberlains and army officers beheld them, all were seized with surprise, notably by seeing the handmaids, who each and every would ravish the reason of an anchorite. And albeit the royal chamberlains and officials were men of family, the sons of grandees and emirs, yet they could not but especially wonder at the costly dresses of the girls and the platters borne upon their heads, nor could they gaze at them open-eyed by reason of the exceeding brilliance and radiance. Then the nabobs went in and reported to the King, who forthright bade admit them to the presence chamber, and Aladdin's mother went in with them.

When they stood before the Sultan, all saluted him with every sign of respect and worship and prayed for his glory and prosperity. Then they set down from their heads the bowls at his feet and, having removed the brocade covers, rested with arms crossed behind them. The Sultan wondered with exceeding wonder, and was distraught by the beauty of the handmaids and their loveliness, which passed praise. And his wits were wildered when he considered the golden bowls brimful of gems which captured man's vision, and he was perplexed at the marvel until he became like the dumb, unable to utter a syllable for the excess of his wonder. Also his sense was stupefied the more when he bethought him that within an hour or so all these treasures had been collected. Presently he commanded the slave girls to enter, with what loads they bore, the dower of the Princess, and when they had done his bidding, Aladdin's mother came forward and said to the Sultan: "O my lord, this be not much wherewith to honor the Lady Badr al-Budur, for that she meriteth these things multiplied times manifold."

Hereat the sovereign turned to the Minister and asked: "What sayest thou, O Wazir? Is not he who could produce such wealth in a time so brief, is he not, I say, worthy to become the Sultan's son-in-law and take the King's daughter to wife?" Then the Minister (although he marveled at these riches even more than did the Sultan), whose envy was killing him and growing greater hour by hour, seeing his liege lord satisfied with the moneys and the dower and yet being unable to fight against fact, made answer, "'Tis not worthy of her." Withal he fell to devising a device against the King, that he might withhold the Lady Badr al-Budur from Aladdin, and accordingly he continued: "O my liege, the treasures of the universe all of them are not worth a nail paring of thy daughter. Indeed thy Highness hath prized these things overmuch in comparison with her."

When the King heard the words of his Grand Wazir, he knew that the speech was prompted by excess of envy, so, turning to the mother of Aladdin, he said: "O woman, go to thy son and tell him that I have accepted of him the dower and stand to my bargain, and that my daughter be his bride and he my son-in-law. Furthermore, bid him at once make act of presence that I may become familiar with him. He shall see naught from me save all honor and consideration, and this night shall be the beginning of the marriage festivities. Only, as I said to thee, let him come to me and tarry not." Thereupon Aladdin's mother returned home with the speed of the storm winds that she might hasten her utmost to congratulate her son, and she flew with joy at the thought that her boy was about to become son-in-law to the Sultan.

After her departure the King dismissed the Divan and, entering the palace of the Princess, bade them bring the bowls and the handmaids before him and before her, that she also might inspect them. But when the Lady Badr al-Budur considered the jewels, she waxed distraught and cried: "Meseemeth that in the treasuries of the world there be not found one jewel rivaling these jewels." Then she looked at the handmaids and marveled at their beauty and loveliness, and knew that all this came from her new bridegroom, who had sent them in her service. So she was gladdened, albeit she had been grieved and saddened on account of her former husband, the Wazir's son, and she rejoiced with exceeding joy when she gazed upon the damsels and their charms. Nor was her sire, the Sultan, less pleased and inspirited when he saw his daughter relieved of an her mourning and melancholy, and his own vanished at the sight of her enjoyment. Then he asked her: "O my daughter, do these things divert thee? Indeed I deem that this suitor of thine be more suitable to thee than the son of the Wazir, and right soon, Inshallah! O my daughter, thou shalt have fuller joy with him."

Such was the case with the King, but as regards Aladdin, as soon as he saw his mother entering the house with face laughing for stress of joy he rejoiced at the sign of glad tidings and cried: "To Allah alone be lauds! Perfected is an I desired." Rejoined his mother: "Be gladdened at my good news, O my son, and hearten thy heart and cool thine eyes for the winning of thy wish. The Sultan hath accepted thine offering- I mean the moneys and the dower of the Lady Badr al-Budur, who is now thine affianced bride. And this very night, O my child, is your marriage and thy first visit to her, for the King, that he might assure me of his word, hath proclaimed to the world thou art his son-in-law, and promised this night to be the night of going in. But he also said to me, 'Let thy son come hither forthright that I may become familiar with him and receive him with all honor and worship.' And now here am I, O my son, at the end of my labors. Happen whatso may happen, the rest is upon thy shoulders."

Thereupon Aladdin arose and kissed his mother's hand and thanked her, enhancing her kindly service. Then he left her and, entering his chamber, took the lamp and rubbed it, when, lo and behold! its slave appeared and cried: "Adsum! Ask whatso thou wantest." The young man replied: "'Tis my desire that thou take me to a hammam whose like is not in the world. Then fetch me a dress so costly and kingly that no royalty ever owned its fellow." The Marid replied, "I hear and I obey," and carried him to baths such as were never seen by the Kings of the Chosroes, for the building was all of alabaster and camelian, and it contained marvelous limnings which captured the sight, and the great hall was studded with precious stones. Not a soul was therein, but when Aladdin entered, one of the Jann in human shape washed him and bathed him to the best of his desire. Aladdin after having been washed and bathed, left the baths and went into the great hall, where he found that his old dress had been removed and replaced by a suit of the most precious and princely. Then he was served with sherbets and ambergrised coffee, and after drinking he arose and a party of black slaves came forward and clad him in the costliest of clothing, then perfumed and fumigated him. It is known that Aladdin was the son of a tailor, a pauper, yet now would none deem him to be such- nay, all would say: "This be the greatest that is of the progeny of the kings. Praise be to Him Who changeth and Who is not changed!"

Presently came the Jinni and, lifting him up, bore him to his home, and asked, "O my lord, tell me, hast thou aught of need?" He answered: "Yes, 'tis my desire that thou bring me eight and forty Mamelukes, of whom two dozen shall forego me and the rest follow me, the whole number with their war chargers and clothing and accouterments. And all upon them and their steeds must be of naught save of highest worth and the costliest, such as may not be found in treasuries of the kings. Then fetch me a stallion fit for the riding of the Chosroes and let his furniture, all thereof, be of gold crusted with the finest gems. Fetch me also eight and forty thousand dinars, that each white slave may carry a thousand gold pieces. 'Tis now my intent to fare to the, Sultan, so delay thou not, for that without an these requisites whereof I bespake thee I may no visit him. Moreover, set before me a dozen slave girls unique in beauty and dight with the most magnificent dresses, that they wend with my mother to the royal palace, and let every handmaid be robed in raiment that befitteth Queen's wearing." The slave replied, "To hear is to obey," and, disappearing for an eye twinkling, brought all he was bidden bring, and led by hand a stallion whose rival was not amongst the Arabian Arabs, and its saddlecloth was of splendid brocade gold-in-wrought.

Thereupon, without stay or delay, Aladdin sent for his mother and gave her the garments she should wear and committed to her charge the twelve slave girls forming her suite to the palace. Then he sent one of the Mamelukes whom the Jinni had brought to see if the Sultan had left the seraglio or not. The white slave went forth lighter than the lightning and, returned in like haste, said, "O my lord, the Sultan awaiteth thee!" Hereat Aladdin arose and took horse, his Mamelukes riding a-van and arear of him, and they were such that all must cry, "Laud to the Lord Who created them and clothed them with such beauty and loveliness!" And they scattered gold amongst the crowd in front of their master, who surpassed them all in comeliness and nor needest thou ask concerning the sons of the kings- praise be to the Bountiful, the Eternal! All this was of the virtues of the wonderful lamp, which whoso possessed, him it gifted with fairest favor and finest figure, with wealth and with wisdom. The folk admired Aladdin's liberality and exceeding generosity, and all were distraught seeing his charms and elegance, his gravity and his good manners. They glorified the Creator for this noble creation, they blessed him each and every, and albeit they knew him for the son of Such-a-one, the tailor, yet no man envied him- nay, all owned that he deserved his great good fortune.

Now the Sultan had assembled the lords of the land and, informing them of the promise he had passed to Aladdin

touching the marriage of his daughter, had bidden them
await his approach and then go forth, one and all, to meet
him and greet him. Hereupon the emirs and wazirs, the
chamberlains, the nabobs and the army officers, took their
stations expecting him at the palace gate. Aladdin would
fain have dismounted at the outer entrance, but one of the
nobles, whom the King had deputed for such duty,
approached him and said, "O my lord, 'tis the royal
command that thou enter riding thy steed, nor dismount
except at the Divan door." Then they all forewent him in a
body and conducted him to the appointed place, where they
crowded about him, these to hold his stirrup and those
supporting him on either side whilst others took him by the
hands and helped him dismount. After which all the emirs
and nobles preceded him into the Divan and led him close
up to the royal throne.

Thereupon the Sultan came down forthright from his seat of
estate and, forbidding him to buss the carpet, embraced and
kissed and seated him to the right of and beside himself.
Aladdin did whatso is suitable in the case of the kings of
salutation and offering of blessings, and said: "O our lord
the Sultan, indeed the generosity of thy Highness demanded
that thou deign vouchsafe to me the hand of thy daughter,
the Lady Badr al-Budur, albeit I undeserve the greatness of
such gift, I being but the humblest of thy slaves. I pray
Allah grant thee prosperity and perpetuance, but in very
sooth, O King, my tongue is helpless to thank thee for the
fullness of the favor, passing all measure, which thou hast
bestowed upon me. And I hope of thy Highness that thou
wilt give me a piece of ground fitted for a pavilion which
shall besit thy daughter, the Lady Badr al-Budur." The
Sultan was struck with admiration when he saw Aladdin in

his princely suit and looked upon him and considered his beauty and loveliness, and noted the Mamelukes standing to serve him in their comeliness and seemlihed. And still his marvel grew when the mother of Aladdin approached him in costly raiment and sumptuous, clad as though she were a queen, and when he gazed upon the twelve handmaids standing before her with crossed arms and with all worship and reverence doing her service. He also considered the eloquence of Aladdin and his delicacy of speech, and he was astounded thereat, he and all his who were present at the levee.

Thereupon fire was kindled in the Grand Wazir's heart for envy of Aladdin until he was like to die. And it was worse when the Sultan, after hearing the youth's succession of prayers and seeing his high dignity of demeanor, respectful withal, and his eloquence and elegance of language, clasped him to his bosom and kissed him and cried, "Alas, O my son, that I have not enjoyed thy converse before this day!" He rejoiced in him with mighty great joy and straightway bade the music and the bands strike up. Then he arose and taking the yotith, led him into the palace, where supper had been prepared, and the eunuchs at once laid the tables. So the sovereign sat down and seated his son-in-law on his right side, and the wazirs and high officials and lords of the land took places each according to his degree, whereupon the bands played and a mighty fine marriage feast was dispread in the palace. The King now applied himself to making friendship with Aladdin and conversed with the youth, who answered him with all courtesy and eloquence, as though he had been bred in the palaces of the kings or he had lived with them his daily life. And the more the talk was prolonged between them, the more did the Sultan's pleasure and delight increase, hearing his son-in-law's readiness of reply and his sweet flow of language.

But after they had eaten and drunken and the trays were removed, the King bade summon the kazis and witnesses, who presently attended and knitted the knot and wrote out the contract writ between Aladdin and the Lady Badr al-Budur. And presently the bridegroom arose and would have fared forth, when his father-in-law withheld him and asked: "Whither away, O my child? The bride fetes have begun and the marriage is made and the tie is tied and the writ is written." He replied: "O my lord the King, 'tis my desire to edify, for the Lady Badr al-Budur, a pavilion befitting her station and high degree, nor can I visit her before so doing. But, Inshallah! the building shall be finished within the shortest time, by the utmost endeavor of thy slave and by the kindly regard of thy Hihgness. And although I do (yes indeed!) long to enjoy the society of the Lady Badr al-Budur, yet 'tis incumbent of me first to serve her, and it becometh me to set about the work forthright." "Look around thee, O my son," replied the Sultan, "for what ground thou deemest suitable to thy design, and do thou take all things into thy hands. But I deem the best for thee will be yonder broad plain facing my palace, and if it please thee, build thy pavilion thereupon." "And this," answered Aladdin, "is the sum of my wishes, that I may be near-hand to thy Highness.

So saying, he farewelled the King and took horse, with his Mamelukes riding before him and behind him, and all the world blessed him and cried, "By Allah he is deserving," until such time as he reached his home. Then he alighted from his stallion and repairing to his chamber, rubbed the lamp and behold, the slave stood before him and said, "Ask, O my lord, whatso thou wantest," and Aladdin rejoined: "I require thee of a service grave and important which thou must do for me, and 'tis that thou build me with all urgency a pavillion fronting the palace of the Sultan. And it must be a marvel for it shall be provided with every requisite, such as royal furniture and so forth." The slave replied, "To hear is to Obey," and evanished, and before the next dawn brake returned to Aladdin and said: "O my lord, the pavilion is finished to the fullest of thy fancy, and if thou wouldst inspect it, arise forthright and fare with me."

Accordingly he rose up, and the slave carried him in the space of an eye glance to the pavilion, which when looked upon it struck him with surprise at such building, all its stones being of jasper and alabaster, Sumaki marble and mosaicwork. Then the slave led him into the treasury, which was full of all manner of gold and silver and costly gems, not to be counted or computed, priced or estimated. Thence to another place, where Aladdin saw all requisites for the table, plates and dishes, spoons and ladles, basins and covers, cups and tasses, the whole of precious metal. Thence to the kitchen, where they found the kitcheners provided with their needs and cooking batteries, likewise golden and silvern. Thence to a warehouse piled up with chests full-packed of royal raiment, stuffs that captured the reason, such as gold-wrought brocades from India and China and kimcobs or orfrayed cloths. Thence to many apartments replete with appointments which beggar description. Thence to the stables containing coursers whose like was not to be met with amongst the kings of the universe. And lastly they went to the harness rooms all hung with housings, costly saddles, and other furniture,

193

everywhere studded with pearls and precious stones. And all this was the work of one night.

Aladdin was wonder-struck and astounded by that magnificent display of wealth, which not even the mightiest monarch on earth could produce, and more so to see his pavilion fully provided with eunuchs and handmaids whose beauty would reduce a saint. Yet the Prime marvel of the pavilion was an upper kiosque or belvedere of four and twenty windows all made of emeralds and rubies and other gems, and one window remained unfinished at the requirement of Aladdin, that the Sultan might prove him impotent to complete it. When the youth had inspected the whole edifice, he was pleased and gladdened exceedingly. Then, turning to the slave, he said: "I require of thee still one thing which is yet wanting and whereof I had forgotten to tell thee." "Ask, O my lord, thy want," quoth the servitor, and quoth the other: "I demand of thee a carpet of the primest brocade all gold-inwrought which, when unrolled and outstretched, shall extend hence to the Sultan's palace, in order that the Lady Badr al-Budur may, when coming hither, pace upon it and not tread common earth." The slave departed for a short while and said on his return, "O my lord, verily that which thou demandest is here." Then he took him and showed him a carpet, which wildered the wits, and it extended from palace to pavillion. And after this the servitor bore off Aladdin and set him down in his own home.

Now day was brightening, so the Sultan rose from his sleep and throwing open the casement, looked out and espied opposite his palace a palatial pavilion ready edified. Thereupon he fell to rubbing his eyes and opening them their widest and considering the scene, and he soon was

194

certified that the new edifice was mighty fine, and grand enough to bewilder the wits. Moreover, with amazement as great he saw the carpet dispread between palace and pavilion. Like their lord, also the royal doorkeepers and the household, one and all, were dazed and amazed at the spectacle. Meanwhile the Wazir came in, and as he entered, espied the newly builded pavilion and the carpet, whereat he also wondered. And when he went in to the Sultan, the twain fell to talking on this marvelous matter with great surprise at a sight which distracted the gazer and attracted the heart. They said finally, "In very truth, of this pavilion we deem that none of the royalties could build its fellow," and the King, turning to the Minister, asked him: "Hast thou seen now that Aladdin is worthy to be the husband of the Princess, my daughter? Hast thou looked upon and considered this right royal building, this magnificence of opulence, which thought of man cannot contain?" But the Wazir in his envy of Aladdin replied: "O King of the Age, indeed this foundation and this building and this opulence may not be save by means of magic, nor can any man in the world, be he the richest in good or the greatest in governance, avail to found and finish in a single night such edifice as this." The Sultan rejoined: "I am surprised to see in thee how thou dost continually harp on evil opinion of Aladdin, but I hold that 'tis caused by thine envy and jealousy. Thou wast present when I gave him the ground at his own prayer for a place whereon he might build a pavilion wherein to lodge my daughter, and I myself favored him with a site for the same, and that too before thy very face. But however that be, shall one who could send me as dower for the Princess such store of such stones whereof the kings never obtained even a few, shall he, I say, be unable to edify an edifice like this?" When the Wazir heard the Sultan's words, he knew that his lord loved Aladdin exceedingly, so his envy and malice increased. only, as he could do nothing against the youth, he sat silent, and impotent to return a reply.

But Aladdin, seeing that it was broad day and the appointed time had come for his repairing to the Place (where his wedding was being celebrated and the emirs and wazirs and grandees were gathered together about the Sultan to be present at the ceremony), arose and rubbed the lamp, and when its slave appeared and said, "O my lord, ask whatso thou wantest, for I stand before thee and at thy service," said he: "I mean forthright to seek the palace, this day being my wedding festival, and I want thee to supply me with ten thousand dinars." The slave evanished for an eye twinkling and returned bringing the moneys, when Aladdin took horse with his Mamelukes a-van and arear and passed on his way, scattering as he went gold pieces upon the lieges until all were fondly affected toward him and his dignity was enhanced. But when he drew near the palace, and the emirs and agas and army officers who were standing to await him noted his approach, they hastened straightway to the King and gave him the tidings thereof, whereupon the Sultan rose and met his son-in-law and, after embracing and kissing him, led him, still holding his hand, into his own apartment, where he sat down and seated him by his right side.

The city was all decorated and music rang through the palace and the singers sang until the King bade bring the noon meal, when the eunuchs and Mamelukes hastened to spread the tables and trays which are such as are served to the kings. Then the Sultan and Aladdin and the lords of the land and the grandees of the realm took their seats and ate and drank until they were satisfied. And it was a mighty fine wedding in city and palace, and the high nobles all rejoiced therein and the commons of the kingdom were equally gladdened, while the governors of provinces and nabobs of districts flocked from far regions to witness Aladdin's marriage and its processions and festivities. The Sultan also marveled in his mind to look at Aladdin's mother and recall to mind how she was wont to visit him in pauper plight while her son could command an this opulence and magnificence. And when the spectators who crowded the royal palace to enjoy the wedding feasts looked upon Aladdin's pavilion and beauties of the building, they were seized with an immense surprise, that so vast an edifice as this could be reared on high during a single night, and they blessed the youth and cried: "Allah gladden him: By Allah, he deserveth all this! Allah bless his days!"

When dinner was done, Aladdin rose and, farewelling the Sultan, took horse with his Mamelukes and rode to his own pavilion, that he might prepare to receive therein his bride, the Lady Badr al-Budur. And as he passed, all the folk shouted their good wishes with one voice and their words were: "Allah gladden thee! Allah increase thy glory! Allah grant thee length of life!" while immense crowds of people gathered to swell the marriage procession, and they conducted him to his new home, he showering gold upon them during the whole time. When he reached his pavilion, he dismounted and walked in and sat him down on the divan, whilst his Mamelukes stood before him with arms afolded. Also after a short delay they brought him sherbets, and when these were drunk, he ordered his white slaves and handmaids and eunuchs and all who were in the pavilion to make ready for meeting the Lady Badr al-Budur. Moreover, as soon as midafternoon came and the air had cooled and the great heat of the sun was abated, the Sultan bade his army officers and emirs and wazirs go down into the maydan plain, whither he likewise rode. And Aladdin also took horse with his Mamelukes, he mounting a stallion whose like was not among the steeds of the, Arab al-Arba, and he showed his horsemanship in the hippodrome, and so played with the jarid that none could withstand him, while his bride sat gazing upon him from the latticed balcony of her bower and, seeing in him such beauty and cavalarice, she fell headlong in love of him and was like to fly for joy. And after they had ringed their horses on the maydan and each had displayed whatso he could of horsemanship, Aladdin proving himself the best man of all, they rode in a body to the Sultan's palace and the youth also returned to his own pavilion.

But when it was evening, the wazirs and nobles took the bridegroom and, falling in, escorted him to the royal hamman (known as the Sultani), when he was bathed. and perfumed. As soon as he came out he donned a dress more magnificent than the former and took horse with the emirs and the soldier officers riding before him and forming a grand cortege, wherein four of the wazirs bore naked swords round about him. All the citizens and the strangers and the troops marched before him in ordered throng carrying wax candles and kettledrums and pipes and other instruments of mirth and merriment, until they conducted him to his pavilion. Here he alighted and, walking in, took his seat and seated the wazirs and emirs who had escorted him, and the Mamelukes brought sherbets and sugared drinks, which they also passed to the people who had followed in his train. It was a world of folk whose tale might not be told. Withal Aladdin bade his Mamelukes stand without the pavilion doors and shower gold upon the crowd.

When the Sultan returned from the maydan plain to his palace, he ordered the household, men as well as women, straightway to form a cavalcade for his daughter, with all ceremony, and bear her to her bridegroom's pavilion. So the nobles and soldier officers who had followed and escorted the bridegroom at once mounted, and the handmaids and eunuchs went forth with wax candles and made a mighty fine procession for the Lady Badr al-Budur, and they paced on preceding her till they entered the pavilion of Aladdin, whose mother walked beside the bride. In front of the Princess also fared the wives of the wazirs and emirs, grandees and notables, and in attendance on her were the eight and forty slave girls presented to her aforetime by her bridegroom, each hending in hand a huge cierge scented with camphor and ambergris and set in a candlestick of gem-studded gold. And reaching Aladdin's pavilion, they led her to her bower in the upper story and changed her robes and enthroned her. Then, as soon as the displaying was ended, they accompanied her to Aladdin's apartments, and presently he paid her the first visit. Now his mother was with the bride, and when the bridegroom came up and did off her veil, the ancient dame fell to considering the beauty of the Princess and her loveliness, and she looked around at the pavilion, which was all litten up by gold and gems besides the manifold candelabra of precious metals encrusted with emeralds and jacinths, so she said in her mind: "Once upon a time I thought the Sultan's palace mighty fine, but this pavilion is a thing apart. Nor do I deem that any of the greatest kings of Chosroes attained in his day to aught like thereof. Also am I certified that all the world could not build anything evening it." Nor less did the Lady Badr al-Budur fall to gazing at the pavilion and marveling for its magnificence.

Then the tables were spread and they all ate and drank and were gladdened after which fourscore damsels came before them, each holding in hand an instrument of mirth and merriment. Then they deftly moved their finger tips and touched the strings, smiting them into song most musical most melancholy, till they rent the hearts of the hearers. Hereat the Princess increased in marvel, and quoth she to herself, "In all my life ne'er heard I songs like these," till she forsook food, the better to listen. And at last Aladdin poured out for her wine and passed it to her with his own hand. So great joy and jubilee went round amongst them, and it was a notable night, such a one as Iskandar, Lord of the Two Horns, had never spent in his time. When they had finished eating and drinking and the tables were removed from before them, Aladdin arose and went in to his bride.

As soon as morning morrowed he left his bed, and the treasurer brought him a costly suit and a mighty fine, of the most sumptuous robes worn by the kings. Then, after drinking coffee flavored with ambergris, he ordered the horses be saddled and, mounting with his Mamelukes before and behind him, rode to the Sultan's palace, and on his entering its court the eunuchs went in and reported his coming to their lord. When the Sultan heard of Aladdin's approach, he rose up forthright to receive him and embraced and kissed him as though he were his own son. Then, seating him on his right, he blessed and prayed for him, as did the wazirs and emirs, the lords of the land and the grandees of the realm. Presently the King commanded bring the morning meal, which the attendants served up, and all broke their fast together, and when they had eaten and drunken their sufficiency and the tables were removed by the eunuchs, Aladdin turned to the Sultan and said: "O my lord, would thy Highness deign honor me this day at dinner in the house of the Lady Badr al-Budur, thy beloved daughter, and come accompanied by all thy Ministers and grandees of the reign?" The King replied (and he was delighted with his son-in-law), "Thou art surpassing in liberality, O my son!"

Then he gave orders to all invited and rode forth with them (Aladdin also riding beside him) till they reached the pavilion, and as he entered it and considered its construction, its architecture and its stonery, all jasper and camelian, his sight was dazed and his wits were amazed at such grandeur and magnificence of opulence. Then, turning to the Minister, he thus addressed him: "What sayest thou? Tell me, hast thou seen in all thy time aught like this amongst the mighties of earth's monarchs for the abundance of gold and gems we are now beholding?" The Grand Wazir replied: "O my lord the King, this be a feat which cannot be accomplished by might of monarch amongst Adam's sons, nor could the collected peoples of the universal world build a palace like unto this,- nay, even builders could not be found to make aught resembling it, save (as I said to thy Highness) by force of sorcery." These words certified the King that his Minister spake not except in envy and jealousy of Aladdin, and would stablish in the royal mind that all this splendor was not made of man, but by means of magic and with the aid of the black art. So quoth he to him: "Suffice thee so much, O Wazir. Thou hast none other word to speak, and well I know what cause urgeth thee to say this say."

Then Aladdin preceded the Sultan till he conducted him to the upper kiosque, where he saw its skylights, windows, and latticed casements and jalousies wholly made of emeralds and rubies and other costly gems, whereat his mind was perplexed and his wits were bewildered and his thoughts were distraught.

Presently he took to strolling round the kiosque and solacing himself with these sights which captured the vision, till he chanced to cast a glance at the window which Aladdin by design had left unwrought and not finished like the rest. And when he noted its lack of completion, he cried, "Woe and wellaway for thee, O window, because of thine imperfection," and, turning to his Minister, he asked, "Knowest thou the reason of leaving incomplete this window and its framework?" The Wazir said: "O my lord, I conceive that the want of finish in this window resulteth from thy Highness having pushed on Aladdin's marriage, and he lacked the leisure to complete it." Now at that time Aladdin had gone in to his bride, the Lady Badr al-Budur, to inform her of her father's presence, and when he returned, the King asked him: "O my son, what is the reason why the window of this kiosque was not made perfect?" "O King of the Age, seeing the suddenness of my wedding," answered he, "I failed to find artists for finishing it." Quoth the Sultan, "I have a mind to complete it myself," and quoth Aladdin: "Allah perpetuate thy glory, O thou the King. So shall thy memory endure in thy daughter's pavilion."

The Sultan forthright bade summon jewelers and goldsmiths, and ordered them he supplied from the treasury with all their needs of gold and gems and noble ores, and when they were gathered together, he commanded them to complete the work still wanting in the kiosque window. Meanwhile the Princess came forth to meet her sire, the Sultan, who noticed as she drew near her smiling face, so he embraced her and kissed her, then led her to the pavilion, and all entered in a body. Now this was the time of the noonday meal and one table had been spread for the sovereign, his daughter, and his son-in-law and a second for the wazirs, the lords of the land, the grandees of the realm, the chief officers of the host, the chamberlains and the nabobs. The King took seat between the Princess and her husband, and when he put forth his hand to the food and tasted it, he was struck with surprise by the flavor of the dishes and their savory and sumptuous cooking. Moreover, there stood before him the fourscore damsels, each and every saying to the full moon, "Rise that I may seat myself in thy stead!" All held instruments of mirth and merriment, and they tuned the same and deftly moved their finger tips and smote the srings into song most musical, most melodious, which expanded the mourner's heart. Hereby the Sultan was gladdened, and time was good to him, and for high enjoyment he exclaimed, "In very sooth the thing is beyond the compass of King and Caesar."

Then they fell to eating and drinking, and the cup went round until they had drunken enough, when sweetmeats and fruits of sorts and other such edibles were served, the dessert being laid out in a different salon, whither they removed and enjoyed of these pleasures their sufficiency. Presently the Sultan arose that he might see if the produce of his jewelers and goldsmiths favored that of the pavilion. So he went upstairs to them and inspected their work and how they had wrought, but he noted a mighty great difference, and his men were far from being able to make anything like the rest of Aladdin's pavilion. They informed him how all the gems stored in the lesser Treasury had been brought to them and used by them, but that the whole had proved insufficient. Wherefor he bade open the greater Treasury, and gave the workmen all they wanted of him. Moreover, he allowed them, an it sufficed not, to take the jewels wherewith Aladdin had gifted him. They carried off the whole and pushed on their labors, but they found the gems fail them, albeit had they not finished half the part wanting to the kiosque window. Herewith the King commanded them to seize all the precious stones owned by the wazirs and grandees of the realm, but although they did his bidding, the supply still fell short of their requirements.

Next morning Aladdin arose to look at the jewelers' work and remarked that they had not finished a moiety of what was wanting to the kiosque window. So he at once ordered them to undo all they had done and restore the jewels to their owners. Accordingly they pulled out the precious stones and sent the Sultan's to the Sultan and the wazirs' to the wazirs. Then the jewelers went to the King and told him of what Aladdin had bidden, so he asked them: "What said he to you, and what was his reason, and wherefore was he not content that the window be finished, and why did he undo the work ye wrought?" They answered, "O our lord, we know not at all, but he bade us deface whatso we had done." Hereupon the Sultan at once called for his horse, and mounting, took the way pavillonward, when Aladdin, after dismissing the goldsmiths and jewelers had retired into his closet and had rubbed the lamp. Hereat straightway its servitor appeared to him and said: "Ask whatso thou wantest. Thy slave is between thy hands," and said Aladdin,

"'Tis my desire that thou finish the window which was left unfinished." The Marid replied, "On my head be it, and also upon mine eyes!" Then he vanished, and after a little while returned, saying, "O my lord, verily that thou commandedst me do is completed." So Aladdin went upstairs to the kiosque and found the whole window in wholly finished state, and whilst he was he was still considering it, behold, a castrato came in to him and said: "O my lord, the Sultan hath ridden forth to visit thee and is passing through the pavilion gate."

So Aladdin at once went down and received his father-in-law. The Sultan, on sighting his son-in-law, cried to him: "Wherefore, O my child, hast thou wrought on this wise and sufferedst not the jewelers to complete the kiosque window, leaving in the pavilion an unfinished place?" Aladdin replied: "O King of the Age, I left it not imperfect save for a design of mine own, nor was I incapable of perfecting it, nor could I purpose that thy Highness should honor me with visiting a pavilion wherein was aught of deficiency. And that thou mayest know I am not unable to make it perfect, let thy Highness deign walk upstairs with me and see if anything remain to be done therewith or not." So the Sultan went up with him and, entering the kiosque, fell to looking right and left, but he saw no default at all in any of the windows- nay, he noted that all were perfect. So he marveled at the sight and embraced Aladdin and kissed him, saying: "O my son, what be this singular feat? Thou canst work in a single night what in months the jewelers could not do. By Allah, I deem thou hast nor brother nor rival in this world." Quoth Aladdin: "Allah prolong thy life and preserve thee to perpetuity! Thy slave deserveth not this encomium." And quoth the King: "By Allah, O my child, thou meritest all praise for a feat whereof all the artists of the world were incapable." Then the Sultan came down and entered the apartments of his daughter, the Lady Badr al-Budur, to take rest beside her, and he saw her joyous exceedingly at the glory and grandeur wherein she was. Then, after reposing awhile, he returned to his palace.

Now Aladdin was wont every day to thread the city streets with his Mamelukes riding a-van and arear of him showering rightward and leftward gold upon the folk, and all the world, stranger and neighbor, far and near, were fulfilled of his love for the excess of his liberality and generosity. Moreover, he increased the pensions of the poor Religious and the paupers, and he would distribute alms to them with his own hand, by which good deed he won high renown throughout the realm and most of the lords of the land and emirs would eat at his table, and men swore not at all save by his precious life. Nor did he leave faring to the chase and the maydan plain and the riding of horses and playing at javelin play in presence of the Sultan. And whenever the Lady Badr al-Budur beheld him disporting himself on the backs of steeds, she loved him much the more, and thought to herself that Allah had wrought her abundant good by causing to happen whatso happened with the son of the Wazir and by preserving her virginity intact for her true bridegroom, Aladdin. Aladdin won for himself day by day a fairer fame and a rarer report, while affection for him increased in the hearts of all the lieges and he waxed greater in the eyes of men.

Moreover, it chanced that in those days certain enemies took horse and attacked the Sultan, who armed and accoutered an army to repel them and made Aladdin commander thereof. So he marched with his men, nor ceased marching until he drew near the foe, whose forces were exceeding many, and presently when the action began, he bared his brand and charged home upon the enemy. Then battle and slaughter befell and violent was the hurly-burly, but at last Aladdin broke the hostile host and put all to flight, slaying the best part of them and pillaging their coin and cattle, property and possessions, and he despoiled them of spoils that could not be counted nor computed. Then he returned victorious after a noble victory and entered the capital, which had decorated herself in his honor, of her delight in him. And the Sultan went forth to meet him and giving him joy, embraced him and kissed him. And throughout the kingdom was held high festival with great joy and gladness. Presently the sovereign and his son-in-law repaired to the pavilion, where they were met by the Princess Badr al-Budur, who rejoiced in her husband and, after kissing him between the eyes, led him to her apartments. After a time the Sultan also came and they sat down while the slave girls brought them sherbets and confections, which they ate and drank. Then the Sultan commanded that the whole kingdom be decorated for the triumph of his son-in-law and his victory over the invader, and the subjects and soldiery and all the people knew only Allah in Heaven and Aladdin on earth, for that their love, won by his liberality, was increased by his noble horsemanship and his successful battling for the country and putting to flight the foe.

Such then was the high fortune of Aladdin, but as regards the Maghrabi, the magician, after returning to his native country he passed all this space of time in bewailing what he had borne of toil and travail to will the lamp, and mostly that his trouble had gone vain and that the morsel when almost touching his lips had flown from his grasp. He pondered all this and mourned and reviled Aladdin for the excess of his rage against him, and at times he would exclaim: "For this bastard's death underground I am well satisfied, and hope only that some time or other I may obtain the lamp, seeing how 'tis yet safe." Now one day of the days he struck a table of sand and dotted down the figures and carefully considered their consequence, then he transferred them to paper that he might study them and make sure of Aladdin's destruction and the safety of the lamp preserved beneath the earth. Presently he firmly stablished the sequence of the figures, mothers as well as daughters, but still he saw not the lamp. Thereupon rage overrode him and he made another trial to be assured of Aladdin's death, but he saw him not in the enchanted treasure.

Hereat his wrath still grew, and it waxed greater when he ascertained that the youth had issued from underground and was now upon earth's surface alive and alert. Furthermore, that he had become owner of the lamp, for which he had himself endured such toil and travail and troubles as man may not bear save for so great an object. Accordingly quoth he to himself: "I have suffered sore pains and penalties which none else could have endured for the lamp's sake in order that other than that I may carry it off, and this accursed hath taken it without difficulty. And who knoweth an he wot the virtues of the lamp, than whose owner none in the world should be wealthier? There is no help but that I work for his destruction." He then struck another geomantic table and, examining the figures, saw that the lad had won for himself unmeasurable riches and had wedded the daughter of his King, so of his envy and jealousy he was fired with the flame of wrath, and rising without let or stay, he equipped himself and set forth for China land, where he arrived in due season.

Now when he had reached the King's capital wherein was Aladdin, he alighted at one of the khans, and when he had rested from the weariness of wayfare, he donned his dress and went down to wander about the streets, where he never passed a group without hearing them prate about the pavilion and its grandeur and vaunt the beauty of Aladdin and his lovesomeness, his liberality and generosity, his fine manners and his good morals. Presently he entered an establishment wherein men were drinking a certain warm beverage, and going up to one of those who were loud in their lauds, he said to him, "O fair youth, who may be the man ye describe and commend?" "Apparently thou art a foreigner, O man," answered the other, "and thou comest from a far country. But even this granted, how happeneth it thou hast not heard of the Emir Aladdin, whose renown, I fancy, hath filled the universe, and whose pavilion, known by report to far and near, is one of the wonders of the world? How, then, never came to thine ears aught of this or the name of Aladdin (whose glory and enjoyment Our Lord increase!) and his fame?" The Moorman replied: "The sum of my wishes is to look upon this pavilion, and if thou wouldest do me a favor, prithee guide me thereunto, for I am a foreigner." The man rejoined, "To hear is to obey," and, foregoing him, pointed out Aladdin's pavilion, whereupon the Moroccan fell to considering it, and at once understood that it was the work of the lamp. So he cried: "Ah! Ah! needs must I dig a pit for this accursed, this son of a snip, who could not earn for himself even an evening meal. And if the Fates abet me, I will assuredly destroy his

209

life and send his mother back to spinning at her wheel, e'en as she was wont erewhiles to do."

So saying, he returned to his caravanserai in a sore state of grief and melancholy and regret bred by his envy and hate of Aladdin. He took his astrological gear and geomantic table to discover where might he the lamp, and he found that it was in the pavilion and not upon Aladdin's person. So he rejoiced thereat with joy exceeding and exclaimed: "Now indeed 'twill he an easy task to take the life of this accursed and I see my way to getting the lamp." Then he went to a coppersmith and said to him: "Do thou make me a set of lamps, and take from me their full price and more, only I would have thee hasten to finish them." Replied the smith, "Hearing and obeying," and fell a-working to keep his word. And when they were ready, the Moorman paid him what price he required, then, taking them, he carried them to the khan and set them in a basket. Presently he began wandering about the highways and market streets of the capital crying aloud: "Ho! Who will exchange old lamps for new lamps?" But when the folk heard him cry on this wise, they derided him and said, "Doubtless this man is Jinnmad, for that he goeth about offering new for old." And a world followed him, and the children of the quarter caught him up from place to place, laughing at him the while, nor did he forbid them or care for their maltreatment. And he ceased not strolling about the streets till he came under Aladdin's pavilion, where he shouted with his loudest voice, and the boys screamed at him: "A madman! A madman!"

Now Destiny had decreed that the Lady Badr al-Budur be sitting in her kiosque, whence she heard one crying like a crier, and the children bawling at him. Only she understood not what was going on, so she gave orders to one of her slave girls, saying, "Go thou and see who 'tis that crieth, and what be his cry." The girl fared forth and looked on, when she beheld a man crying, "Ho! Who will exchange old lamps for new lamps?" and the little ones pursuing and laughing at him. And as loudly laughed the Princess when this strange case was told to her. Now Aladdin had carelessly left the lamp in his pavilion without hiding it and locking it up in his strongbox, and one of the slave girls who had seen it said: "O my lady, I think to have noticed in the apartment of my lord Aladdin an old lamp, so let us give it in change for a new lamp to this man, and see if his cry he truth or lie." Whereupon the Princess said to the slave girl, "Bring the old lamp which thou saidst to have seen in thy lord's apartment."

Now the Lady Badr al-Budur knew naught of the lamp and of the specialities thereof which had raised Aladdin, her spouse, to such high degree and grandeur, and her only end and aim was to understand by experiment the mind of a man who would give in exchange the new for the old. So the handmaid fared forth and went up to Aladdin's apartment and returned with the lamp to her lady, who, like all the others, knew nothing of the Maghrabi's cunning tricks and his crafty device. Then the Princess bade an aga of the eunuchry go down and barter the old lamp for a new lamp. So he obeyed her bidding and, after taking a new lamp from the man, he returned and laid it before his lady, who looking at it and seeing that it was brand-new, fell to laughing at the Moorman's wits.

But the Moroccan, when he held the article in hand and recognized it for the lamp of the enchanted treasury, at once placed it in his breast pocket and left all the other lamps to the folk who were bartering, of him. Then he went forth running till he was clear of the city, when he walked leisurely over the level grounds, and he took patience until night fell on him in desert ground, where was none other but himself. There he brought out the lamp, when suddenly appeared to him the Marid, who said: "Adsum! Thy slave between thy hands is come. Ask of me whatso thou wantest." "'Tis my desire," the Moorman replied, "that thou upraise from its present place Aladdin's pavilion, with its inmates and all that be therein, not forgetting myself, and set it down upon my own land, Africa. Thou knowest my town, and I want the building placed in the gardens hard by it." The Marid slave replied: "Hearkening and obedience. Close thine eyes and open thine eyes, whenas thou shalt find thyself together with the pavilion in thine own country." This was done, and in an eye twinkling the Moroccan and the pavilion, with all therein, were transported to the African land.

Such then was the work of the Maghrabi, the magician, but now let us return to the Sultan and his son-in-law. It was the custom of the King, because of his attachment to and his affection for his daughter, every morning when he had shaken off sleep to open the latticed casement and look out therefrom, that he might catch sight of her abode. So that day he arose and did as he was wont. But when he drew near the latticed casement of his palace and looked out at Aladdin's pavilion, he saw naught- nay, the site was smooth as a well-trodden highway and like unto what it had been aforetime, and he could find nor edifice nor offices. So astonishment clothed him as with a garment, and his wits were wildered and he began to rub his eyes, lest they he dimmed or darkened, and to gaze intently. But at last he was certified that no trace of the pavilion remained, nor sign of its being, nor wist he the why and the wherefore of its disappearance. So his surprise increased and he smote hand upon hand and the tears trickled down his cheeks over his beard, for that he knew not what had become of his daughter.

Then he sent out officials forthright and summoned the Grand Wazir, who at once attended, and seeing him in this piteous plight, said: "Pardon, O King of the Age, may Allah avert from thee every ill! Wherefore art thou in such sorrow?" Exclaimed the sovereign, "Methinketh thou wettest not my case." And quoth the Minister: "Oh no wise, O our lord. By Allah, I know of it nothing at all." "Then," resumed the Sultan, "'tis manifest thou hast not looked this day in the direction of Aladdin's pavilion." "True, O my lord," quoth the Wazir. "It must still be locked and fast shut," and quoth the King: "Forasmuch as thou hast no inkling of aught, arise and look out at the window and see Aladdin's pavilion, whereof thou sayest 'tis locked and fast shut." The Minister obeyed his bidding, but could not see anything, or pavilion or other place. So with mind and thoughts sore perplexed he returned to his liege lord, who asked him: "Hast now learned the reason of my distress, and noted yon locked-up palace and fast shut?" Answered the Wazir: "O King of the Age, erewhile I represented to thy Highness that this pavilion and these matters be all magical." Hereat the Sultan, fired with wrath, cried, "Where be Aladdin?" and the Minister replied, "He hath gone a-hunting," when the King commanded without stay or delay sundry of his agas and army officers to go and bring to him his son-in-law chained and with pinioned elbows.

So they fared forth until they found Aladdin, when they

said to him: "O our lord Aladdin, excuse us, nor be thou wroth with us, for the King hath commanded that we carry thee before him pinioned and fettered, and we hope pardon from thee, because we are under the royal orders which we cannot gainsay." Aladdin, hearing these words, was seized with surprise, and not knowing the reason of this, remained tonguetied for a time, after which he turned to them and asked: "O assembly, have you naught of knowledge concerning the motive of the royal mandate? Well I wot my soul to be innocent, and that I never sinned against King or against kingdom." "O our lord," answered they, "we have no inkling whatever."

So Aladdin alighted from his horse and said to them: "Do ye whatso the Sultan bade you do, for that the King's command is upon the head and the eyes." The agas, having bound Aladdin in bonds and pinioned his elbows behind his back, haled him in chains and carried him into the city. But when the lieges saw him pinioned and ironed, they understood that the Sultan purposed to strike off his head, and forasmuch as he was loved of them exceedingly, all gathered together and seized their weapons, then, swarming out of their houses, followed the soldiery to see what was to do. And when the troops arrived with Aladdin at the palace, they went in and informed the Sultan of this, whereat he forthright commanded the sworder to cut off the head of his son-in-law.

Now as soon as the subjects were aware of this order, they barricaded the gates and closed the doors of the palace and sent a message to the King saying: "At this very moment we will level thine abode over the heads of all it containeth, and over thine own, if the least hurt or harm befall Aladdin." So the Wazir went in and reported to the Sultan:

"O King of the Age, thy commandment is about to seal the roll of our lives, and 'twere more suitable that thou pardon thy son-in-law, lest there chance to us a sore mischance, for that the lieges do love him far more than they love us." Now the Sworder had already dispread the carpet of blood and, having seated Aladdin thereon, had bandaged his eyes. Moreover, he had walked round him three several times awaiting the last orders of his lord, when the King looked out of the window and saw his subjects, who had suddenly attacked him, swarming up the walls intending to tear them down. So forthright he bade the Sworder stay his hand from Aladdin and commanded the crier fare forth to the crowd and cry aloud that he had pardoned his son-in-law and received him back into favor.

But when Aladdin found himself free and saw the Sultan seated on his throne, he went up to him and said: "O my lord, inasmuch as thy Highness hath favored me throughout my life, so of thy grace now deign let me know the how and the wherein I have sinned against thee." "O traitor," cried the King, "unto this present I knew not any sin of thine." Then, turning to the Wazir, he said: "Take him and make him look out at the window, and after let him tell us where be his pavilion." And when the royal order was obeyed, Aladdin saw the place level as a well-trodden road, even as it had been ere the base of the building was laid, nor was there the faintest trace of edifice. Hereat he was astonished and perplexed, knowing not what had occurred. But when he returned to the presence, the King asked him: "What is it thou hast seen? Where is thy pavilion, and where is my daughter, the core of my heart, my only child, than whom I have none other?" Aladdin answered, "O King of the Age, I wot naught thereof nor aught of what hath befallen," and the Sultan rejoined: "Thou must know, O Aladdin, I have pardoned thee only that thou go forth and look into this affair and inquire for me concerning my daughter. Nor do thou ever show thyself in my presence except she be with thee, and if thou bring her not, by the life of my head I will cut off the head of thee." The other replied: "To hear is to obey. Only vouchsafe me a delay and respite of some forty days, after which, an I produce her not, strike off my head and do with me whatso thou wishest." The Sultan said to Aladdin: "Verily, I have granted thee thy request, a delay of forty days. But think not thou canst fly from my hand, for I would bring thee back even if thou wert above the clouds instead of being only upon earth's surface." Replied Aladdin: "O my lord the Sultan, as I said to thy Highness, an I fail to bring her within the term appointed, I will present myself for my head to he stricken off."

Now when the folk and the lieges all saw Aladdin at liberty, they rejoiced with joy exceeding and were delighted for his release, but the shame of his treatment and bashfulness before his friends and the envious exultation of his foes had bowed down Aladdin's head. So he went forth a wandering through the city ways, and he was perplexed concerning his case and knew not what had befallen him. He lingered about the capital for two days, in saddest state, wotting not what to do in order to find his wife and his pavilion, and during this time sundry of the folk privily brought him meat and drink. When the two days were done, he left the city to stray about the waste and open lands outlying the walls, without a notion as to whither he should wend. And he walked on aimlessly until the path led him beside a river, where, of the stress of sorrow that overwhelmed him, he abandoned himself to despair and thought of casting himself into the water. Being, however, a good Moslem who professed the unity of the Godhead, he feared Allah in his soul, and standing upon the margin, he prepared to perform the wuzu ablution.

But as he was bailing up the water in his right hand and rubbing his fingers, it so chanced that he also rubbed the ring. Hereat its Marid appeared, and said to him: "Adsum! Thy thrall between thy hands is come. Ask of me whatso thou wantest." Seeing the Marid, Aladdin rejoiced with exceeding joy and cried: "O Slave, I desire of thee that thou bring before me my pavilion and therein my wife, the Lady Badr al-Budur, together with all and everything it containeth." "O my lord," replied the Marid, "'tis right hard upon me that thou demandest a service whereto I may not avail. This matter dependeth upon the Slave of the Lamp, nor dare I even attempt it." Aladdin rejoined: "Forasmuch as the matter is beyond thy competence, I require it not of thee, but at least do thou take me up and set me down beside my pavilion in what land soever that may be." The slave exclaimed, "Hearing and obeying, O my lord," and uplifting him high in air, within the space of an eye glance set him down beside his pavilion in the land of Africa, and upon a spot facing his wife's apartment.

Now this was at fall of night, yet one look enabled him to recognize his home, whereby his cark and care were cleared away and he recovered trust in Allah after cutting off all his hope to look upon his wife once more. Then he fell to pondering the secret and mysterious favors of the Lord (glorified he His omnipotence!), and how after despair had mastered him the ring had come to gladden him, and how when all his hopes were cut off, Allah had deigned bless him with the services of its slave. So he rejoiced and his melancholy left him. Then, as he had passed four days without sleep for the excess of his cark and care and sorrow and stress of thought, he drew near his pavilion and slept under a tree hard by the building, which (as we mentioned) had been set down amongst the gardens outlying the city of Africa. He slumbered till morning showed her face, and when awakened by the warbling of the small birds, he arose and went down to the bank of the river which flowed thereby into the city, and here he again washed hands and face and after finished his wuzu ablution. Then he prayed the dawn prayer, and when he had ended his orisons he returned and sat down under the windows of the Princess's bower.

Now the Lady Badr al-Budur, of her exceeding sorrow for severance from her husband and her sire, the Sultan, and for the great mishap which had happened to her from the Maghrabi, the magician, the accursed, was wont to rise during the murk preceding dawn and to sit in tears, inasmuch as she could not sleep o' nights and had forsworn meat and drink. Her favorite slave girl would enter her chamber at the hour of prayer salutation in order to dress her, and this time, by decree of Destiny, when she threw open the window to let her lady comfort and console herself by looking upon the trees and rills, and she herself peered out of the lattice, she caught sight of her master sitting below, and informed the Princess of this, saying: "O my lady! O my lady! Here's my lord Aladdin seated at the foot of the wall!" So her mistress arose hurriedly and gazing from the casement, saw him, and her husband, raising his head, saw her, so she saluted him and he saluted her, both being like to fly for joy. Presently quoth she, "Up and come in to me by the private postern, for now the accursed is not here," and she gave orders to the slave girl, who went down and opened for him. Then Aladdin passed through it and was met by his wife, when they embraced and exchanged kisses with all delight until they wept for overjoy.

After this they sat down, and Aladdin said to her: "O my lady, before all things 'tis my desire to ask thee a question. 'Twas my wont to place an old copper lamp in such a part of my pavilion. What became of that same?" When the Princess heard these words, she sighed and cried, "O my dearling, 'twas that very lamp which garred us fall into this calamity!" Aladdin asked her, "How befell the affair?" and she answered by recounting to him all that passed, first and last, especially how they had given in exchange an old lamp for a new lamp, adding: "And next day we hardly saw one another at dawn before we found ourselves in this land, and he who deceived us and took the lamp by way of barter informed me that he had done the deed by might of his magic and by means of the lamp; that he is a Moorman from Africa; and that we are now in his native country."

When the Lady Badr al-Budur ceased speaking, Aladdin resumed: "Tell me the intent of this accursed in thy respect, also what he sayeth to thee and what he his will of thee." She replied: "Every day he cometh to visit me once and no more. He would woo me to his love, and he sueth that I take him to spouse in lieu of thee and that I forget thee and he consoled for the loss of thee. And he telleth me that the Sultan, my sire, hath cut off my husband's head, adding that thou, the son of pauper parents, wast by him enriched. And he sootheth me with talk, but he never seeth aught from me save weeping and wailing, nor hath he heard from me one sugar-sweet word." Quoth Aladdin: "Tell me where he hath placed the lamp, an thou know anything thereof," and quoth she: "He beareth it about on his body alway, nor is it possible that he leave it for a single hour. Moreover, once when he related what I have now recounted to thee, he brought it out of his breast pocket and allowed me to look upon it." When Aladdin heard these words, he joyed with exceeding joy and said: "O my lady, do thou lend ear to me. 'Tis my design to go from thee forthright and to return only after doffing this my dress, so wonder not when thou see me changed, but direct one of thy women to stand by the private postern alway, and whenever she espy me coming, at once to open. And now I will devise a device whereby to slay this damned loon."

Herewith he arose and, issuing from the pavilion door, walked till he met on the way a fellah, to whom he said, "O man, take my attire and give me thy garments." But the peasant refused, so Aladdin stripped him of his dress perforce and donned it, leaving to the man his own rich gear by way of gift. Then he followed the highway leading to the neighboring city and entering it, went to the perfumers' bazaar, where he bought of one some rarely potent bhang, the son of a minute, paying two dinars for two drachms thereof, and he returned in disguise by the same road till he reached the pavilion. Here the slave girl opened to him the private postern, wherethrough he went in to the Lady Badr al-Budur, and said: "Hear me! I desire of thee that thou dress and dight thyself in thy best and thou cast off all outer show and semblance of care. Also when the accursed, the Maghrabi, shall visit thee, do thou receive him with a 'Welcome and fair welcome,' and meet him with smiling face and invite him to come and sup with thee.

Moreover, let him note that thou hast forgotten Aladdin, thy beloved, likewise thy father, and that thou hast learned to love him with exceeding love, displaying to him all manner joy and pleasure. Then ask him for wine, which must be red, and pledge him to his secret in a significant draught. And when thou hast given him two or three cups full and hast made him wax careless, then drop these drops into his cup and fill it up with wine. No sooner shall he drink of it than he will fall upon his back senseless as one dead." Hearing these words, the Princess exclaimed: "'Tis exceedingly sore to me that I do such deed, withal must I do it that we escape the defilement of this accursed who tortured me by severance from thee and from my sire. Lawful and right therefore is the slaughter of this accursed."

Then Aladdin ate and drank with his wife what hindered his hunger, then, rising without stay or delay, fared forth the pavilion. So the Lady Badr al-Budur summoned the tirewoman, who robed and arrayed her in her finest raiment and adorned her and perfumed her. And as she was thus, behold, the accursed Maghrabi entered. He joyed much seeing her in such case and yet more when she confronted him, contrary to her custom, with a laughing face, and his love longing increased, and his desire to have her. Then she took him and, seating him beside her, said: "O my dearling, do thou (an thou be willing) come to me this night and let us sup together. Sufficient to me hath been my sorrow, for were I to sit mourning through a thousand years or even two thousand, Aladdin would not return to me from the tomb. And I depend upon thy say of yesterday; to wit, that my sire, the Sultan, slew him in his stress of sorrow for serverance from me.

"Nor wonder thou an I have changed this day from what I

was yesterday, and the reason thereof is I have determined upon taking thee to friend and playfellow in lieu of and succession to Aladdin, for that now I have none other man but thyself. So I hope for thy presence this night, that we may sup together and we may carouse and drink somewhat of wine each with other, and especially 'tis my desire that thou cause me taste the wine of thy natal soil, the African land, because belike 'tis better than aught of the wine of China we drink. I have with me some wine, but 'tis the growth of my country and I vehemently wish to taste the wine produced by thine."

When the Maghrabi saw the love lavisht upon him by the Lady Badr al-Budur, and noted her change from the sorrowful, melancholy woman she was wont to be, he thought that she had cut off her hope of Aladdin, and he joyed exceedingly and said to her: "I hear and obey, O my lady, whatso thou wishest and all thou biddest. I have at home a jar of our country wine, which I have carefully kept and stored deep in earth for a space of eight years, and I will now fare and fill from it our need and will return to thee in all haste." But the Princess, that she might wheedle him the more and yet more, replied: "O my darling, go not thou, leaving me alone, but send one of the eunuchs to fill for us thereof, and do thou remain sitting beside me, that I may find in thee my consolation." He rejoined: "O my lady, none wotteth where the jar be buried save myself, nor will I tarry from thee." So saying, the Moorman went out, and after a short time he brought back as much wine as they wanted, whereupon quoth the Princess to him: "Thou hast been at pains and trouble to serve me, and I have suffered for thy sake, O my beloved." Quoth he: "On no wise, O eyes of me. I hold myself enhonored by thy service."

Then the Lady Badr al-Budur sat with him at table, and the twain fell to eating, and presently the Princess expressed a wish to drink, when the handmaid filled her a cup forthright and then crowned another for the Moroccan. So she drank to his long life and his secret wishes, and he also drank to her life. Then the Princess, who was unique in eloquence and delicacy of speech, fell to making a cup companion of him and beguiled him by addressing him in the sweetest terms of hidden meaning. This was done only that he might become more madly enamored of her, but the Maghrabi thought that it resulted from her true inclination for him, nor knew that it was a snare set up to slay him. So his longing for her increased, and he was dying of love for when he saw her address him in such tenderness of words and thoughts, and his head began to swim and an the world seemed as nothing in his eyes. But when they came to the last of the supper and the wine had mastered his brains and the Princess saw this in him, she said: "With us there be a custom throughout our country, but I know not an it be the usage of yours or not." The Moorman replied, "And what may that be?" So she said to him: "At the end of supper each lover in turn taketh the cup of the beloved and drinketh it off." And at once she crowned one with wine and bade the handmaid carry to him her cup, wherein the drink was blended with the bhang.

Now she had taught the slave girl what to do, and all the handmaids and eunuchs in the pavilion longed for the sorcerer's slaughter and in that matter were one with the Princess. Accordingly the damsel handed him the cup and he, when he heard her words and saw her drinking from his cup and passing hers to him and noted all that show of love, fancied himself Iskandar, Lord of the Two Horns. Then said she to him, the while swaying gracefully to either side and putting her hand within his hand: "O my life, here is thy cup with me and my cup with thee, and on this wise do lovers drink from each other's cups." Then she bussed the brim and drained it to the dregs, and again she kissed its lip and offered it to him. Thereat he flew for joy and, meaning to do the like, raised her cup to his mouth and drank off the whole contents, without considering whether there was therein aught harmful or not. And forthright he rolled upon his back in deathlike condition and the cup dropped from his grasp, whereupon the Lady Badr al-Budur and the slave girls ran hurriedly and opened the pavilion door to their lord Aladdin, who, disguised as a fellah, entered therein.

He went up to the apartment of his wife, whom he found still sitting at table, and facing her lay the Maghrabi as one slaughtered. So he at once drew near to her and kissed her and thanked her for this. Then, rejoicing with joy exceeding, he turned to her and said: "Do thou with thy handmaids betake thyself to the inner rooms and leave me alone for the present, that I may take counsel touching mine affair." The Princess hesitated not but went away at once, she and her women. Then Aladdin arose, and after locking the door upon them, walked up to the Moorman and put forth his hand to his breast pocket and thence drew the lamp, after which he unsheathed his sword and slew the villain. Presently he rubbed the lamp and the Marid slave appeared and said: "Adsum, O my lord! What is it thou wantest?" "I desire of thee," said Aladdin, "that thou take up my pavilion from this country and transport it to the land of China and there set it down upon the site where it was whilom, fronting the palace of the Sultan." The Marid replied, "Hearing and obeying, O my lord."

Then Aladdin went and sat down with his wife and throwing his arms round her neck, kissed her and she kissed him, and they set in converse what while the Jinni transported the pavilion and all therein to the place appointed. Presently Aladdin bade the handmaids spread the table before him, and he and the Lady Badr al-Budur took seat thereat and fell to eating and drinking, in all joy and gladness, till they had their sufficiency, when, removing to the chamber of wine and cup converse, they sat there and caroused in fair companionship and each kissed other with all love liesse. The time had been long and longsome since they enjoyed aught of pleasure, so they ceased not doing, thus until the wine sun arose in their heads and sleep gat hold of them, at which time they went to their bed in all ease and comfort. Early on the next morning Aladdin woke and awoke his wife, and the slave girls came in and donned her dress and prepared her and adorned her whilst her husband arrayed himself in his costliest raiment, and the twain were ready to fly for joy at reunion after parting. Moreover, the Princess was especially joyous and gladsome because on that day she expected to see her beloved father.

Such was the case of Aladdin and the Lady Badr al-Budur, but as regards the Sultan, after he drove away his son-in-law he never ceased to sorrow for the loss of his daughter, and every hour of every day he would sit and weep for her as women weep, because she was his only child and he had none other to take to heart. And as he shook off sleep morning after morning he would hasten to the window and throw it open and peer in the direction where formerly stood Aladdin's pavilion and pour forth tears until his eyes were dried up and their lids were ulcered. Now on that day he arose at dawn and, according to his custom, looked out, when lo and behold! he saw before him an edifice, so he rubbed his eyes and considered it curiously, when he became certified that it was the pavilion of his son-in-law. So he called for a horse without let or delay, and as soon as his beast was saddled, he mounted and made for the place, and Aladdin, when he saw his father-in-law approaching, went down and met him halfway, then, taking his hand, aided him to step upstairs to the apartment of his daughter. And the Princess, being as earnestly desirous to see her sire, descended and greeted him at the door of the staircase fronting the ground-floor hall. Thereupon the King folded her in his arms and kissed her, shedding tears of joy, and she did likewise, till at last Aladdin led them to the upper saloon, where they took seats and the Sultan fell to asking her case and what had betided her.

The Lady Badr al-Budur began to inform the Sultan of all which had befallen her, saying: "O my father, I recovered not life save yesterday when I saw my husband, and he it was who freed me from the thraldom of that Maghrabi, that magician, that accursed, than whom I believe there be none viler on the face of earth. And but for my beloved, I had never escaped him, nor hadst thou seen me during the rest of my days. But mighty sadness and sorrow gat about me, O my father, not only for losing thee but also for the loss of a husband under whose kindness I shall be all the length of my life, seeing that he freed me from that fulsome sorcerer." Then the Princess began repeating to her sire everything that happened to her, and relating to him how the Moorman had tricked her in the guise of a lamp-seller who offered in exchange new for old, how she had given him the lamp whose worth she knew not, and how she had bartered it away only to laugh at the lampman's folly.

"And next morning, O my father," she continued, "we found ourselves and whatso the pavilion contained in Africa land, till such time as my husband came to us and devised a device whereby we escaped. And had it not been for Aladdin's hastening to our aid, the accursed was determined to enjoy me perforce." Then she told him of the bhang drops administered in wine to the African and concluded: "Then my husband returned to me, and how I know not, but we were shifted from Africa land to this place." Aladdin in his turn recounted how, finding the wizard dead-drunken, he had sent away his wife and her women from the poluted place into the inner apartments; how he had taken the lamp from the sorcerer's breast pocket, whereto he was directed by his wife; how he had slaughtered the villain; and finally how, making use of the lamp, he had summoned its slave and ordered him to transport the pavilion back to its proper site, ending his tale with: "And, if thy Highness have any doubt anent my words, arise with me and look upon the accursed magician." The King did accordingly and, having considered the Moorman, bade the carcass be carried away forthright and burned and its ashes scattered in air.

Then he took to embracing Aladdin and, kissing him, said: "Pardon me, O my son, for that I was about to destroy thy life through the foul deeds of this damned enchanter, who cast thee into such pit of peril. And I may be excused, O my child, for what I did by thee, because I found myself forlorn of my daughter, my only one, who to me is dearer than my very kingdom. Thou knowest how the hearts of parents yearn unto their offspring, especially when like myself they have but one and none other to love." And on this wise the

Sultan took to excusing himself and kissing his son-in-law. Aladdin said to the Sultan: "O King of the time, thou didst naught to me contrary to Holy Law, and I also sinned not against thee, but all the trouble came from that Maghrabi, the impure, the magician." Thereupon the Sultan bade the city be decorated, and they obeyed him and held high feast and festivities. He also commanded the crier to cry about the streets saying: "This day is a mighty great fate, wherein public rejoicings must be held throughout the realm, for a full month of thirty days, in honor of the Lady Badr al-Budur and her husband Aladdin's return to their home."

On this wise befell it with Aladdin and the Maghrabi, but withal the King's son-in-law escaped not wholly from the accursed, albeit the body had been burnt and the ashes scattered in air. For the villain had a brother yet more villainous than himself, and a greater adept in necromancy, geomancy, and astromancy. And even as the old saw saith, "A bean and 'twas split," so each one dwelt in his own quarter of the globe that he might fill it with his sorcery, his fraud, and his treason. Now one day of the days it fortuned that the Moorman's brother would learn how it fared with him, so he brought out his sandboard and dotted it and produced the figures which, when he had considered and carefully studied them, gave him to know that the man he sought was dead and housed in the tomb. So he grieved and was certified of his disease, but he dotted a second time seeking to learn the manner of the death and where it bad taken place. So he found that the site was the China land and that the mode was the foulest of slaughter. Furthermore, that he who did him die was a young man Aladdin hight. Seeing this, he straightway arose and equipped himself for wayfare, then he set out and cut across the wilds and wolds and heights for the space of many a month until he reached China and the capital of the Sultan wherein was the slayer of his brother.

He alighted at the so-called strangers' khan and, hiring himself a cell, took rest therein for a while, then he fared forth and wandered about the highways that he might discern some path which would aid him unto the winning of his ill-minded wish; to wit, of wreaking upon Aladdin blood revenge for his brother. Presently he entered a coffeehouse, a fine building which stood in the market place and which collected a throng of folk to play, some at the mankalah, others at the backgammon, and others at the chess and what not else. There he sat down and listened to those seated beside him, and they chanced to be conversing about an ancient dame and a holy, by name Fatimah, who dwelt away at her devotions in a hermitage without the town, and this she never entered save only two days each month. They mentioned also that she had performed many saintly miracles, which when the Maghrabi, the necromancer, heard he said in himself: "Now have I found that which I sought. Inshallah- God willing- by means of this crone will I will to my wish."

The necromancer went up to the folk who were talking of the miracles performed by the devout old woman and said to one of them: "O my uncle, I heard you an chatting about the prodigies of a certain saintess named Fatimah. Who is she, and where may be her abode?" "Marvelous!" exclaimed the man. "How canst thou be in our city and yet never have heard about the miracles of the Lady Fatimah? Evidently, O thou poor fellow, thou art a foreigner, since the fastings of this devotee and her asceticism in worldly matters and the beauties of her piety never came to thine ears." The Moorman rejoined: "'Tis true, O my lord. Yes, I am a stranger, and came to this your city only yesternight. And I hope thou wilt inform me concerning the saintly miracles of this virtuous woman and where may be her wone, for that I have fallen into a calamity, and 'tis my wish to visit her and crave her prayers, so haply Allah (to Whom be honor and glory!) will, through her blessings, deliver me from mine evil." Hereat the man recounted to him the marvels of Fatimah, the devotee, and her piety and the beauties of her worship, then, taking him by the hand, went with him without the city and showed him the way to her abode, a cavern upon a hillock's head. The necromancer acknowledged his kindness in many words and, thanking him for his good offices, returned to his cell in the caravanserai.

Now by the fiat of Fate on the very next day Fatimah came down to the city, and the Maghrabi, the necromancer, happened to leave his hostelry a-morn, when he saw the folk swarming and crowding. Wherefore he went up to discover what was to do, and found the devotee standing a-middlemost the throng, and all who suffered from pain or sickness flocked to her soliciting a blessing, and praying for her prayers, and each and every she touched became whole of his illness. The Moroccan, the necromancer, followed her about until she returned to her antre. Then, awaiting till the evening evened, he arose and repaired to a vintner's store, where he drank a cup of wine. After this he fared forth the city, and finding the devotee's cavern, entered it and saw her lying prostrate with her back upon a strip of matting. So he came forward and mounted upon her belly, then he drew his dagger and shouted at her, and when she awoke and opened her eyes, she espied a Moorish man with an unsheathed poniard sitting upon her middle as though about to kill her.

She was troubled and sore terrified, but he said to her: "Hearken! And thou cry out or utter a word, I will slay thee at this very moment. Arise now and do all I bid thee." Then he sware to her an oath that if she obeyed his orders, whatever they might be, he would not do her die. So saying, he rose up from off her and Fatimah also arose, when he said to her, "Give me thy gear and take thou my habit," whereupon she gave him her clothing and head fillets, her face kerchief and her mantilla. Then quoth he, "'Tis also requisite that thou anoint me with somewhat shall make the color of my face like unto thine." Accordingly she went into the inner cavern, and bringing out a gallipot of ointment, spread somewhat thereof upon her palm and with it besmeared his face until its hue favored her own. Then she gave him her staff and, showing him how to walk and what to do when he entered the city, hung her rosary around his neck. Lastly she handed to him a mirror and said, "Now look! Thou differest from me in naught," and he saw himself Fatimah's counterpart as thou she had never gone or come. But after obtaining his every object he falsed his oath and asked for a cord, which she brought to him. Then he seized her and strangled her in the cavern, and presently, when she was dead, haled the corpse outside and threw it into a pit hard by and went back to sleep in her cavern. And when broke the day, he rose, and repairing to the town, took his stand under the walls of Aladdin's pavilion.

Hereupon flocked the folk about him, all being certified that he was Fatimah, the devotee, and he fell to doing whatso she was wont to do. He laid hands on these in pain and recited for those a chapter of the Koran and made orisons for a third. Presently the thronging of the folk and the clamoring of the crowd were heard by the Lady Badr al-Budur, who said to her handmaidens. "Look what is to do, and what he the cause of this turmoil!" Thereupon the aga of the eunuchry fared forth to see what might be the matter and, presently returning, said: "O my lady, this clamor is caused by the Lady Fatimah, and if thou be pleased to command, I will bring her to thee. So shalt thou gain through her a blessing." The Princess answered: "Go bring her, for since many a day I am always hearing of her miracles and her virtues, and I do long to see her and get a blessing by her intervention, for the folk recount her manifestations in many cases of difficulty."

The aga went forth and brought in the Moroccan, the necromancer, habited in Fatimah's clothing, and when the wizard stood before the Lady Badr al-Budur, he began at first sight to bless her with a string of prayers, nor did any one of those present doubt at all but that he was the devotee herself. The Princess arose and salaamed to him, then, seating him beside her, said: "O my Lady Fatimah, 'tis my desire that thou abide with me alway, so might I be blessed through thee, and also learn of thee the paths of worship and piety and follow thine example making for salvation." Now all this was a foul deceit of the accursed African, and he designed furthermore to complete his guile, so he continued: "O my Lady, I am a poor woman and a religious that dwelleth in the desert, and the like of me deserveth not to abide in the palaces of the kings." But the Princess replied: "Have no care whatever, O my Lady Fatimah. I will set apart for thee an apartment of my pavilion that thou mayest worship therein, and none shall ever come to trouble thee. Also thou shalt avail to worship Allah in my place better than in thy cavern." The Moroccan rejoined: "Hearkening and obedience, O my lady. I will not oppose thine order, for that the commands of the children of the kings may not be gainsaid nor renounced. Only I hope of thee that my eating and my drinking and sitting may be within my own chamber, which shall be kept wholly private. Nor do I require or desire the delicacies of diet, but do thou favor me by sending thy handmaid every day with a bit of bread and a sup of water, and, when I feel fain of food, let me eat by myself in my own room."

Now the accursed hereby purposed to avert the danger of haply raising his face kerchief at mealtimes, when his intent might be baffled by his beard and mustachios discovering him to be a man. The Princess replied: "O my Lady Fatimah, be of good heart, naught shall happen save what thou wishest. But now arise and let me show thee the apartment in the palace which I would prepare for thy sojourn with us." The Lady Badr al-Budur arose, and taking the necromancer who had disguised himself as the devotee, ushered him in to the place which she had kindly promised him for a home, and said: "O my Lady Fatimah, here thou shalt dwell with every comfort about thee and in all privacy and repose, and the place shall be named after thy name." Whereupon the Maghrabi acknowledged her kindness and prayed for her. Then the Princess showed him the jalousies and the jeweled kiosque with its four and twenty windows, and said to him, "What thinkest thou, O my Lady Fatimah, of this marvelous pavilion?" The Moorman replied: "By Allah, O my daughter, 'tis indeed passing fine and wondrous exceedingly, nor do I deem that its fellow is to be found in the whole universe. But alas for the lack of one thing which would enhance its beauty and decoration!" The

Princess asked her: "O my Lady Fatimah, what lacketh it, and what be this thing would add to its adornment? Tell me thereof, inasmuch as I was wont to believe it wholly perfect." The Moroccan answered: "O my lady, all it wanteth is that there he hanging from the middle of the dome the egg of a fowl called the roc, and were this done, the pavilion would lack its peer all the world over." The Princess asked, "What he this bird, and where can we find her egg?" and the Moroccan answered, "O my lady, the roc is indeed a giant fowl which carrieth off camels and elephants in her pounces and flieth away with them, such is her stature and strength. Also this fowl is mostly found in Mount Kaf, and the architect who built this pavilion is able to bring thee one of her eggs."

They then left such talk, as it was the hour for the noonday meal, and when the handmaid had spread the table, the Lady Badr alBudur sent down to invite the accursed African to eat with her. But he accepted not, and for a reason he would on no wise consent- nay, he rose and retired to the room which the Princess had assigned to him and whither the slave girls carried his dinner. Now when evening evened, Aladdin returned from the chase and met his wife, who salaamed to him, and he clasped her to his bosom and kissed her. Presently, looking at her face, he saw thereon a shade of sadness, and he noted that, contrary to her custom, she did not laugh, so he asked her: "What hath betided thee, O my dearling? Tell me, hath aught happened to trouble thy thoughts?" "Nothing whatever," answered she. "But, O my beloved, I fancied that our pavilion lacked naught at all. However, O eyes of me, O Aladdin, were the dome of the upper story hung with an egg of the fowl called roc, there would be naught like it in the universe." Her husband rejoined: "And for this trifle thou art saddened, when 'tis the easiest of all matters to me! So cheer thyself, and whatever thou wantest, 'tis enough thou inform me thereof, and I will bring it from the abysses of the earth in the quickest time and at the earliest hour."

Aladdin, after refreshing the spirits of his Princess by promising her all she could desire, repaired straightway to his chamber and taking the lamp, rubbed it, when the Marid appeared without let or delay saying, "Ask whatso thou wantest." Said the other: "I desire thee to fetch me an egg of the bird roc, and do thou hang it to the dome crown of this my pavilion." But when the Marid heard these words, his face waxed fierce and he shouted with a mighty loud voice and a frightful, and cried: "O denier of kindly deeds, sufficeth it not for thee that I and all the Slaves of the Lamp are ever at thy service, but thou must also require me to bring thee our Liege Lady for thy pleasure, and hang her up at thy pavilion dome for the enjoyment of thee and thy wife? Now, by Allah, ye deserve, thou and she, that I reduce you to ashes this very moment and scatter you upon the air. But inasmuch as ye twain be ignorant of this matter, unknowing its inner from its outer significance, I will pardon you, for indeed ye are but innocents. The offense cometh from that accursed necromancer, brother to the Maghrabi, the magician, who abideth here representing himself to be Fatimah, the devotee, after assuming her dress and belongings and murthering her in the cavern. Indeed he came hither seeking to slay thee by way of blood revenge for his brother, and 'tis he who taught thy wife to require this matter of me."

So saying, the Marid evanished. But when Aladdin heard these words, his wits fled his head and his joints trembled at the Marid's terrible shout. But he empowered his purpose and, arising forthright, issued from his chamber and went into his wife's. There he affected an ache of head, for that he knew how famous was Fatimah for the art and mystery of healing all such pains. And when the Lady Badr alBudur saw him sitting hand to head and complaining of unease, she asked him the cause and he answered, "I know of none other save that my head acheth exceedingly." Hereupon she straightway bade summon Fatimah, that the devotee might impose her hand upon his head, and Aladdin asked her, "Who may this Fatimah be?" So she informed him that it was Fatimah, the devotee, to whom she had given a home in the pavilion. Meanwhile the slave girls had fared forth and summoned the Maghrabi, and when the accursed made act of presence, Aladdin rose up to him and, acting like one who knew naught of his purpose, salaamed to him as though he had been the real Fatimah and, kissing the hem of his sleeve, welcomed him and entreated him with honor, and said: "O my Lady Fatimah, I hope thou wilt bless me with a boon, for well I wot thy practice in the healing of pains. I have gotten a mighty ache in my head." The Moorman, the accursed, could hardly believe that he heard such words, this being all that he desired. The necromancer, habited as Fatimah, the devotee, came up to Aladdin that he might place hand upon his head and heal his ache. So he imposed one hand and, putting forth the other under his gown, drew a dagger wherewith to slay him. But Aladdin watched him and, taking patience till he had wholly unsheathed the weapon, seized him with a forceful grip and, wrenching the dagger from his grasp, plunged it deep into his heart.

When the Lady Badr al-Budur saw him do on this wise, she

shrieked and cried out: "What hath this virtuous and holy woman done that thou hast charged thy neck with the heavy burthen of her blood shed wrongfully? Hast thou no fear of Allah that thou killest Fatimah, this saintly woman, whose miracles are far-famed?" "No," replied Aladdin, "I have not killed Fatimah. I have slain only Fatimah's slayer, he that is the brother of the Maghrabi, the accursed, the magician, who carried thee off by his black art and transported my pavilion to the Africa land. And this damnable brother of his came to our city and wrought these wiles, murthering Fatimah and assuming her habit, only that he might avenge upon me his brother's blood. And he also 'twas who taught thee to require of me a roc's egg, that my death might result from such requirement. But an thou doubt my speech, come forward and consider the person I have slain." Thereupon Aladdin drew aside the Moorman's face kerchief and the Lady Badr al-Budur saw the semblance of a man with a full heard that well-nigh covered his features.

She at once knew the truth, and said to her husband, "O my beloved, twice have I cast thee into death risk!" But he rejoined: "No harm in that, O my lady. By the blessing of your loving eyes, I accept with all joy all things thou bringest me." The Princess, hearing these words, hastened to fold him in her arms and kissed him, saying: "O my dearling, all this is for my love to thee and I knew naught thereof, but indeed I do not deem lightly of thine affection." So Aladdin kissed her and strained her to his breast, and the love between them waxed but greater. At that moment the Sultan appeared, and they told him all that had happened, showing him the corpse of the Maghrabi, the necromancer, when the King commanded the body to be burned and the ashes scattered on air, even as had befallen the wizard's brother.

And Aladdin abode with his wife, the Lady Badr al-Budur, in all pleasure and joyaunce of life, and thenceforward escaped every danger, and after a while, when the Sultan deceased, his son-in-law was seated upon the throne of the kingdom. And he commanded and dealt justice to the lieges so that all the folk loved him, and he lived with his wife in all solace and happiness until there came to him the Destroyer of delights and the Severer of societies.

IV.   The Ebony Horse

There was once in times of yore and ages long gone before, a great and puissant King, of the kings of the Persians, Sabur by name, who was the richest of all the kings in store of wealth and dominion and surpassed each and every in wit and wisdom. He was generous, openhanded and beneficent, and he gave to those who sought him and repelled not those who resorted to him, and he comforted the brokenhearted and honorably entreated those who fled to him for refuge.

Moreover, he loved the poor and was hospitable to strangers and did the oppressed justice upon the oppressor. He had three daughters, like full moons of shining light or flower gardens blooming bright, and a son as he were the moon. And it was his wont to keep two festivals in the twelvemonth, those of the Nau-Roz, or New Year, and

Mihrgan, the Autumnal Equinox, on which occasions he threw open his palaces and gave largess and made proclamation of safety and security and promoted his chamberlains and viceroys. And the people of his realm came in to him and saluted him and gave him joy of the holy day, bringing him gifts and servants and eunuchs.

Now he loved science and geometry, and one festival day as he sat on his kingly throne there came in to him three wise men, cunning artificers and past masters in all manner of craft and inventions, skilled in making things curious and rare, such as confound the wit, and versed in the knowledge of occult truths and perfect in mysteries and subtleties. And they were of three different tongues and countries: the first a Hindi or Indian, the second a Roumi or Greek, and the third a Farsi or Persian. The Indian came forward and, prostrating himself before the King, wished him joy of the festival and laid before him a present befitting his dignity; that is to say, a man of gold, set with precious gems and jewels of price and hending in hand a golden trumpet. When Sabur saw this, he asked, "O sage, what is the virtue of this figure?" and the Indian answered: "O my lord, if this figure be set at the gate of thy city, it will be a guardian over it; for if an enemy enter the place, it will blow this clarion against him and he will be seized with a palsy and drop down dead." Much the King marveled at this and cried, "By Allah, O sage, an this thy word be true, I will grant thee thy wish and thy desire."

Then came forward the Greek and, prostrating himself before the King, presented him with a basin of silver in whose midst was a peacock of gold, surrounded by four and twenty chicks of the same metal. Sabur looked at them and turning to the Greek, said to him, "O sage, what is the virtue of this peacock?" "O my lord," answered he, "as often as an hour of the day or night passeth, it pecketh one of its young and crieth out and flappeth its wing, till the four and twenty hours are accomplished. And when the month cometh to an end, it will open its mouth and thou shalt see the crescent therein." And the King said, "An thou speak sooth, I will bring thee to thy wish and thy desire."

Then came forward the Persian sage and, prostrating himself before the King, presented him with a horse of the blackest ebony wood inlaid with gold and jewels, and ready harnessed with saddle, bridle, and stirrups such as befit kings, which when Sabur saw, he marveled with exceeding marvel and was confounded at the beauty of its form and the ingenuity of its fashion. So he asked, "What is the use of this horse of wood, and what is its virtue and what the secret of its movement?" and the Persian answered, "O my lord, the virtue of this horse is that if one mount him, it will carry him whither he will and fare with its rider through the air and cover the space of a year in a single day."

The King marveled and was amazed at these three wonders, following thus hard upon one another on the same day, and turning to the sage, said to him: "By Allah the Omnipotent, and our Lord the Beneficent, who created all creatures and feedeth them with meat and drink, an thy speech be veritable and the virtue of thy contrivance appear, I will assuredly give thee whatsoever thou lustest for and will bring thee to thy desire and thy wish!" Then he entertained the sages three days, that he might make trial of their gifts, after which they brought the figures before him and each took the creature he had wroughten and showed him the mystery of its movement. The trumpeter blew the trump, the peacock pecked its chicks, and the Persian sage mounted the ebony horse, whereupon it soared with him high in air and descended again. When King Sabur saw all this, he was amazed and perplexed and felt like to fly for joy and said to the three sages: "Now I am certified of the truth of your words and it behooveth me to quit me of my promise. Ask ye, therefore, what ye will, and I will give you that same."

Now the report of the King's daughters had reached the sages, so they answered: "If the King be content with us and accept of our gifts and allow us to prefer a request to him, we crave of him that he give us his three daughters in marriage, that we may be his sons-inlaw, for that the stability of kings may not be gainsaid." Quoth the King, "I grant you that which you wish and you desire," and bade summon the kazi forthright, that he might marry each of the sages to one of his daughters. Now it fortuned that the Princesses were behind a curtain, looking on, and when they heard this, the youngest considered her husband-to-be and behold, he was an old man, a hundred years of age, with hair frosted, forehead drooping, eyebrows mangy, ears slitten, beard and mustachios stained and dyed, eyes red and goggle, cheeks bleached and hollow, flabby nose like a brinjall or eggplant, face like a cobblees apron, teeth overlapping and lips like camel's kidneys, loose and pendulous- in brief, a terror, a horror, a monster, for he was of the folk of his time the unsightliest and of his age the frightfulest. Sundry of his grinders had been knocked out and his eyeteeth were like the tusks of the Jinni who frighteneth poultry in henhouses.

Now the girl was the fairest and most graceful of her time, more elegant than the gazelle, however tender, than the gentlest zephyr blander, and brighter than the moon at her full, for amorous fray right suitable, confounding in graceful sway the waving bough and outdoing in swimming gait the pacing roe,- in fine, she was fairer and sweeter by far than all her sisters. So when she saw her suitor, she went to her chamber and strewed dust on her head and tore her clothes and fell to buffeting her face and weeping and walling. Now the Prince, her brother, Kamar al-Akmar, or the Moon of Moons hight, was then newly returned from a journey and, hearing her weeping and crying, came in to her (for he loved her with fond affection, more than his other sisters) and asked her: "What aileth thee? What hath befallen thee? Tell me, and conceal naught from me." So she smote her breast and answered: "O my brother and my dear one, I have nothing to hide. If the palace be straitened upon thy father, I will go out, and if he be resolved upon a foul thing, I will separate myself from him, though he consent not to make provision for me, and my Lord will provide." Quoth he, "Tell me what meaneth this talk and what hath straitened thy breast and troubled thy temper." "O my brother and my dear one," answered the Princess, "know that my father hath promised me in marriage to a wicked magician who brought him as a gift a horse of black wood, and hath bewitched him with his craft and his egromancy. But as for me, I will none of him, and would, because of him, I had never come into this world!"

Her brother soothed her and solaced her, then fared to his sire and said: "What be this wizard to whom thou hast given my youngest sister in marriage, and what is this present which he hast brought thee, so that thou hast killed my sister with chagrin? It is not right that this should be." Now the Persian was standing by, and when he heard the Prince's words, he was mortified and filled with fury, and the King said, "O my son, an thou sawest this horse, thy wit would be confounded and thou wouldst be amated with amazement." Then he bade the slaves bring the horse before him and they did so, and, when the Prince saw it, it pleased him. So (being an accomplished cavalier) he mounted it forthright and struck its sides with the shovelshaped stirrup irons. But it stirred not, and the King said to the sage, "Go show him its movement, that he also may help thee to win thy wish."

Now the Persian bore the Prince a grudge because he willed not he should have his sister, so he showed him the pin of ascent on the right side of the horse and saying to him, "Trill this," left him. Thereupon the Prince trilled the pin and lo! the horse forthwith soared with him high in ether, as it were a bird, and gave not over flying till it disappeared from men's espying, whereat the King was troubled and perplexed about his case and said to the Persian, "O Sage, look how thou mayst make him descend." But he replied, "O my lord, I can do nothing, and thou wilt never see him again till Resurrection Day, for he, of his ignorance and pride, asked me not of the pin of descent, and I forgot to acquaint him therewith." When the King heard this, he was enraged with sore rage, and bade bastinado the sorcerer and clap him in jail, whilst he himself cast the crown from his head and beat his face and smote his breast. Moreover, he shut the doors of his palaces and gave himself up to weeping and keening, he and his wife and daughters and all the folk of the city, and thus their joy was turned to annoy and their gladness changed into sore affliction and sadness.

Thus far concerning them, but as regards the Prince, the horse gave not over soaring with him till he drew near the sun, whereat he gave himself up for lost and saw death in the sides, and was confounded at his case, repenting him of having mounted the horse and saying to himself: "Verily, this was a device of the sage to destroy me on account of my youngest sister. But there is no Majesty and there is no Might save in Allah, the Glorious, the Great! I am lost without recourse, but I wonder, did not he who made the ascent pin make also a descent pin?" Now he was a man of wit and knowledge and intelligence, so he fell to feeling all the parts of the horse, but saw nothing save a screw like a cock's head on its right shoulder and the like on the left, when quoth he to himself, "I see no sip save these things like button."

Presently he turned the right-hand pin, whereupon the horse flew heavenward with increased speed. So he left it, and looking at the sinister shoulder and finding another pin, he wound it up and immediately the steed's upward motion slowed and ceased and it began to descend, little by little, toward the face of the earth, while the rider became yet more cautious and careful of his life. And when he saw this and knew the uses of the horse, his heart was filled with joy and gladness and he thanked Almighty Allah for that He had deigned deliver him from destruction. Then he began to turn the horse's head whithersoever he would, making it rise and fall at pleasure, till he had gotten complete mastery over its every movement. He ceased not to descend the whole of that day, for that the steed's ascending flight had borne him afar from the earth, and as he descended, he diverted himself with viewing the various cities and countries over which he passed and which he knew not, never having seen them in his life.

Amongst the rest, he decried a city ordered after the fairest fashion in the midst of a verdant and riant land, rich in trees and streams, with gazelles pacing daintily over the plains, whereat he fell a-musing and said to himself, "Would I knew the name of yon town and in what land it is!" And he took to circling about it and observing it right and left. By this time, the day began to decline and the sun drew near to its downing, and he said in his mind, "Verily I find no goodlier place to night in than this city, so I will lodge here, and early on the morrow I will return to my kith and kin and my kingdom and tell my father and family what hath passed and acquaint him with what mine eyes have seen.

Then he addressed himself to seeking a place wherein he might safely bestow himself and his horse and where none should descry him, and presently, behold, he espied a-middlemost of the city a palace rising high in upper air surrounded by a great wall with lofty crenelles and battlements, guarded by forty black slaves clad in complete mail and armed with spears and swords, bows and arrows. Quoth he, "This is a goodly place," and turned the descent pin, whereupon the horse sank down with him like a weary bird, and alighted gently on the terrace roof of the palace. So the Prince dismounted and ejaculating "Alhamdolillah-praise be to Allah," he began to go round about the horse and examine it, saying: "By Allah, he who fashioned thee with these perfections was a cunning craftsman, and if the Almighty extend the term of my life and restore me to my country and kinsfolk in safety and reunite me with my father, I will assuredly bestow upon him all manner bounties and benefit him with the utmost beneficence."

By this time night had overtaken him and he sat on the roof till he was assured that all in the palace slept, and indeed hunger and thirst were sore upon him for that he had not tasted food nor drunk water since he parted from his sire.

So he said within himself, "Surely the like of this palace will not lack of victual," and, leaving the horse above, went down in search of somewhat to eat. Presently he came to a staircase and, descending it to the bottom, found himself in a court paved with white marble and alabaster, which shone in the light of the moon. He marveled at the place and the goodliness of its fashion, but sensed no sound of speaker and saw no living soul and stood in perplexed surprise, looking right and left and knowing not whither he should wend. Then said he to himself, "I may not do better than return to where I left my horse and pass the night by it, and as soon as day shall dawn I will mount and ride away."

However, as he tarried talking to himself, he espied a light within the palace, and making toward it, found that it came from a candle that stood before a door of the harem, at the head of a sleeping eunuch, as he were one of the Ifrits of Solomon or a tribesman of the Jinn, longer than lumber and broader than a bench. He lay before the door, with the pommel of his sword gleaming in the flame of the candle, and at his head was a bag of leather hanging from a column of granite. When the Prince saw this, he was affrighted and said, "I crave help from Allah the Supreme! O mine Holy One, even as Thou hast already delivered me from destruction, so vouchsafe me strength to quit myself of the adventure of this palace!" So saying, he put out his hand to the budget and taking it, carried it aside and opened it and found in it food of the best.

He ate his fill and refreshed himself and drank water, after which he hung up the provision bag in its place and drawing the eunuch's sword from its sheath, took it, whilst the slave slept on, knowing not whence Destiny should come to him. Then the Prince fared forward into the palace and ceased not till he came to a second door, with a curtain drawn before it. So he raised the curtain and, behold, on entering he saw a couch of the whitest ivory inlaid with pearls and jacinths and jewels, and four slave girls sleeping about it. He went up to the couch, to see what was thereon, and found a young lady lying asleep, chemised with her hair as she were the full moon rising over the eastern horizon, with flower-white brow and shining hair parting and cheeks like blood-red anemones, and dainty moles thereon. He was amazed at her as she lay in her beauty and loveliness, her symmetry and grace, and he recked no more of death.

So he went up to her, trembling in every nerve, and, shuddering with pleasure, kissed her on the right cheek, whereupon she awoke forthright and opened her eyes, and seeing the Prince standing at her head, said to him, "Who art thou, and whence comest thou?" Quoth he, "I am thy slave and thy lover." Asked she, "And who brought thee hither?" and he answered, "My Lord and my fortune." Then said Shams al-Nahar (for such was her name) "Haply thou art he who demanded me yesterday of my father in marriage and he rejected thee, pretending that thou wast foul of favor. By Allah, my sire lied in his throat when he spoke this thing, for thou art not other than beautiful." Now the son of the King of Hind had sought her in marriage, but her father had rejected him for that he was ugly and uncouth, and she thought the Prince was he. So when she saw his beauty and grace (for indeed he was like the radiant moon) the syntheism of love gat hold of her heart as it were a flaming fire, and they fell to talk and converse.

Suddenly, her waiting women awoke and, seeing the Prince with their mistress, said to her, "O my lady, who is this with thee?" Quoth she: "I know not. I found him sitting by me when I woke up. Haply 'tis he who seeketh me in marriage of my sire." Quoth they, "O my lady, by Allah the All-Father, this is not he who seeketh thee in marriage, for he is hideous and this man is handsome and of high degree. Indeed, the other is not fit to be his servant." Then the handmaidens went out to the eunuch, and finding him slumbering, awoke him, and he started up in alarm. Said they, "How happeth it that thou art on guard at the palace and yet men come in to us whilst we are asleep?" When the black heard this, he sprang in haste to his sword, but found it not, and fear took him, and trembling. Then he went in, confounded, to his mistress and seeing the Prince sitting at talk with her, said to him, "O my lord, art thou man or Jinni?" Replied the Prince: "Woe to thee, O unluckiest of slaves. How darest thou even the sons of the royal Chosroes with one of the unbelieving Satans?" And he was as a raging lion.

Then he took the sword in his hand and said to the slave, "I am the King's son-in-law, and he hath married me to his daughter and bidden me go in to her." And when the eunuch heard these words he replied, "O my lord, if thou be indeed of kind a man as thou avouchest, she is fit for none but for thee, and thou art worthier of her than any other." Thereupon the eunuch ran to the King, shrieking loud and rending his raiment and heaving dust upon his head. And when the King heard his outcry, he said to him: "What hath befallen thee? Speak quickly and be brief, for thou hast fluttered my heart." Answered the eunuch, "O King, come to thy daughter's succor, for a devil of the Jinn, in the likeness of a King's son hath got possession of her, so up and at him!"

When the King heard this, he thought to kill him and said, "How camest thou to be careless of my daughter and let this demon come at her?" Then he betook himself to the Princess's palace, where he found her slave women standing to await him, and asked them, "What is come to my daughter?" "O King," answered they, "slumber overcame us and when we awoke, we found a young man sitting upon her couch in talk with her, as he were the full moon. Never saw we aught fairer of favor than he. So we questioned him of his case and he declared that thou hadst given him thy daughter in marriage. More than this we know not, nor do we know if he be a man or a Jinni, but he is modest and well-bred, and doth nothing unseemly or which leadeth to disgrace."

Now when the King heard these words, his wrath cooled, and he raised the curtain little by little and looking in, saw sitting at talk with his daughter a Prince of the goodliest, with a face like the full moon for sheen. At this sight he could not contain himself, of his jealousy for his daughter's honor, and putting aside the curtain, rushed in upon them drawn sword in hand like a furious Ghul. Now when the Prince saw him he asked the Princess, "Is this thy sire?" and she answered, "Yes." Whereupon he sprang, to his feet and, seizing his sword, cried out at the King with so terrible a cry that he was confounded. Then the youth would have fallen on him with the sword, but the King, seeing that the Prince was doughtier than he, sheathed his scimitar and stood till the young man came up to him, when he accosted him courteously and said to him, "O youth, art thou a man or a Jinni?" Quoth the Prince: "Did I not respect thy right as mine host and thy daughter's honor, I would spill thy blood! How darest thou fellow me with devils, me that am a Prince of the sons of the royal Chosroes, who, had they wished to take thy kingdom, could shake thee like an earthquake from thy glory and thy dominions, and spoil thee of all thy possessions?"

Now when the King heard his words, he was confounded with awe and bodily fear of him and rejoined: "If thou indeed be of the sons of the Kings, as thou pretendest, how cometh it that thou enterest my palace without my permission, and smirchest mine honor, making thy way to my daughter and feigning that thou art her husband and claiming that I have given her to thee to wife, I that have slain kings and king's sons who sought her of me in marriage? And now who shall save thee from my might and majesty when, if I cried out to my slaves and servants and bade them put thee to the vilest of deaths, they would slay thee forthright? Who shall deliver thee out of my hand?"

When the Prince heard this speech of the King, he answered: "Verily, I wonder at thee and at the shortness and denseness of thy wit! Say me, canst covet for thy daughter a mate comelier than myself, and hast ever seen a stouter-hearted man or one better fitted for a Sultan or a more glorious in rank and dominion than I?" Rejoined the King: "Nay, by Allah! But I would have had thee, O youth, act after the custom of kings and demand her from me to wife before witnesses, that I might have married her to thee publicly. And now, even were I to marry her to thee privily, yet hast thou dishonored me in her person." Rejoined the Prince: "Thou sayest sooth, O King, but if thou summon thy slaves and thy soldiers and they fall upon me and slay me, as thou pretendest, thou wouldst but publish thine own disgrace, and the folk would be divided between belief in thee and disbelief in thee. Wherefore, O King, thou wilt do well, meseemeth, to turn from this thought to that which I shall counsel thee." Quoth the King, "Let me hear what thou hast to advise," and quoth the Prince:

"What I have to propose to thee is this: Either do thou meet me in combat singular, I and thou, and he who slayeth his adversary shall be held the worthier and having a better title to the kingdom; or else let me be this night, and whenas dawns the morn, draw out against me thy horsemen and footmen and servants, but first tell me their number." Said the King, "They are forty thousand horse, besides my own slaves and their followers, who are the like of them in number." Thereupon said the Prince: "When the day shall break, do thou array them against me and say to them: 'This man is a suitor to me for my daughter's hand, on condition that he shall do battle singlehanded against you all; for he pretendeth that he will overcome you and put you to the rout, and indeed that ye cannot prevail against him.' After which, leave me to do battle with them. If they slay me, then is thy secret the surer guarded and thine honor the better warded, and if I overcome them and see their backs, then is it the like of me a king should covet to his son-in-law."

So the King approved of his opinion and accepted his proposition, despite his awe at the boldness of his speech and amaze at the pretensions of the Prince to meet in fight his whole host, such as he had described it to him, being at heart assured that he would perish in the fray and so he should be quit of him and freed from the fear of dishonor. Thereupon he called the eunuch and bade him go to his Wazir without stay and delay and command him to assemble the whole of the army and cause them don their arms and armor and mount their steeds. So the eunuch carried the King's order to the Minister, who straightway summoned the captains of the host and the lords of the realm and bade them don their harness of derring-do and mount horse and sally forth in battle array.

Such was their case, but as regards the King, he sat a long while conversing with the young Prince, being pleased with his wise speech and good sense and fine breeding. And when it was daybreak, he returned to his palace and, seating himself on his throne, commanded his merry men to mount, and bade them saddle one of the best of the royal steeds with handsome selle and housings and trappings and bring it to the Prince. But the youth said, "O King, I will not mount horse till I come in view of the troops and review them." "Be it as thou wilt," replied the King. Then the two repaired to the parade ground where the troops were drawn up, and the young Prince looked upon them and noted their great number. After which the King cried out to them, saying: "Ho, all ye men, there is come to me a youth who seeketh my daughter in marriage, and in very sooth never have I seen a goodlier than he- no, nor a stouter of heart nor a doughtier of arm, for he pretendeth that he can overcome you singlehanded, and force you to flight and that, were ye a hundred thousand in number, yet for him would ye be but few. Now when he chargeth down on you, do ye receive him upon point of pike and sharp of saber, for indeed he hath undertaken a mighty matter."

Then quoth the King to the Prince, "Up, O my son, and do thy devoir on them." Answered he: "O King, thou dealest not justly and fairly by me. How shall I go forth against them, seeing that I am afoot and the men be mounted?" The King retorted, "I bade thee mount, and thou refusedst, but choose thou which of my horses thou wilt." Then he said,

"Not one of thy horses pleaseth me, and I will ride none but that on which I came." Asked the King, "And where is thy horse?" "Atop of thy palace." "In what part of my palace?" "On the roof." Now when the King heard these words, he cried: "Out on thee! This is the first sip thou hast given of madness. How can the horse be on the roof.? But we shall at once see if thou speak truth or lies." Then he turned to one of his chief officers and said to him, "Go to my palace and bring me what thou findest on the roof." So all the people marveled at the young Prince's words, saying one to other, "How can a horse come down the steps from the roof.? Verily this is a thing whose like we never heard."

In the meantime the King's messenger repaired to the palace and, mounting to the roof, found the horse standing there, and never had he looked on a handsomer. But when he drew near and examined it, he saw that it was made of ebony and ivory. Now the officer was accompanied by other high officers, who also looked on, and they laughed to one another, saying: "Was it of the like of this horse that the youth spake? We cannot deem him other than mad. However, we shall soon see the truth of his case. Peradventure herein is some mighty matter, and he is a man of high degree." Then they lifted up the horse bodily, carrying it to the King, set it down before him. And all the lieges flocked round to look at it, marveling at the beauty of its proportions and the richness of its saddle and bridle. The King also admired it, and wondered at it with extreme wonder, and he asked the Prince, "O youth, is this thy horse?" He answered, "Yes, O King, this is my horse, and thou shalt soon see the marvel it showeth." Rejoined the King, "Then take and mount it," and the Prince retorted, "I will not mount till the troops withdraw afar from it."

So the King bade them retire a bowshot from the horse, whereupon quoth its owner: "O King, see thou, I am about to mount my horse and charge upon thy host and scatter them right and left and split their hearts asunder." Said the King, "Do as thou wilt, and spare not their lives, for they will not spare thine." Then the Prince mounted, whilst the troops ranged themselves in ranks before him, and one said to another, "When the youth cometh between the ranks, we will take him on the points of our pikes and the sharps of our sabers." Quoth another: "By Allah, this is a mere misfortune. How shall we slay a youth so comely of face and shapely of form?" And a third continued: "Ye will have hard work to get the better of him, for the youth had not done this but for what he knew of his own prowess and pre-eminence of valor."

Meanwhile, having settled himself in his saddle, the Prince turned the pin of ascent whilst an eyes were strained to see what he would do, whereupon the horse began to heave and rock and sway to and fro and make the strangest of movements steed ever made, till its belly was filled with air and it took flight with its rider and soared high into the sky. When the King saw this, he cried out to his men, saying: "Woe to you! Catch him, catch him, ere he 'scape you!" But his Wazirs and viceroys said to him: "O King, can a man overtake the flying bird? This is surely none but some mighty magician or Marid of the, Jinn, or devil, and Allah save thee from him! So praise thou the Almighty for deliverance of thee and of all thy host from his hand."

Then the King returned to his palace after seeing the feat of the Prince, and going in to his daughter, acquainted her with what had befallen them both on the parade ground. He found her grievously afflicted for the Prince and bewailing her separation from him, wherefore she fell sick with violent sickness and took to her pillow. Now when her father saw her on this wise, he pressed her to his breast and kissing her between the eyes, said to her: "O my daughter, praise Allah Almighty and thank Him for that He hath delivered us from this crafty enchanter, this villian, this low fellow, this thief who thought only of seducing thee!" And he repeated to her the story of the Prince and how he had disappeared in the firmament, and he abused him and cursed him, knowing not how dearly his daughter loved him. But she paid no heed to his words and did but redouble in her tears and wails, saying to herself, "By Allah, I will neither eat meat nor drain drink till Allah reunite me with him!" Her father was greatly concerned for her case and mourned much over her plight, but for all he could do to soothe her, love longing only increased on her.

Thus far concerning the King and Princess Shams al-Nahar, but as regards Prince Kamar al-Akmar, when he had risen high in air, he turned his horse's head toward his native land, and being alone, mused upon the beauty of the Princess and her loveliness. Now he had inquired of the King's people the name of the city and of its King and his daughter, and men had told him that it was the city of Sana'a. So he journeyed with all speed till he drew near his father's capital and, making an airy circuit about the city, alighted on the roof of the King's palace, where he left his horse whilst he descended into the palace, and seeing its threshold strewn with ashes, thought that one of his family was dead. Then he entered, as of wont, and found his father and mother and sisters clad in mourning raiment of black, all pale of faces and lean of frames. When his sire descried him and was assured that it was indeed his son, he cried out with a great cry and fell down in a fit, but after a time, coming to himself, threw himself upon him and embraced him, clipping him to his bosom and rejoicing in him with exceeding joy and extreme gladness. His mother and sisters heard this, so they came in, and seeing the Prince, fell upon him, kissing him and weeping and joying with exceeding joyance.

Then they questioned him of his case, so he told them all that had past from first to last, and his father said to him, "Praised be Allah for thy safety, O coolth of my eyes and core of my heart!" Then the King bade hold high festival, and the glad tidings flew through the city. So they beat drums and cymbals and, doffing the weed of mourning, they donned the gay garb of gladness and decorated the streets and markets, whilst the folk vied with one another who should be the first to give the King joy, and the King proclaimed a general pardon, and opening the prisons, released those who were therein prisoned. Moreover, he made banquets for the people, with great abundance of eating and drinking, for seven days and nights, and all creatures were gladsomest. And he took horse with his son and rode out with him, that the folk might see him and rejoice.

After a while the Prince asked about the maker of the horse, saying, "O my father, what hath fortune done with him?" and the King answered: "Allah never bless him nor the hour wherein I set eyes on him! For he was the cause of thy separation from us, O my son, and he hath lain in jail since the day of thy disappearance." Then the King bade release him from prison and, sending for him, invested him in a dress of satisfaction and entreated him with the utmost favor and munificence, save that he would not give him his

256

daughter to wife. Whereat the sage raged with sore rage and repented of that which he had done, knowing that the Prince had secured the secret of the steed and the manner of its motion. Moreover, the King said to his son: "I reck thou wilt do well not to go near the horse henceforth, and more especially not to mount it after this day; for thou knowest not its properties, and belike thou art in error about it."

Now the Prince had told his father of his adventure with the King of Sana'a and his daughter, and he said, "Had the King intended to kill thee, he had done so, but thine hour was not yet come." When the rejoicings were at an end, the people returned to their places and the King and his son to the palace, where they sat down and fell to eating, drinking, and making merry. Now the King had a handsome handmaiden who was skilled in playing the lute, so she took it and began to sweep the strings and sing thereto before the King and his son of separation of lovers, and she chanted the following verses:

"Deem not that absence breeds in me aught of forgetfulness.
What should remember I did you fro' my remembrance
wane?
Time dies but never dies the fondest love for you we bear,
And in your love I'll die and in your love I'll arise again."

When the Prince heard these verses, the fires of longing flamed up in his heart, and pine and passion redoubled upon him. Grief and regret were sore upon him and his bowels yeamed in him for love of the King's daughter of Sana'a. So he rose forthright and, escaping his father's notice, went forth the palace to the horse and mounting it, turned the pin of ascent, whereupon birdlike it flew with him high in air and soared toward the upper regions of the sky. In early morning his father missed him, and going up to the pinnacle of the palace in great concern, saw his son rising into the firmament, whereat he was sore afflicted and repented in all penitence that he had not taken the horse and hidden it. And he said to himself, "By Allah, if but my son returned to me, I will destroy the horse, that my heart may be at rest concerning my son." And he fell again to weeping and bewailing himself.

Such was his case, but as regards the Prince, he ceased not flying on through air till he came to the city of Sana'a and alighted on the roof as before. Then he crept down stealthily and, finding the eunuch asleep, as of wont, raised the curtain and went on little by little till he came to the door of the Princess's alcove chamber and stopped to listen, when lo! he heard her shedding plenteous tears and reciting verses, whilst her women slept round her. Presently, overhearing her weeping and wailing, quoth they, "O our mistress, why wilt thou mourn for one who mourneth not for thee?" Quoth she, "O ye little of wit, is he for whom I mourn of those who forget or who are forgotten?" And she fell again to wailing and weeping, till sleep overcame her.

Hereat the Prince's heart melted for her and his gall bladder was like to burst, so he entered and, seeing her lying asleep without covering, touched her with his hand, whereupon she opened her eyes and espied him standing by her. Said he, "Why all this crying and mourning?" And when she knew him, she threw herself upon him and took him around the neck and kissed him and answered, "For thy sake and because of my separation from thee." Said he, "O my lady, I have been made desolate by thee all this long time!" But she replied, "'Tis thou who hast desolated me, and hadst thou tarried longer, I had surely died!" Rejoined he: "O my lady, what thinkest thou of my case with thy father, and how he dealt with me? Were it not for my love of thee, O temptation and seduction of the Three Worlds, I had certainly slain him and made him a warning to all beholders, but even as I love thee, so I love him for thy sake." Quoth she: "How couldst thou leave me? Can my life be sweet to me after thee?" Quoth he: "Let what hath happened suffice. I am now hungry, and thirsty." So she bade her maidens make ready meat and drink, and they sat eating and drinking and conversing till night was well-nigh ended; and when day broke he rose to take leave of her and depart ere the eunuch should awake.

Shams al-Nahar asked him, "Whither goest thou?" and he answered, "To my father' house, and I plight thee my troth that I will come to thee once in every week." But she wept and said: "I conjure thee, by Allah the Almighty, take me with thee whereso thou wendest and make me not taste anew the bitter gourd of separation from thee." Quoth he, "Wilt thou indeed go with me?" and quoth she, "Yes." "Then," said he, "arise, that we depart." So she rose forthright and going to a chest, affayed herself in what was richest and dearest to her of her trinkets of gold and jewels of price, and she fared forth, her handmaids recking naught. So he carried her up to the roof of the palace and, mounting the ebony horse, took her up behind him and made her fast to himself, binding her with strong bonds. After which he turned the shoulder pin of ascent and the horse rose with him high in air.

When her slave women saw this, they shrieked aloud and told her father and mother, who in hot haste ran to the palace roof and looking up, saw the magical horse flying away with the Prince and Princess. At this the King was troubled with ever-increasing trouble and cried out, saying, "O King's son, I conjure thee, by Allah, have ruth on me and my wife and bereave us not of our daughter!" The Prince made him no reply, but, thinking in himself that the maiden repented of leaving father and mother, asked her, "O ravishment of the age, say me, wilt thou that I restore thee to thy mother and father?" Whereupon she answered: "By Allah, O my lord, that is not my desire. My only wish is to be with thee, wherever thou art, for I am distracted by the love of thee from all else, even from my father and mother." Hearing these words, the Prince joyed with great joy, and made the horse fly and fare softly with them, so as not to disquiet her. Nor did they stay their flight till they came in sight of a green meadow, wherein was a spring of running water. Here they alighted and ate and drank, after which the Prince took horse again and set her behind him, binding her in his fear for her safety, after which they fared on till they came in sight of his father's capital.

At this, the Prince was filled with joy and bethought himself to show his beloved the seat of his dominion and his father's power and dignity and give her to know that it was greater than that of her sire. So he set her down in one of his father's gardens without the city where his parent was wont to take his pleasure, and carrying her into a domed summerhouse prepared there for the King, left the ebony horse at the door and charged the damsel keep watch over it, saying, "Sit here till my messenger come to thee, for I go now to my father to make ready a palace for thee and show thee my royal estate." She was delighted when she heard these words and said to him, "Do as thou wilt," for she thereby understood that she should not enter the city but with due honor and worship, as became her rank.

Then the Prince left her and betook himself to the palace of the King his father, who rejoiced in his return and met him and welcomed him, and the Prince said to him: "Know that I have brought with me the King's daughter of whom I told thee, and have left her without the city in such a garden and come to tell thee, that thou mayest make ready the procession of estate and go forth to meet her and show her the royal dignity and troops and guards." Answered the King, "With joy and gladness," and straightway bade decorate the town with the goodliest adornment. Then he took horse and rode out in all magnificence and majesty, he and his host, high officers, and household, with drums and kettledrums, fifes and clarions and all manner instruments, whilst the Prince drew forth of his treasuries jewelry and apparel and what else of the things which kings hoard and made a rare display of wealth-and splendor. Moreover he got ready for the Princess a canopied litter of brocades, green, red, and yellow, wherein he set Indian and Greek and Abyssinian slave girls. Then he left the litter and those who were therein and preceded them to the pavilion where he had set her down, and searched but found naught, neither Princess nor horse.

When he saw this, he beat his face and rent his raiment and began to wander round about the garden as he had lost his wits, after which he came to his senses and said to himself: "How could she have come at the secret of this horse, seeing I told her nothing of it? Maybe the Persian sage who made the horse hath chanced upon her and stolen her away, in revenge for my father's treatment of him." Then he sought the guardians of the garden and asked them if they had seen any pass the precincts, and said: "Hath anyone come in here? Tell me the truth and the whole truth, or I will at once strike off your heads." They were terrified by his threats, but they answered with one voice, "We have seen no man enter save the Persian sage, who came to gather healing herbs." So the Prince was certified that it was indeed he that had taken away the maiden, and abode confounded and perplexed concerning his case. And he was abashed before the folk and, turning to his sire, told him what had happened and said to him: "Take the troops and march them back to the city. As for me, I will never return till I have cleared up this affair."

When the King heard this, he wept and beat his breast and said to him: "O my son, calm thy choler and master thy chagrin and come home with us and look what Idng's daughter thou wouldst fain have, that I may marry thee to her." But the Prince paid no heed to his words and farewelling him, departed, whilst the King returned to the city, and their joy was changed into sore annoy. Now, as Destiny issued her decree, when the Prince left the Princess in the garden house and betook himself to his father's palace for the ordering of his affair, the Persian entered the garden to pluck certain simples and, scenting the sweet savor of musk and perfumes that exhaled from the Princess and impregnated the whole place, followed it till he came to the pavilion and saw standing at the door the horse which he had made with his own hands. His heart was filled with joy and gladness, for he had bemourned its loss much since it had gone out of his hand. So he went up to it and, examining its every part, found it whole and sound, whereupon he was about to mount and ride away when he bethought himself and said, "Needs must I first look what the Prince hath brought and left here with the horse." So he entered the pavilion and seeing the Princess sitting there, as she were the sun shining sheen in the sky serene, knew her at the first glance to be some highborn lady, and doubted not but the Prince had brought her thither on the horse and left her in the pavilion whilst he went to the city to make ready for her entry in state procession with all splendor.

Then he went up to her and kissed the earth between her hands, whereupon she raised her eyes to him and, finding him exceedingly foul of face and favor, asked, "Who art thou?", and he answered, "O my lady, I am a messenger sent by the Prince, who hath bidden me bring thee to another pleasance nearer the city, for that my lady the Queen cannot walk so far and is unwilling, of her joy in thee, that another should forestall her with thee." Quoth she, "Where is the Prince?" and quoth the Persian, "He is in the city, with his sire, and forthwith he shall come for thee in great state." Said she: "O thou! Say me, could he find none handsomer to send to me?" Whereat loud laughed the sage and said: "Yea verily, he hath not a Mameluke as ugly as I am, but, O my lady, let not the ill favor of my face and the foulness of my form deceive thee. Hadst thou profited of me as hath the Prince, verily thou wouldst praise my affair. Indeed, he chose me as his messenger to thee because of my uncomeliness and loathsomeness in his jealous love of thee. Else hath he Mamelukes and Negro slaves, pages, eunuchs, and attendants out of number, each goodlier than other."

Whenas she heard this, it commended itself to her reason and she believed him, so she rose forthright and, putting her hand in his, said, "O my father, what hast thou brought me to ride?" He replied, "O my lady thou shalt ride the horse thou camest on," and she, "I cannot ride it by myself."

Whereupon he smiled and knew that he was her master and said, "I will ride with thee myself." So he mounted and, taking her up behind him, bound her to himself with firm bonds, while she knew not what he would with her. Then he turned the ascent pin, whereupon the belly of the horse became full of wind and it swayed to and fro like a wave of the sea, and rose with them high in air, nor slackened in its flight till it was out of sight of the city. Now when Shams al-Nahar saw this, she asked him: "Ho, thou! What is become of that thou toldest me of my Prince, making me believe that he sent thee to me?" Answered the Persian, "Allah damn the Prince! He is a mean and skinflint knave." She cried: "Woe to thee! How darest thou disobey thy lord's commandment?" Whereto the Persian replied: "He is no lord of mine. Knowest thou who I am?" Rejoined the Princess, "I know nothing of thee save what thou toldest me," and retorted he: "What I told thee was a trick of mine against thee and the King's son. I have long lamented the loss of this horse which is under us, for I constructed it and made myself master of it. But now I have gotten firm hold of it and of thee too, and I will burn his heart even as he hath burnt mine, nor shall he ever have the horse again- no, never! So be of good cheer and keep thine eyes cool and clear, for I can be of more use to thee than he. And I am generous as I am wealthy. My servants and slaves shall obey thee as their mistress. I will robe thee in finest raiment and thine every wish shall be at thy will."

When she heard this, she buffeted her face and cried out, saying: "Ah, wellaway! I have not won my beloved and I have lost my father and mother!" And she wept bitter tears over what had befallen her, whilst the sage fared on with her, without ceasing, till he came to the land of the Greeks and alighted in a verdant mead, abounding in streams and trees. Now this meadow lay near a city wherein was a King of high puissance, and it chanced that he went forth that day to hunt and divert himself. As he passed by the meadow, he saw the Persian standing there, with the damsel and the horse by his side, and before the sage was ware, the King's slaves fell upon him and carried him and the lady and the horse to their master, who, noting the foulness of the man's favor and his loathsomeness and the beauty of the girl and her loveliness, said, "O my lady, what kin is this oldster to thee?" The Persian made haste to reply, saying, "She is my wife and the daughter of my father's brother." But the lady at once gave him the lie and said: "O King, by Allah, I know him not, nor is he my husband. Nay, he is a wicked magician who hath stolen me away by force and fraud." Thereupon the King bade bastinado the Persian, and they beat him till he was well-nigh dead, after which the King commanded to carry him to the city and cast him into jail; and, taking from him the damsel and the ebony horse (though he knew not its properties nor the secret of its motion), set the girl in his seraglio and the horse amongst his hoards.

Such was the case with the sage and the lady, but as regards Prince Kamar al-Akmar, he garbed himself in traveling gear and taking what he needed of money, set out tracking their trail in very sorry plight, and journeyed from the country to country and city to city seeking the Princess and inquiring after the ebony horse, whilst all who heard him marveled at him and deemed his talk extravagant. Thus he continued doing a long while, but for all his inquiry and quest, he could hit on no news of her. At last he came to her father's city of Sana'a and there asked for her, but could get no tidings of her and found her father mourning her loss. So he turned back and made for the land of the Greeks, continuing to inquire concerning the twain as he went till, as chance would have it, he alighted at a certain khan and saw a company of merchants sitting at talk. So he sat down near them and heard one say, "O my friends, I lately witnessed a wonder of wonders." They asked, "What was that?" and he answered: "I was visiting such a district in such a city (naming the city wherein was the Princess), and I heard its people chatting of a strange thing which had lately befallen. It was that their King went out one day hunting and coursing with a company of his courtiers and the lords of his realm, and issuing from the city, they came to a green meadow where they espied an old man standing, with a woman sitting hard by a horse of ebony. The man was foulest foul of face and loathly of form, but the woman was a marvel of beauty and loveliness and elegance and perfect grace, and as for the wooden horse, it was a miracle- never saw eyes aught goodlier than it nor more gracious than its make." Asked the others, "And what did the King with them?" and the merchant answered; "As for the man, the King seized him and questioned him of the damsel and he pretended that she was his wife and the daughter of his paternal uncle, but she gave him the lie forthright and declared that he was a sorcerer and a villian. So the King took her from the old man and bade beat him and cast him into the trunk house. As for the ebony horse, I know not what became of it."

When the Prince heard these words, he drew near to the merchant and began questioning him discreetly and courteously touching the name of the city and of its King, which when he knew, he passed the night full of joy. And as soon as dawned the day he set out and traveled sans surcease till he reached that city. But when he would have entered, the gatekeepers laid hands on him, that they might bring him before the King to question him of his condition and the craft in which he skilled and the cause of his coming thither- such being the usage and custom of their ruler. Now it was suppertime when he entered the city, and it was then impossible to go in to the King or take counsel with him respecting the stranger. So the guards carried him to the jail, thinking to lay him by the heels there for the night. But when the warders saw his beauty and loveliness, they could not find it in their hearts to imprison him. They made him sit with them without the walls, and when food came to them, he ate with them what sufficed him.

As soon as they had made an end of eating, they turned to the Prince and said, "What countryman art thou?" "I come from Fars," answered he, "the land of the Chosroes." When they heard this, they laughed and one of them said: "O Chosroan, I have heard the talk of men and their histories and I have looked into their conditions, but never saw I or heard I a bigger liar than the Chosroan which is with us in the jail." Quoth another, "And never did I see aught fouler than his favor or more hideous than his visnomy." Asked the Prince, "What have ye seen of his lying?" and they answered: "He pretendeth that he is one of the wise! Now the King came upon him as he went a-hunting, and found with him a most beautiful woman and a horse of the blackest ebony- never saw I a handsomer. As for the damsel, she is with the King, who is enamored of her and would fain marry her. But she is mad, and were this man a leech, as he claimeth to be, he would have healed her, for the King doth his utmost to discover a cure for her case and a remedy for her disease, and this whole year past hath he spent treasures upon physicians and astrologers on her account, but none can avail to cure her. As for the horse, it is in the royal hoard house, and the ugly man is here with us in prison, and as soon as night falleth, he weepeth and bemoaneth himself and will not let us sleep."

When the warders had recounted the case of the Persian egromancer they held in prison and his weeping and wailing, the Prince at once devised a device whereby he might compass his desire, and presently the guards of the gate, being minded to sleep, led him into the jail and locked the door. So he overheard the Persian weeping and bemoaning himself in his own tongue, and saying: "Alack, and alas for my sin, that I sinned against myself and against the King's son, in that which I did with the damsel, for I neither left her nor won my will of her! All this cometh of my lack of sense, in that I sought for myself that which I deserved not and which befitted not the like of me. For whoso seeketh what suiteth him not at all, falleth with the like of my fall." Now when the King's son heard this, he accosted him in Persian, saying: "How long will this weeping and wailing last? Say me, thinkest thou that hath befallen thee that which never befell other than thou?"

Now when the Persian heard this, he made friends with him and began to complain to him of his case and misfortunes. And as soon as the morning morrowed, the warders took the Prince and carried him before their King, informing him that he had entered the city on the previous night, at a time when audience was impossible. Quoth the King to the Prince, "Whence comest thou, and what is thy name and trade, and why hast thou traveled hither?" He replied: "As to my name, I am called in Persian Harjah. As to my country, I come from the land of Fars, and I am of the men of art and especially of the art of medicine and healing the sick and those whom the Jinns drive mad. For this I go round about all countries and cities, to profit by adding knowledge to my knowledge, and whenever I see a patient I heal him, and this is my craft." Now when the King heard this, he rejoiced with exceeding joy and said, "O excellent sage, thou hast indeed come to us at a time when we need thee." Then he acquainted him with the case of the Princess, adding, "If thou cure her and recover her from her madness, thou shalt have of me everything thou seekest." Replied the Prince, "Allah save and favor the King. Describe to me all thou hast seen of her insanity, and tell me how long it is since the access attacked her, also how thou camest by her and the horse and the sage."

So the King told him the whole story, from first to last, adding, "The sage is in jail." Quoth the Prince, "O auspicious King, and what hast thou done with the horse?" Quoth the King, "O youth, it is with me yet, laid up in one of my treasure chambers." Whereupon said the Prince within himself: "The best thing I can do is first to see the horse and assure myself of its condition. If it be whole and sound, all will be well and end well. But if its motor works be destroyed, I must find some other way of delivering my beloved." Thereupon he turned to the King and said to him: "O King, I must see the horse in question. Haply I may find in it somewhat that will serve me for the recovery of the damsel." "With all my heart," replied the King, and taking him by the hand, showed him into the place where the horse was. The Prince went round about it, examining its condition, and found it whole and sound, whereat he rejoiced greatly and said to the King: "Allah save and exalt the King! I would fain go in to the damsel, that I may see how it is with her, for I hope in Allah to heal her by my healing hand through means of the horse." Then he bade them take care of the horse and the King carried him to the Princess's apartment, where her lover found her wringing her hands and writhing and beating herself against the ground, and tearing her garments to tatters as was her wont. But there was no madness of Jinn in her, and she did this but that none might approach her.

When the Prince saw her thus, he said to her, "No harm shall betide thee, O ravishment of the Three Worlds," and went on to soothe her and speak her fair, till he managed to whisper, "I am Kamar al-Akmar," whereupon she cried out with a loud cry and fell down fainting for excess of joy. But the King thought this was epilepsy brought on by her fear of him, and by her suddenly being startled. Then the Prince put his mouth to her ear and said to her: "O Shams al-Nahar, O seduction of the universe, have a care for thy life and mine and be patient and constant; for this our position needeth sufferance and skillful contrivance to make shift for our delivery from this tyrannical King. My first move will be now to go out to him and tell him that thou art possessed of a Jinn and hence thy madness, but that I will engage to heal thee and drive away the evil spirit if he will at once unbind thy bonds. So when he cometh in to thee, do thou speak him smooth words, that he may think I have cured thee, and all will be done for us as we desire." Quoth she, "Hearkening and obedience," and he went out to the King in joy and gladness, and said to him: "O august King, I have, by thy good fortune, discovered her disease and its remedy, and have cured her for thee. So now do thou go in to and speak her softly and treat her kindly, and promise her what thou desirest of her be accomplished to thee."

Thereupon the King went in to her, and when she saw him, she rose and kissing the ground before him, bade him welcome and said, "I admire how thou hast come to visit thy handmaid this day." Whereat he was ready to fly for joy and bade the waiting women and the eunuchs attend her and carry her to the hammam and make ready for her dresses and adornment. So they went in to her and saluted her, and she returned their salaams with the goodliest language and after the pleasantest fashion. Whereupon they clad her in royal apparel and, clasping a collar of jewels about her neck, carried her to the bath and served her there. Then they brought her forth as she were the full moon, and when she came into the King's presence, she saluted him and kissed ground before him. Whereupon he joyed in her with joy exceeding and said to the Prince: "O Sage, O Philosopher, all this is of thy blessing. Allah increase to us the benefit of thy healing breath!" The Prince replied: "O King, for the completion of her cure it behooveth that thou go forth, thou and all thy troops and guards, to the place where thou foundest her, not forgetting the beast of black wood which was with her. For therein is a devil, and unless I exorcise him, he will return to her and afflict her at the head of every month." "With love and gladness," cried the King, "O thou Prince of all philosophers and most learned of all who see the light of day."

Then he brought out the ebony horse to the meadow in question and rode thither with all his troops and the Princess, little weeting the purpose of the Prince. Now when they came to the appointed place, the Prince, still habited as a leech, bade them set the Princess and the steed as far as eye could reach from the King and his troops, and said to him: "With thy leave, and at thy word, I will now proceed to the fumigations and conjurations, and here imprison the adversary of mankind, that he may never more return to her. After this, I shall mount this wooden horse, which seemeth to be made of ebony, and take the damsel up behind me, whereupon it will shake and sway to and fro and fare forward till it come to thee, when the affair will be at an end. And after this thou mayest do with her as thou wilt." When the King heard his words, he rejoiced with extreme joy, so the Prince mounted the horse, and taking the damsel up behind him, whilst the King and his troops watched him, bound her fast to him. Then he turned the ascending pin and the horse took flight and soared with them high in air, till they disappeared from every eye.

After this the King abode half the day expecting their return, but they returned not. So when he despaired of them, repenting him greatly of that which he had done and grieving sore for the loss of the damsel, he went back to the city with his troops. He then sent for the Persian who was in prison and said to him: "O thou traitor, O thou villain, why didst thou hide from me the mystery of the ebony horse? And now a sharper hath come to me and hath carried it off, together with a slave girl whose ornaments are worth a mint of money, and I shall never see anyone or anything of them again!" So the Persian related to him all his past, first and last, and the King was seized with a fit of by which well-nigh ended his life. He shut himself up in his palace for a while, mourning and afflicted. But at last his Wazirs came in to him and applied themselves to comfort him, saying: "Verily, he who took the damsel is an enchanter, and praised be Allah who hath delivered thee from his craft and sorcery!" And they ceased not from him till he was comforted for her loss.

Thus far concerning the King, but as for the Prince, he continued his career toward his father's capital in joy and cheer, and stayed not till he alighted on his own palace, where he set the lady in safety. After which he went in to his father and mother and saluted them and acquainted them with her coming, whereat they were filled with solace and gladness. Then he spread great banquets for the townsfolk and they held high festival a whole month, at the end of which time he went in to the Princess and they took their joy of each other with exceeding joy. But his father brake the ebony horse in pieces and destroyed its mechanism for flight.

Moreover, the Prince wrote a letter to the Princess's father, advising him of all that had befallen her and informing him how she was now married to him and in all health and happiness, and sent it by a messenger, together with costly presents and curious rarities. And when the messenger arrived at the city which was Sana'a and delivered the letter and the presents to the King, he read the missive and rejoiced greatly thereat and accepted the presents, honoring and rewarding the bearer handsomely. Moreover, he forwarded rich gifts to his son-in-law by the same messenger, who returned to his master and acquainted him with what had passed, whereat he was much cheered. And after this the Prince wrote a letter every year to his father-in-law and sent him presents till, in course of time, his sire King Sabur deceased and he reigned in his stead, ruling justly over his lieges and conducting himself well and righteously toward them, so that the land submitted to him and his subjects did him loyal service. And Kamar al-Akmar and his wife Shams al-Nahar abode in the enjoyment of all satisfaction and solace of life till there came to them the Destroyer of delights and Sunderer of societies, the Plunderer of palaces, the Caterer for cemeteries, and the Garnerer of graves. And now glory be to the Living One who dieth not and in whose hand is the dominion of the worlds visible and invisible!

(The End)

Made in the USA
Las Vegas, NV
28 May 2021

23825967R00159